'Paddy Crewe's excellent second book will be one of the best things that you read all year'
Observer

'Remarkable ... Crewe's sensitivity to the tentacles of neglect in his characters is phenomenal. Time and again he captures a deep human truth'
Sunday Times

'Crewe recounts in lavish, unhurried prose [the protagonists'] respective childhoods, their abrupt coming together, their gradual drifting apart, and the love that keeps the two connected throughout like a magnetic thread ... There's an earnestness to the writing, yet it's a heart scorcher just the same. Read it and indulge'
Daily Mail

'Effective and moving ... Crewe's prose sings'
Financial Times

'This slow-burn love story is gorgeously written, with two characters you won't forget easily'
Good Housekeeping

'*True Love* is a perfect read if you're looking for a character-driven novel with split narratives or a coming-of-age story that is both heartbreaking and uplifting, reminiscent of Sally Rooney's work'
Press Association

'Invokes this sense of melancholy with true deftness ... Crewe's unabashed desire to move his readers is to be genuinely commended ... A full-throated, heart-on-sleeve piece of storytelling'
Guardian

www.penguin.co.uk

'Paddy Crewe writes with a lyrical, lonely prose that's full of the kind of tenderness which both frightens and saves us'
Minnie Driver

'Empathetic, honest, compelling. I'll read anything Paddy Crewe writes'
Bonnie Garmus, author of
Lessons in Chemistry

'*True Love* had me from its gorgeous, lyrical opening to its transcendent final pages. Paddy Crewe is an exceptionally gifted writer'
Louise Kennedy, author of *Trespasses*

'Pulls you in, holds you fast. A mesmerising tale of love and the depth of loneliness'
Claire Daverley, author of
Talking at Night

'Paddy Crewe brings out the longing, the fire and the strange melancholy of love in the tale of Keely and Finn where love is ripped away, rebuilt and found again. A love story in the truest sense, told with stinging insight and moments of quiet beauty'
Scott Preston, author of
The Borrowed Hills

'A gorgeous, compulsive, lionhearted book which I was caught up by and rolled along with over the course of a single breathless weekend. Beautiful and clever'
Nick Blackburn,
author of *The Reactor*

'Brilliant – a wonderful, powerful, urgent writer'
David Almond, author of *Skellig*

Paddy Crewe was born in Middlesbrough and studied at Goldsmiths. His debut novel, *My Name is Yip*, was shortlisted for the Betty Trask, the Wilbur Smith, a South Bank Sky Arts Award and The Authors' Club Best First Novel Award, and longlisted for the Walter Scott Prize.

True Love

PADDY CREWE

PENGUIN BOOKS

TRANSWORLD PUBLISHERS

UK | USA | Canada | Ireland | Australia
India | New Zealand | South Africa

Transworld is part of the Penguin Random House group of companies
whose addresses can be found at global.penguinrandomhouse.com.

Penguin Random House UK, One Embassy Gardens,
8 Viaduct Gardens, London SW11 7BW

penguin.co.uk

First published in Great Britain in 2024 by Doubleday
an imprint of Transworld Publishers
Penguin paperback edition published 2025

001

Typeset in 11.65/16pt Adobe Caslon Pro by Jouve (UK), Milton Keynes.
Printed and bound in Great Britain by Clays Ltd, Elcograf S.p.A.

The authorized representative in the EEA is Penguin Random House Ireland,
Morrison Chambers, 32 Nassau Street, Dublin D02 YH68.

A CIP catalogue record for this book is available from the British Library

ISBN: 978-1-804-99373-6

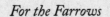
For the Farrows

PART ONE

SEACOALER

1

THE BLACK CRUNCH AND SHIFT OF SQUANDERED coal beneath the horse. It travels up into Keg's thighs, into the sway of her narrow hips. Wind lifts her fringe and stiffens her cheeks, whips a shimmer to the surface of her soft blue eyes. The grey sky above her remains solid, unmoving. It is a single pane of native cloud, a leaden weight under which the world toils, bending backs until they're as knotted as wands of driftwood.

Keg knows the measure of this suffering. She has seen it in everyone here at the camp, in the stooped and blighted figure of her own da. But there are also those days when the sky can span blue and cloudless as far as she can see, and there arrives the feeling inside her that something bigger is at work, that there's something else out there waiting for her. She has tried to explain it, to dress it in words, but the feeling shrugs off everything she throws at it, refuses to be made into a thing she can handle, a thing she can own.

The salt-stiff leather of the reins twines around her pale fingers. She pats Immy's neck, runs a palm down the coarse spill of her mane. The poor beast's getting old now. She's spent most of her days lugging her da in the cart behind her, the waves of the sea crashing against her strong, muscled legs, spindrift frosting her shivering flanks, the tide snaring the shag of her fetlocks with seaweed. Keg can still remember when Immy's coat was sleek and white, when she would frisk about in the marbled surf and her da would shout for her to still herself, broadening his stance so as not to topple into the water. But by the end of each day her coat would be streaked black by the coal and now, all these years later, she's turned a permanent ashy grey.

Keg brings her to a stop, looks down the track to the beach where she can see a portion of the sea, washing green and grey and raking its white nails up and down the black shore.

She's looking for Welty. Her da has told her that her brother is down here, warned her that if she doesn't go and fetch him and bring him back for his tea, then there'll not be a bite left for either of them.

She'd thought he'd be here at the very eastern edge of the camp, where the gravel gives way to stands of dry grass and a gentle roll of dun-coloured dunes, stacks of smoke from the power station towering darkly in the distance. He likes to bring his toys down here, to drive his little cars over the rough ground, to dig holes with sticks and bury his favourite stones and shells.

But he's nowhere to be seen.

She heels Immy's flanks and moves her on. The light is now waning, the sky just beginning to purple at its fringes.

4

The wind is also picking up, sharpening the blade of itself, skimming along the length of her body. She can hear the sea over the brow of the dune, its vast, unending roar. She'll be able to hear it from her bed in the caravan tonight. Sometimes it comforts her, and lulls her into a deep and dreamless sleep; but she's looked at the maps at school, has seen the sheer size of it, and it can frighten her, too. The depth and the darkness. All that space, and almost none of it known.

How is anything truly known? This is one of those thoughts that she sometimes has, that seems to be both too big and too small. Whenever she feels like she's close to an answer, it either throws a shadow over her so vast that she loses her way, or it slips between her fingers, and she's left staring down into nothing but the cracked furrows of her palms. The older she gets, the more she's coming to understand that this will always be the case, that the world doesn't owe her any explanations.

Salt whitens the corners of her mouth. Her tongue slips from between her teeth, dabs at her lips. They're softer and fuller than they were last year. She's been practising kissing at night in bed, making sure that Welty is asleep, and then slipping the shoulder of her pyjama top down and working her lips against the smooth skin there. Mostly she imagines no one in particular, but sometimes the face of a boy comes into her mind. She has seen him only twice, both times sitting on the wall near the shop in town, his pale ankles showing from beneath the cuffs of his trousers, the laces of his black boots frayed and dangling, his swinging heels knocking loose little showers of mortar. She doesn't know his name but she thinks about him, and when she does she feels a warmth spread down her neck and across her chest. She senses that there's something worth taking note of in this summoning of another body, a quiet, elusive power that'll be revealed to her in time, but not quite yet.

She's been called Keg since she was a baby. Her real name is Keely, but she was once so round and chubby, and had so quickly established a preference for rolling rather than crawling, that her da said she looked like the kegs of beer that would be delivered on a morning to the pub and lowered down into the cellar. Once he'd started calling her it, everyone else wanted to follow, and now there isn't a single person who doesn't.

Her mam was yet to get sick in those first years. There are photographs of her holding Keg on her lap, of the pair of them lying on the floor together next to heaps of crumpled-up wrapping paper. Both of them are smiling. Life is moving as it should, with many good years ahead. This is what their faces say.

But now, at twelve, Keg is stick thin, with long, angular legs and arms, and straight blonde hair that hangs limply over her eyes and shoulders, down the notched length of her spine. Her da tells her to eat more, shovels steaming piles of food on to her plate, which she does her very best to finish. But it doesn't matter how much she eats; she remains skin and bones, and when she reaches up to adjust the nozzle of the shower, which never offers any more than a dribble of water, she can feel her skin tauten over her ribs, and she might run her knuckles over them – sometimes fiercely, sometimes gently – as if they are the ossified strings of an instrument only she can play and hear.

SHE STARTS TO CALL out her brother's name. At first she uses the name she's responsible for coining: Welty. But when he doesn't respond, she switches to his real name: William.

It's not unusual that he should be hard to find. He's a small, feral creature, always on the move. He's seldom clean and his hair – a much darker shade than Keg's – is kept long at the back, though their da cuts his fringe for him every few weeks so that it doesn't hang over his eyes. He, too, is thin and bony, a collection of sharp angles that jut from the cuffs of jeans and jumpers, that press against the soft, washed fabric of his T-shirts.

Keg thinks of his shoulder blades, how often she's seen him in summer with his shirt off and tucked in the waistband of his shorts, hunched over a rock pool or braid of kelp. He will hear her coming and turn, the wind in his dark hair, his shoulder blades rearing up, freckled by the sun, like beautifully smooth stones.

She calls out again, but this time the wind snatches her voice away immediately. It's starting to really blow now, tugging at her clothes and hair, trying to bully her from her seat. If Immy weren't so old and wise she might start to baulk, but this isn't the first storm she's seen. She knows the punishing brunt of this wind, has fended the sting of driving rain, sleet, snow; and not once has she ever complained.

Keg has seen such weather before as well, has seen worse

than this. Once, when she was very small, she'd woken to the crack of thunder directly overhead. It had been so loud that she'd screamed, but she hadn't been able to hear her own voice, and she'd felt panicked, thinking that she'd lost it somehow, that it had been stolen from her and she'd never be able to speak again.

And the wind – it had been so strong that the caravan had rocked from side to side, as if it might tip right over. She'd left her own bed and groped through the darkness of her small room, only for it to be suddenly lit by the livid stitchwork of lightning outside her small, rattling window, and she'd looked down to see her hands, both of them blue and quaking before her.

Her mam and da were sat up in bed. They smiled when she came in, both laughed when she declared her worry about the caravan tipping over. Welty was feeding at her mam's breast, suckling away and making queer little noises, no different from one of the pups Keg had seen in the last litter born in the camp. When she'd asked to sleep beside her mam, her mam had moved over and left a spot of warmth for Keg to curl up in. She'd burrowed down under the covers, the flashes of lightning still reaching her, until she'd drifted off to sleep and woken hours later to buttery shafts of sunlight, and the briny air pouring through the window.

So she has seen worse.

And yet she can't keep herself from beginning to feel uneasy. The light has changed again. Moments ago, there was a purple hue to the sky, but now it's lowered even further and turned a deep, murky green. It reminds Keg of one of the deep puddles she and Welty sometimes find tucked between the folds of the dunes in summer, old rainwater that they like to stir up with sticks until the mud mushrooms up at them in great roiling clouds.

She calls her brother's name, Welty, William, as if there are two people she's looking for. But again the wind swipes her voice away. She turns to look back at the camp. She can still make out the carts and the old tyres slumped about; she can see the few rusted cars and horse trailers, the heaps of dung, the crates and the corrugated sheds; and then the fleet of caravans, theirs with its one broken window patched over with a flattened cereal box, the aerial on the roof bending beneath the push of the wind.

THERE ARE A GOOD few families in the camp now, people who've moved here from every nook and cranny of the country. Plenty of the men had once been coal miners. Mick and Gordon and Stookie and Harvo – all of them were once down the mines. But they found the camp and they found the coal that the tides and the currents wash back onto the beach. Coal is what they know, what they've always known; it's as much a part of them as anything else, the way it blackens their pale skins and can never be fully washed away.

And then there are the women: the backbone of the camp, always on the move, feeding and nursing the children, cooking and grafting and fixing up the caravans. They, too, will take to the beach and darken their hands with coal from time to time. Work is something that has lived in them long since they can remember, a ragged, brooding creature that demands the grind of their muscle and bone. But even in their barbed talk and lilting gossip, there is a tender burr of compassion, the words they stitch and weave between themselves like the nests that birds build for their young. Because they are the canniest of protectors, and their capacity for hope is vast; even if it cracks beneath the weight of longing, of loss, it can be renewed in the slow, dark hours of a single night, so that when they wake and rise and look out into the cold light of morning, they know nothing other than to carry on with what it is they must do.

Some newcomers in the camp are welcome, some are not. New arrivals must always be treated with a degree of suspicion. Because the camp is a family. At least this is what Mick often tells Keg. With his large, belted overcoat, his coarse sideburns and his pitted nose, he's shorter than their da but he's broader, and his hands are as rough as quoins of sandstone.

Mick and his wife, Evelyn, have three children, all too young for Keg to take any interest in. Evelyn is large boned with soft features. Her face is always red and sometimes strands of her auburn hair lie dark and flat with sweat against the ruddy expanse of her brow. She's kind, and blessed with a warmth that seems to envelop everyone she comes into contact with. Should anyone have an injury, it's to Mick and Evelyn's caravan that they go.

There's Elsie and Ruth, the partners of Stookie and Harvo. They're younger than Evelyn, and Keg thinks Ruth particularly beautiful. She has dark hair, olive skin, a small and perfectly round mole just to the right of one of her eyebrows. Ruth says that her grandparents are from Italy, and she cooks strange food with names that no one can ever pronounce.

Ruth is her favourite because she doesn't talk to Keg like she's a baby. She seems less bothered about providing Keg with care, more with just enjoying her company and treating her like an equal. It was to Ruth that Keg went last year in a state of terror and panic when she'd first started to bleed. With dried tears tightening her cheeks, she'd sat as Ruth explained what was happening to her body, throwing her bloodied underwear in the bin, bringing out a clean pair of her own and showing her how to use the pads that she fetched down from the small closet in her bathroom.

That evening, as Ruth had told her to, Keely had asked her da to include the pads in his next shop. Both of their faces had reddened, and a silence had lasted between them, broken only by the gulls the next morning that wheeled and cackled above the deadened fires and cast around their bright, spun-sugar eyes in search of scraps.

Keg doesn't like hanging around with other kids. She prefers the company of adults, those who seem to have sussed the world out, with their loud voices and hard, uncompromising gestures. They're always telling her to make herself scarce, but if she lingers long enough there's a chance she'll hear something new and thrillingly unfamiliar to her, which she'll then whisk away, and like a puzzle spend weeks obsessively turning over in her head, hoping that she, too, will begin to move with the stolid assurance of someone who understands their purpose, who has finally found their place.

On a night, a fire is lit outside and people gather to stand or sit around it. Dogs chase one another, barking and yipping, brushing against legs as people talk through their days while the children run free in the dark, laughing and screaming. Keg sometimes reluctantly joins in, though only if she's been forced to supervise. All of them know not to go down to the sea. From the moment they take their first steps, they're warned to keep well away from it. Because people drown. Even adults get swept away, dragged out and pulled into the deep, with no chance of surviving.

It's stronger than anything else on earth, their da says, and it doesn't care who it takes.

Keg's da is down at the beach, day in and day out. He and Gordon are in partnership since they both went in on a truck; and after they heap it full of the coal they've gathered, they set out to deliver, weaving awkwardly down the narrow streets of town and the villages beyond, parking up with the rumble of loose chips in the back, then hopping down from the cab to drag the bags they've filled and leave them propped against the doors.

Their da is a tall man with long, powerful arms. His hair always stands on end and has a sprung, loaded quality to it that makes it feel firm to the touch. She's always liked how he has to stoop slightly when he's walking around in the caravan, the simian roll and swing of his hanging fists. His features are sharp and there's a kink in his nose that he says is from when he broke it as a boy. In certain lights, it can give him a vaguely menacing quality, but when he smiles his eyes crease and the blue in them seems to leap out at whoever he happens to be looking at. Kindness, she supposes, is what he radiates. She's forever being told that she has these same eyes, that she's her da's daughter.

Neither Keg nor Welty truly know what he was like before their mam died. Keg was only five and Welty just coming up for one. Her memories of those times swim in and out of focus. For the most part, she thinks she's recalled everything about her mam; but then there are some times when her mam's face arrives, unbidden – when she's at school or picking down on the beach, or riding in the cart back to camp with Welty jostling beside her – and she'll find that she has another memory, something just surrendered to the light, and she'll stow it away with the others, hoarding and protecting each of them with her own bristling, maternal zeal.

More consistently tangible, though, is the smell of her mam, her touch. Keg can recall sitting on her lap and fingering the thick weave of her jumper, then leaning into her neck to breathe in her scent, which was always strongest there. She can remember the pinch of her mam's hands beneath her armpits as she was lifted up on to the counter in the kitchen, a tissue held up to her nose as she was asked to blow.

Sometimes, when she's out on the beach, Keg will suddenly be able to smell her, and on instinct she'll pivot sharply, as if she might find her mam simply standing there, as if she has not been gone all these years but just a few short minutes. She doesn't know where the smell comes from, whether her body conjures it from a space deep within that holds on to such things; or if those who have died leave an enduring trace of themselves, some phantom vapour that can be occasionally realized by entering the body of those they'd once loved.

Either way, it never makes her sad. She likes it, likes how it makes her think about the world and her life, a strain of magic that's worth savouring all the more for how little she understands of it. She feels as if her da is no different from those early days, and yet she knows deep down that he must be. And she knows, even if it's never been clear to her how, that she must be different as well.

Welty was too young; he has no memories of their mam at all, but he likes to talk about her, particularly on a night when they're in bed. They share the same tiny room. Keg has a proper bed with a pinewood frame, but since they never have any money to spare, da and Gordon made Welty a bed from one of the old pallets left out in the camp, cutting bits away and lashing other bits together, and then finally painting it blue.

Even though he's so much younger, Keg nearly always goes to bed at the same time as Welty. She likes to read a story to him, to see the way his face changes as the words reach him. Sometimes he'll drift off right away, the day having taken its toll on his young, innocent body. Other times, he won't appear tired at all but bright-eyed, restless, and he'll spit out a volley of questions about their mam.

She remembers one night in particular. It was late, their da long gone to bed, but she could tell that Welty was still awake. She could hear him tossing and turning in his grey twist of sheets on the floor below her, and she'd reached over to the small bedside table between them and switched on the lamp.

Immediately he'd sprung up, resting on his elbow, his dark hair mussed and hanging over his eyes slitted against the light.

What's wrong? she'd asked him.

I'm thinking about Mam, he'd said.

What about her?

A small crease between his eyes darkened at the question, and his lips had twisted to one side in the way he sometimes does when he's thinking hard.

Did she have enough time? he asked.

Enough time for what?

To love me, he said. Did she have enough time to love me like she did you and Da?

He'd never asked this question before, and Keely wondered at his mind, at the thoughts which must swirl and pick at him, just as in her own.

Of course she loved you, she said. Mam loved you the moment you were born. That's how it works. It doesn't take any time to love your kid. It just happens.

Welty had lain down then on his back and looked up at the ceiling, at the two wings of damp that have been spreading incrementally each year.

Tell me about her, he'd said.

And she had – she'd told him all the little snippets she remembers about their mam, the same way she's done time and time again. She never minds, never grows bored or frustrated, because she feels that with each telling she brings their mam a little closer to the both of them. Sometimes, when she's speaking, she has the feeling that their mam is looking at them. Not down on them, as people always seem to say, but from behind something, or through something, and Keg believes in such moments that this presence, even though she can't see it, is a kind of extension of their mam, the faint pulse of a wish that she's making from wherever she is, asking her to keep Welty safe.

KEG CONSIDERS GOING BACK and telling her da that she can't find Welty. Perhaps he's already back there, lurking around the sheds and talking to Gordon, which he sometimes likes to do. Gordon is like an uncle to the both of them. He's a quiet man with blond hair, pale skin and dark, nut-brown eyes. He's younger than their da by a decade or so, but he possesses what people refer to as an old spirit, which Keg takes to mean he has something of the earth trapped inside him, something that keeps him grounded and true at all times.

It is a sight Keg and Welty know as well as any: Gordon and their da up to their waists in the water, working their long-handled shovels down and then up, down and then up, emptying the black blade into the cart until it's heaped high with glistening chips which Immy can pull on to the beach.

Gordon was with da when he'd given her the instructions to find Welty, both of them sat around the table in the caravan, tapping their cigarettes into the large scallop shell that they use as an ashtray. Gordon had had his lean, sinewy legs crossed at the ankle, and stretched out so far that they nearly reached the curling lino of the kitchen. He takes his boots off by the door and his socks always have holes in them, so that Keg and Welty openly cry out in disgust at the sight of his toes, the yellow horn of his nails and the coarse twists of hair that sprig up out of cracked, greenish skin.

It's Friday, so there is already a small army of empty cans arranged on the table. Neither of them are drunks, not in the way some people from the camp are, going at it every night and sometimes not even sleeping before starting work again. With drink, her da never becomes angry but distant, vaguely melancholy, and Keg can see an ache in him that rises up to the surface, that sits in his eyes and hangs from the corners of his mouth.

For a long time, she has wanted to ask about this sadness of his, so shyly rearing its head and then ducking back into the shadows the instant she fixes an eye on it. It's just that she can never seem to find what words to use. The precariousness of language has occurred to her before, how one moment it will appear so strong and robust, and the next so brittle and distant from the feeling or act it's been tasked to scaffold. Will there ever be anything she can say to him that will bridge this gap between them? Or will it always be here, this span of time and space flickering in the half-light, that they can only glimpse each other across?

But her da and Gordon had been in fine spirits in the caravan – it had been a good day, they'd worked hard, and now they could relax, eat something, drink some more and then retire to their beds and fall asleep the moment their heads touched the pillow. But first she needed to go and find her nuisance of her brother.

He'll be up and down the dunes, her da said. Fetch him back or you'll both bloody starve.

Keg looks down the track at the sea again. Still no sign of him. Welty knows that he isn't to go down to the beach alone. He has his moments of stupidity, but he'd never be so foolish. Keg has had to drag him out of a number of messy situations: the time he'd climbed up on to one of the corrugated sheds and become snagged on a rusted nail, dangling like a puppet with its strings cut; or when he'd badly burned his hand after gripping the exhaust of their da's truck not a minute after they'd returned from a trip into town. He'd been planning to place his lips against it, to blow down it as he'd seen a saxophonist do on the music show they watch on TV, with the expectation that it might make a similar noise. It was Keg who'd had to run cold water over it while he cried, then take him over to see Evelyn and have her bandage it up with some aloe vera.

Keg moves off again, steering Immy on, her hooves picking their way between the sere grasses, punching the arch of her shod hooves into clots of damp sand, weeds shooting greenly through along the berm. The wind tries to shunt her off but she rides Immy without a saddle and leans in close, so that her crotch is pressed against the hard warmth of her back, and her legs lie snug against her flanks, feeling the sprung cage of her ribs, the shift and slide of her muscles. She rides her no other way. A saddle is no more than a separation, an interference between her and Immy. They should both be able to feel the other, know the contours of the other's frame and mood.

Immy's eyes are so dark that Keg has spent minutes at a time just staring into them. Horses are sacred around here. Always have been. They're used every day, and without them they'd all be lost. Without Immy, Keg feels as if she would be a lesser, more muted version of herself. There are certain qualities, qualities that language once again fails to assist her with, that horses have. It is their quiet alertness, the way they seem attuned to certain forces beyond their control, that Keg swears she can feel bleed into her own being, helping bolster her passage through the world, so that she doesn't feel quite so vulnerable to the unknown or the unnamable.

There's a trodden path that cuts through the roll of brown dunes, dipping and rising up so that sometimes the sea disappears, and at others the full acreage of it stretches out. She crests a small rise and pulls Immy to a stop again. She watches the sea, sees how it roils and thrashes beneath the low sky. Its colour: the green of verdigris and the purple of a fresh, smarting bruise. The waves, rising and slapping down, rising and slapping down.

She moves Immy on and calls for Welty again, but there's no use: the wind is too strong. She scans the dunes, hopes to see his dark head of hair spring up somewhere, or see his body crabbed low with his back to her, too busy studying something he's found to know that he's late, that Da's cooking dinner and will be working up a mind to give him a clip round the ear.

She feels it then, a little worm of unease that struts queasily around her stomach. She turns and looks back to the camp again. The dirtied chassis of the caravan has smudged into darkness, but Da or Gordon have flicked the light on, a little square of which glows out from behind the muslin curtain. Everything else – the sheds, the vans, the crates and carts and heaps of wheels – is falling into darkness. Welty isn't normally out this late, isn't normally so hard to find. She should ride back there. She should dig her heels into Immy's side and canter along the trail until she can knuckle the window and warn them of what is unfolding.

But she doesn't.

She feels she knows exactly what her da and Gordon will say. Her da will probably be doing the chips, the peelings strewn around him, standing in his socks at the one gas ring and swaying slightly to a song that's on the radio; Gordon will be slumped at the table, his legs stretched out even further, a can rested in the shallow of his bony chest. They'd not care for any theatrics on a Friday night, not when they're enjoying a bit of relaxation, and she imagines they'll tell her to get back out there, and to hurry up if she and Welty don't want to go hungry for the night.

The uneven click of grit and stones beneath Immy's hooves. Her ears are almost hidden beneath the knotted heap of her mane. She needs to be brushed. She'll get Welty to do it when she finds him. He can stay outside in the cold and the wind and do it while they eat their dinner. He'll whine and moan but she won't let him in until it's done, until he's put Immy back in her stable and fed her as well, and he's promised never to stay out so late again.

The trail dips between two dunes. Keg has to lean back so as not to topple over Immy's head. There's a place at the end of the trail that she knows Welty is very fond of. It's not a cave as such, but that's what Welty calls it, more of a hole that's been carved out of the dunes by the wind and the rain. She'll go to it, and no doubt he'll be there, and his pale face will stare up at her, and he'll say: What? as if he's completely unaware of the darkness that's gathered all around him.

They climb up out of the dip and the sea is there again,

thrashing darkly. The wind skirls around Immy's fetlocks, flings sand in her face so that she tosses her head. The first drops of rain start to fall. They strike the backs of Keg's hands, the nape of her neck, and as she looks out over the sea, at the thin line of the horizon, she can see grey shoals coming down from the low clouds, a twisting curtain that is being pulled across the last of the light.

It's then that she knows Welty isn't in the cave. She knows he's not anywhere on the trail or in the dunes. It's one of those feelings she sometimes gets, that she's had for as long as she can remember – bright, almost blinding pulses of knowledge that strobe through the dark and tangled briar of her thoughts. The shock of it now, her body held and wound tight by this force, this force that has no right to the mastery of her but that she can't help but heed, a weathervane fixed and pointing in one direction by a confluence of screaming winds.

Welty is down on the beach.

She knows it with a terrible fierceness that makes her stomach knot. Her vision dims and flickers like a bulb about to blow. She wheels Immy around, catches a glimpse of both the sea and the smeared flare of light from the camp through the gauzy weave of rain. For a moment, she feels caught between them, trapped in amber, as if she might never move again. Everything will remain as it is, and she finds that she wants this; she wants the world to come to a halt, for time to cease its endless march. But then her heels are nipping into Immy's flanks and they are cantering back along the trail the way they've come.

The rain starts to slant down heavier. It plasters her

fringe to her forehead, runs down her cheeks, drips in a pendulous thread from her chin. She drags the sleeve of her coat across her eyes. She can taste salt. Her hands are cold, the tips of her fingers feeling numbed and yet still burning with a vague, fuzzy pain. Her bottom lifts clear of Immy's back, comes down hard and then is jolted back up again. Taller grasses whip at her boots and shins. The rain is hard and painful, like a scoop of gravel dashed in her face, pinging against her cheeks, her eyelids, her temples.

The lights of the camp are barely visible now through the twist and blur of cloud. No fires lit, no thin pipings of smoke, no groups huddled or sloping off toward the pub. Everyone is inside, buttressed by warmth and sound and light, some faces no doubt peering up at the sky and alive with the dark augurings she is now living. She hopes that one is her da's, that he's searched the darkness of the camp and sensed what she senses, that there's danger in the air.

Keg reaches the little track that she'd looked down only minutes before and steers Immy between its slick banks, her hooves showering sand and stones. Then the grind of the coal on the beach, the sound so crisp to Keg's ear even with the wind that she imagines sparks knifing brightly beneath her. The sea is flinging itself, hissing and foaming and groaning, suddenly all around her: a seductive, implacable beast that will gladly drag her and Immy into its depths.

Immy rears up, flicks her head this way and that. Keg grips the reins, tries to soothe her, looks up and down the beach. She calls for Welty again and again. She stops and leans into the wind to see if she can hear his reply, the soft rising of his voice. But there's nothing. Nothing but the wind, the sea, blood thrumming in her ears. She decides to move up the beach. She doesn't canter but trots. The tide is coming in, washing up the black shore so that Immy's hooves kick and splash through the froth of the surf, through the rubbery sticks of kelp and the knots of seaweed.

Keg's eyes narrow to cut through the gloom. Coal chips are scattered everywhere and there's a large mound of them up ahead where Da and Gordon have unloaded a cart but have left it for the morning. Rocks, their humped and nightmarish shapes, rise up out of the sand and gleam darkly.

Immy's becoming restless. Her eyes rove wildly, showing their whites when she cranes her rain-slick neck. Keg has never known her be like this, so skittish, snapping at the air, sending her tongue looping wildly to lick at the salt caking her nostrils. Even in the failing light, her coat has a greasy, mottled shine to it, like oil sitting on water. By this time she's normally in her stable, dry and warm and expecting her feed. She doesn't mind the rain; she's well used to being wet. It's the wind and the spreading darkness that has her heart hammering so quick and hard that Keg can feel it along the lengths of her shins.

She calls for Welty again but this time she doesn't stop. He has to hear it. There's a small, stubborn flame at the back of her mind that's trying to keep her body calm, that the surge of adrenaline in her bloodstream is threatening to extinguish. It could be that he's already back at the caravan, that he's faffing about at the other end of the camp, playing with Mick and Evelyn's border collie, Axle.

She tells herself these things. She tells herself that she'd be better off turning back now or it'll be her that ends up in trouble, tossed from Immy's back when something spooks her for good and swept out to sea.

But she can't rid herself of that feeling she'd had up on the dunes. That for all the eight years of his life that she's been caring for him, it's never felt like this: he's never been out on his own in weather this bad, in light this poor, with the sea this wild. She's always been able to feel his presence, and has never before known him to stray beyond the compass of her care.

But this feeling isn't inside her anymore. Instead, there's a cold rush of something unknown to her; or it's a sensation that she might have felt once a very long time ago, when she was still small and her mam was in the hospital. When she and her da had visited and seen her in the bed, her face pale and sunken, her eyes shut and her hair all but gone. Keg had had questions to ask her da, so many of them that she'd felt fit to burst; but what had stopped her was the same feeling inside her now, a cold boil at the back of her throat, warning her that whatever she did or said would make no difference, that whatever was happening was beyond her control.

If Welty could just appear, if she could see the small white dial of his face, the dark eyes and the sharp tips of his ears poking out through the mop of his hair – then everything would be all right, the coldness in her throat would vanish. She wouldn't even be angry, wouldn't make him comb out Immy's mane. She would just squeeze him to her, take in the raw, animal scent of him, and then lift him up on to Immy's back, where he would sit in front of her, and she would wrap her arms around his waist, whispering in his ear of all the chips that Da was cooking, that were waiting to be sprinkled with salt and showered in vinegar and red sauce.

Because this is what they've always done: talk to each other. Day in and day out. Even though there's four years between them, there's no one closer to her. No one feels to be an extension of herself in the same way that he does. She loves her da, knows him to be a good, honest man that would do anything in his power to make her happy. But she loves Welty in a different way. There are some days when she looks at him and she's so aware of the way he moves: his body, tight and lithe, is running on the same blood that she has inside of her, and he becomes in these moments a kind of miracle, a kind of saviour. She is him and he is her, and they must be together, always.

Keg is growing more and more frantic, her breath coming fast and shallow, her eyes trapped open. She hasn't done what her mam has asked of her, she hasn't protected him. Her throat burns as she screams out his name. The rain driving, the wind scouring, the sea thundering on to the shore. She digs her heels in hard now so that Immy moves up to a canter, her hooves kicking up a spray, crunching down on to the coal.

And that's when she sees something, something that catches in her vision. Her eyes are pulled toward it with a force that she'll come to remember as feeling almost magnetic. She doesn't know what it is, and yet some small part of her is already aware that she's again entering a different world. She can feel it, a terrible shift that's all around her, the leaving of one kind of life for the beginning of another. Even though there's no visible line, no sign or mark drawn in the sand, she knows she's about to cross into a land she doesn't know, that will look the same in so many ways but will be entirely other.

What she sees are the red and white stripes of Welty's jumper floating in the surf. She hopes that it's just the jumper, that Welty is elsewhere, that he's watching her in just his T-shirt from the dunes, calling her name as she has been his. But it moves stiffly, the arms outstretched, and she feels herself closer to that invisible line again, right in front of her now, dragging her toward it, imploring her to cross it.

She leaps down from Immy.

The biting cold of the water sucks at her legs. It pulls at her, wants to drag her down, but she moves through it; and as she gets closer to the red and white stripes, her eyes start to make out the rest of him: she sees the back of his head, the dark twist of his hair; she sees the pale flash of his skinny legs where the sea has pulled his cotton bottoms loose.

She's screaming as she reaches out and takes an arm. It's cold and heavy, and she can't bring herself to turn him over. She knows if she sees his face then that'll be all she ever sees.

But she doesn't have to, because her da is suddenly behind her and so is Gordon, and she watches as Welty is lifted up out of the water into their da's arms and he's being carried away through the surf back toward the beach, and so is she, tucked under Gordon's arm, her face buried into the rough wax of his coat, nothing but her own cries and the darkness around her.

2

THERE ARE DAYS WHEN HE GETS UP, WHEN SHE CAN
hear him in the kitchen, the kettle boiling and the butter
scraping over the toast. These are the good days. He'll talk
a little, and he'll tousle her hair when she gets up to join
him. They'll drink a cup of tea together with the radio on,
and they'll stare out the window into the brightening camp.
Almost always, even if there's very little wind, they'll be
able to hear the sea, and they'll each glance at the other's
soft, glazed expression, and they'll know that they're seeing
the same things, the same dark, violent reel of images
behind their eyes.

With just the two of them in the caravan, it seems
almost too big. One day she'd come back and Welty's bed
had been taken out of the room they'd shared. She'd
screamed and found her da, but he'd only held her and
pointed to the scrub at the edge of the camp where a small
fire was nearly burned out. She looked at the thin weave of
smoke and even from where she'd been stood, she'd been

able to see the blue paint curling in the heat and drifting away on the breeze.

Why couldn't we have kept it? she'd asked later that night over the table, her food almost untouched.

Kept what? her da replied.

Her eyes flicked toward the darkling window where the last embers still glowed at the edge of the camp.

His bed, she said.

Her da had sighed, put his knife and fork down, rubbed his coal-blackened hands up and down his face where they left thin, shadowy streaks.

Because it's of no use anymore, he said.

It doesn't have to be of any use, she said.

It does, he returned, pushing his plate away and rising from his seat so fast that the table shook. Everything has to be of use. If it's of no fucking use, then there's no point fucking keeping it.

She'd watched then as he'd stormed out, leaving her alone. She'd scraped his half-full plate into the bin, washed the dishes, sat back at the table and waited for him to return. At some point, she must have fallen asleep, because she remembers hearing him coming back in and lifting her up, too big for him to carry, but her arms and legs instinctively wrapping around him, breathing in the sour lick of booze on his breath as he laid her down in her bed, pulling the duvet over her like she'd used to do with Welty.

Now, without Welty, they can hear each other's every move. They can suddenly feel how the caravan shudders and lurches underfoot. How it creaks and whines in the night, as if Welty's extra weight had been enough to subdue these things, to anchor it and them to the earth fully. But they both know that's not the case, that these were just things neither of them had taken much notice of before, because their minds had always been elsewhere, had been allowed to inhabit different avenues of thought. Because they'd had the possibility of being happy.

Her da had stopped calling her Keg the day after it happened. Suddenly, she was Keely. She'd never been called this before. It was a strange kind of shock to hear her da use it, but she thought she understood why: they came as a pair, Keg and Welty, and so to call her Keg would be to always acknowledge an absence, to be made to confront the brute reality of Welty's no longer existing over and over again.

Gordon soon followed suit, then so did everybody else on the camp. And then so did she. She was now Keely, and after a few weeks Keg grew to seem like a different person to her, not a part of her at all, but a stranger that she'd once met long ago.

She no longer goes to school. The last time she went was when she was thirteen, almost exactly a year after Welty had died. Then she'd just stopped. Her da hadn't said anything about it. Everyone, all of her classmates and even kids in other years, had eventually come to learn of what had happened; she was looked at differently, treated differently, and she couldn't stand it.

Twice, Miss Collins, her English teacher, had come to the camp and knocked on the door of the caravan. The first time, neither she nor her da had been in, but were down on the beach. Mick, his protective instincts bristling, had seen the stranger from the window of his caravan, and he'd gone out and asked what she was after, his large arms folded across his chest. Flustered, Miss Collins explained that she was looking for Keely, that she was a teacher from her school. But Mick hadn't wanted to hear it, and he'd sent her away.

Plenty of people who'd been dismissed by Mick never returned, but Miss Collins came a second time a week or so later. This time, Keely let her in, sat her down at the little table, and she listened as Miss Collins spoke to her about her prospects, about how firmly she believed that she had real potential, that she was aware of the tragedy that had befallen them and how she was terribly, terribly sorry about it. But school was still an opportunity. It was a chance for Keely to explore, to find out what mattered, to live a life of her own choosing.

Her da had stood by the sink, hands thrust deep into the pockets of his faded jeans, and said nothing for the entirety of it all, his face blank and occasionally turning away to look out the window. But Keely had had to stop herself from crying. That somebody should care enough about her to come out here, to find her and say such things – she'd almost been persuaded to return. But when she thought about putting on her uniform again and walking through those stale-smelling corridors; when she thought about all the faces looking at her as she went by, she knew that she'd never go back. And she'd told Miss Collins this, and Miss Collins had nodded, and she'd sipped the tea that Keely's da had made.

Befallen. She'd heard Miss Collins use that word, and in that moment she'd known that she would always remember it. A tragedy had befallen them. It made the whole thing sound unreal, as if it had happened years and years before, in a time when she wasn't alive, in a time that had had nothing to do with her.

Eventually, Miss Collins had left. She said that she'd be back, but Keely had told her not to bother. She wasn't going to change her mind.

But then Keely had seen her the next day walking across the camp, her beige coat flapping in the wind. She was carrying something, a bag that looked heavy and awkward, swinging and knocking against her stockinged legs.

Keely was preparing herself to answer the door, to reiterate more forcefully this time what she'd said the day before. Then she saw Miss Collins walking away. She was no longer carrying the bag but clutching her coat to herself, her head bowed against the wind, her dark hair dragged free of its pinnings.

Keely went to the door and pulled it open. She heard the crackle and whisper of the bag before she saw it tucked by one of the plant pots full of old rainwater. She looked up and caught Miss Collins climbing into her car, shutting the door and then lurching away, the engine rattling noisily and the exhaust pluming smoke that bunched in dark fists before drifting away.

Keely turned back to the bag. Immediately she could see that inside it were books, their sharp corners and angles threatening to pierce the plastic. She felt a small, unexpected thrill to see them, and without knowing why, she furtively lifted up the bag and took it straight to her room, closing the door softly behind her so as not to attract the attention of her da.

Settled on her bed, she searched through them one by one, reading the titles and the descriptions of the stories on the back, occasionally pressing her nose to a page and inhaling the overripe, almost sweet scent of it. They possessed an energy that she could feel, that swelled and filled the room, this room that was no longer their room or our room but her room, and that seemed to have doubled in size now that she no longer had to navigate Welty's bed to reach her own.

She stacked the books up and admired them, then picked one at random and began to read. It had been a long time since she'd last read anything other than the back of the cereal packet, but there, on the very first page, she found her mind drawn away from Welty, away from the pale, lifeless sheen of his skin in the surf.

For the first time since Welty's death, she abandoned the contents of her own mind and entered someone else's. Page after page went by, and she was surprised by how much she could understand, by how much these different lives she was reading about – lives lived long ago, in circumstances utterly divorced from her own – could so precisely skewer her own feelings, were capable of offering truths that thrust greenly up through the scorched landscape of her own mind, and were hers to keep and wield as she pleased.

From that day she read through all of them, and when she got to the last one, she started over again. On the second time through, though, she found them to have changed. They were the same books, with the same covers and the same words inside them, and yet they were radically different. That was when she first stumbled into the delicious snare of written words: they wrapped themselves around her, living, breathing things that forsook their rigid formation on the page and leapt out into her own life, where they followed her from room to room, down onto the beach, crawled out from under the jettisoned chips of coal she stooped to pick up and return to the cart.

Reading began to make her aware of herself without plunging her into dark, endless corridors of introspection, without every door opening out on to the beach, on to the drift of Welty's cold, lifeless body. She had been broken, was no longer whole, but there were pieces of this shattered self that she found could be clumsily, uncleanly put back together, and that seemed to reflect a light that, against all the odds, might yet reveal a way for her to continue on into the future.

NOW IT'S BEEN A year since Miss Collins dropped off the first bag of books, and she's dropped off several more since. Keely's room isn't really big enough for shelves, so she has to stack them along the wall where Welty's bed used to be. Even now, she finds the odd chip of blue paint from the framework of the pallet, and she picks them up and keeps them in a little jar in the drawer of her bedside table.

Her da is curious about the books. She's seen him picking them up, turning them in his coal-smudged hands, then placing them back with his brow furrowed and his eyebrows raised.

One day, he asks her why she reads them. The question takes her by surprise. At first, she can't think how to answer, and the best she can give him is a dismissive, surly shrug.

Because, she says.

He smiles slightly.

Because of what? he replies.

Keely shrugs again and seconds pass in which they only stare at one another. She watches her da's eyes narrow slightly, the corners of his mouth slowly lifting and falling. She knows that he's trying to discern if it's a moment for laughter or solemnity. They have these awkward, halting instances between them more and more of late, where she can feel the power of her own mystery, the sheer alienness of herself through his eyes. And even though she knows it causes him pain, she can't help but relish his confusion. It is addictive, this watching him squirm.

Because they're mine, she says.

Her da's lips flicker upward.

Is that it? he asks.

She nods, but just as he's about to turn away from her, a sentence arrives in her mind. She doesn't want to say it, but it comes loaded with a power all its own, sliding off her tongue and prising apart her teeth.

They take me away, she says.

Her da frowns, still half turned away from her so that she can see the corded muscles in his neck.

From where?

Keely feels a flat rush of heat rise up from the base of her throat. If she were to look in the mirror, she knows she'd find small islands of redness dappling her skin.

From here, she says.

Later that night, she thinks for a long time about what she'd said. Her da had looked at her for a second or two, no longer, and then he'd only nodded and turned away, as if they'd enjoyed nothing more than a routine exchange.

But she sees now, in the dark of her room, that what she'd said was both true and untrue: books do take her away, but they also root her more firmly to her home. And if she indulges the occasional reverie in which her life unfurls elsewhere, in a different place and a different time, then she's also dimly aware of a growing comfort and strength in knowing where she's from, that the land and the people she's grown up with will never be rinsed fully from her blood, no matter what is still to come.

After that day, her da never asks about her reading again, but she knows that he watches her as she reads in the morning and at night, as if she might vanish into the books and never come back.

KEELY IS FIFTEEN NOW. Her body has changed over the past couple of years: her hips have filled out and her breasts, though not as big as Evelyn's or Ruth's, show through the shirts and jumpers she wears. There was something sly about their growth, the way her nipples had become hard and painful to the touch, and then, almost day by day, she'd felt the ghostly weight of them added to her, a presence that she's found both pleasing and disturbing.

Her da, she knows, has struggled with her drift into womanhood. Ever since she'd been born, she's sensed that he's felt her character to be inextricably linked to her body: as a baby, the small, innocent heft of her belly had given rise to her first nickname. And with the hard lines and sharp angles that had followed, he'd been able to see something of her quiet stoicism, her prickly obstinance. But these days, if he occasionally glimpses a half-moon of her hip as she stoops to empty the washing machine, or if she slips out from the bathroom with only her towel wrapped and pinched beneath her armpits, he has the uncanny feeling of watching a stranger, and for a short, vertiginous beat, nothing in his life aligns, and he drifts through time, his mind as glaringly empty as a sheet of sun-struck desert.

So, just as when she'd first started bleeding, it was Ruth she turned to about needing to buy bras for herself, and Ruth had assured her that she'd take her shopping. But Keely still had to ask her da for money, and when he'd asked her what it was for, she'd not been able to lie. He'd handed the note and few coins over, then opened his mouth as if he wanted to say something, but had seemed to think better of it. Instead, he'd done his best to arrange his features – with his lips pursed too tightly, and his increasingly unruly brows lifted – in a way she could tell he hoped to be both accepting and encouraging.

This, to Keely's mind, had been another line to be crossed. A different kind of line to the one she'd crossed when Mam had died, and when she'd found Welty, but a line nonetheless. The world, she's come to realize, is made up of them; she suspects that some people can remain completely ignorant of them for the whole of their lives, while there are others, and she is one of them, who are ever-vigilant, sensitive to certain quirks of atmosphere – the shimmer of light or fall of shadow, the needle of dread or pulse of heat – that forecast the passing of one frame to another.

In this case, she knows she's crossed a line by the way

men look at her when she's in town doing the shopping; or when she's at work; or when she meets up with Sarah, her best friend from school who she still sees every few weeks or so. A man's stare can sometimes make her feel unwashed, and she'll return home with a desperate yearning to shower, as if pungent oil has been smeared all over her skin. But there are other times when she feels, from the very second of her waking up, like she wants to be noticed, and even though there's a grubbiness to most of the men she passes in the street, the looks she receives can lift her out of herself, can make her feel wanted in a way that she doesn't really understand but can't help but seek out.

She's found a job in the shop in town for three days a week: Mondays, Wednesdays and Fridays. It's boring and she has to set off in the dark in winter on her bike, which she rides out of the camp, down the long stretch of grey road and into town. When she gets there, she has to unlock the shop, switch on all the lights and see that all the paperboys have the correct stacks for their routes. Then she has to sort the till, all while trying to warm herself up, because the heating takes an age to kick in, and she normally has to wear gloves until midday if she doesn't want her fingers to fall off.

The customers are mostly kind to her, and she likes to chat and hear about their lives. None of them ask why she's not in school. It's funny, she thinks, how much people will tell you about themselves given the slightest opportunity. Life has a way of simplifying itself when she's here. Everyone just wants to be listened to, if only for a short time, and she does her best to oblige. There's not a great deal more to it than that, and if this realization has on occasion brought with it a kind of ennui, then it's also brought moments she does her best to receive gratefully and to cherish.

Most importantly, the job gives her some money, the majority of which she keeps for herself, but some of which she hands over every week to her da. He'd never ask for it, but she knows it's the right thing to do. His own work out on the beach is getting more and more difficult – not just because he's getting on and the years have made an old man of him before his time, but because, as he often says, it's a way of life that's dying out. The country is changing and times are moving on. The people in charge are not their kind of people. Love, in their eyes, is not a thing that can be extended toward an entire community, but must be kept behind closed doors, reserved for those who have something to offer in return for it.

He says these things with a look of such overwhelming weariness and resignation that it makes Keely ache. She moves over to wherever he might be, leans into his side and takes in the feel of him: the salt and the sweat and the coal. Lately – often, but not often enough – she has the terrible feeling that she's forgetting things, that all the things she's stowed away in her head are being slowly, imperceptibly filched from her.

When she's not at the shop, she gets up with Da and Gordon and heads down to the beach to help out with the day's graft. She rises when they do, just before dawn, and walks to the stables to fetch Immy, who's always ready and waiting for her. She's still as reliable as she ever was; but sometimes Keely can't help but feel she catches a flicker of sadness in her dark eyes that had never been there before, as if she, too, has been changed by the night of Welty's death.

There's no way of being down on the beach without thinking about Welty. She knows it's the same for her da, for Gordon, for everyone else who works there: Mick and Stookie and Harvo. It's a weight they all must carry. There are days when she feels it to be a little lighter, and when she looks out across the sea and sky, she can glimpse that feeling she used to have when she was smaller, of there being something out there waiting for her, something bigger at work.

But then the next day she'll feel the weight to be heavier than it ever was, and she's forced to contend with the fact that loss and grief have no fixed dimension, no logical balance of forces that can be pinned down and held still.

On a night, she listens to her da. She can hear the small reports of his ankles and knees clicking, his muscles and tendons sore from working the shovel in and out of the water, from shaking the coal chips off the blade and into the cart, then stooping down to do it over and over again. These are some of the only times he talks, quietly bemoaning his age and the toll the years are taking on his body. She's grateful for any words, because she knows very well that right around the corner might be a string of bad days, when he can't bring himself to get out of bed.

THE MOMENT SHE OPENS her eyes, she knows: there's no whistling of the kettle, no footsteps, no radio droning softly through the wall. And the air, the first breath that she draws deeply into her lungs, feels heavy, unclean. She knows that he'll be flat on his back, tears streaming from the deep spokes of his scrunched eyes, rolling over his temples and into his hairline, which he's let grow wild and untamed, streaked silver now in places.

She knows she can't stay in bed as well. She knows that Gordon can't do a day of work on his own. They need the money. So she does her best to beat back the heavy air. She gets up and changes and she boils the kettle herself, turns on the radio, opens the curtains and the door and lets the wash of grey dawn light in.

Then she takes coffee to her da, places it amongst the clutter of his bedside table - other mugs of cold tea, an ashtray, a scattering of beer cans - and she sits by his side on the lip of the bed. The room smells of old sweat, sour and oniony, and there's a pall of smoke that hangs and drifts just below the ceiling.

She leans over him and draws the curtains.

It's another day, she always tells him. Look. Look outside and see it.

But he doesn't look. He only stares up at the ceiling, and she knows that he's hating himself. He's wishing himself dead, because on these days he believes that Welty's death is his fault. He should have known. He should have been able to sense that something was wrong. He should have told Welty more times about the danger of the beach.

It doesn't seem to matter how often she tells him that he's not to blame. He doesn't believe her; and, despite the crippling lassitude that can sweep through her in the face of his silence, she understands why – because there are times when she feels exactly the same, when she believes she's to blame, for all the same reasons he does.

Everything that she tells her da she could apply to herself – that Welty knew the dangers, that he'd been told a million times. But it doesn't seem to work like that. Her mind turns on her; it manipulates time, twists logic, cruelly renders every moment of that day into a portent she ought to have taken note of. And once she starts, she can't stop. She obsesses over every detail, feeling her insides burn with the knowledge that even the slightest of incidents could have prevented it all: if she'd tidied away his trainers, then he wouldn't have seen them and decided to go out; if he'd stumbled over a rock and grazed his knee, he would have come back to the caravan demanding a plaster; if the rain had started sooner, he would have been soaked to the skin and slinked into one of the sheds to keep dry.

But none of these things did happen, and so she kisses her da on his creased brow and leaves him lying there. She eats her porridge alone with the radio on, and then she's out the door to meet Gordon. She never needs to explain anything. Gordon knows her da's patterns of grief as well as she does, and he'll swing by later on to see what he can do to rouse him. But until then there's work to be done, it's as simple as that.

No one else down on the beach needs it explained either. They see her da isn't there and they understand. In truth, it doesn't take long for his absence to be forgotten; there's too much going on to think about much else. The many horses and the many carts, the shouts of the men and the slap and grind and rinse of the shovels that plunge time and time again into the waves, the waves that roar and froth and hiss on the black shore.

Lying down in bed won't bring him back, Keely has heard Evelyn say.

If it were up to Mick or Ruth or Evelyn, they'd pay him a visit. They'd march straight in the caravan to fuss and haul him up out of bed.

But her da has told Keely: I don't want visitors.

Tell them I'm fine, he says. Tell no one to knock. Tell them I'll be back out tomorrow.

She's done as he's asked, and she's told everyone that her da just wants to be left alone. For the most part, they honour his wishes; but Ruth will still always bring some food round: lasagne, cacciatore, Bolognese, carbonara. Keely doesn't know what they are or what's in them, but they taste good, and she's always pleased to hear the knock at the door and see Ruth standing with two stained tea towels wrapped around her hands, steam rising up in the chill night air.

EVERYONE IN THE CAMP had attended the funeral. Welty was buried only a few days after it happened, in the cemetery by the little church that looked out across the sea. It hadn't been possible to have him directly next to their mam, though they were a matter of a few feet apart.

There had been a time, perhaps when she was around ten, before Welty had joined Mam in the ground, when Keely had asked their da if they could go and visit their mam's grave frequently. She'd seen something on TV, on one of the soaps that she liked to watch at night with her tea, someone kneeling solemnly beside a headstone and laying pretty-looking flowers down next to it, then stepping back and seeming – with their fingers neatly interleaved at their waist and a knowing smile spreading across their face – to come to some kind of acceptance or understanding of all that had happened.

It became apparent to Keely that there was a physical place connected to her mam, a place that Keely could be, and she hoped that rather than rely on the fleeting presence that survived only in her mind, something more tangible might be established between them, somewhere they could both inhabit.

So for two weekends in a row, their da had taken them to the cemetery in the old truck still rattling with loose chips of coal, a twenty-minute drive beyond the town. Once there, he'd watched on from a slight distance, never getting too close or laying anything down himself, as Keely and Welty had placed a collection of greenery that they'd picked from the dunes and fastened together with an elastic band – clover, lady's bedstraw, sea rocket, kidney vetch, orchids – down beneath the faded lettering of their mam's name and the dates between which her life had been lived.

The little heaps of greenery didn't look as pretty as the flowers on the TV had, but Keely had been happy enough. They were all things that their mam would have seen plenty of, and would surely remind her of her home.

But after those first times, their da had started to become uncomfortable about it, clicking his tongue and shaking his head at the idea of another trip.

You've been enough, he'd said one day when she and Welty were riding in the back of the cart, pressed up against the heap of coal that Immy was lugging toward the camp. His back was to them as he marched up ahead, his hand resting against Immy's neck, not turning as he spoke.

We've only been twice, Keely replied.

Twice is enough, he said. You've done what you wanted.

But the flowers will die or get blown away, she said.

Welty was beside her, his hands and face black and his nose running, but he was still too young to really understand the significance of the conversation. He'd helped gather the flowers from the dunes and he'd had his own little pile to lay down next to their mam, but he hadn't had any true sense of the occasion.

Then the new ones you'll put down will die, their da said, and you'll be forever going back there. Best that you leave off for a while. Your mam knows you love her. She needs her rest.

Keely had fallen silent then, not because she agreed with her da, but because of the strangeness of those last words. It seemed to her that all her mam could ever do was rest, so why would she not welcome a visit from them once a week or so? But she'd not brought it up again, and after a while her mam had returned to living only in her head, and she rarely thought of the grave that must be bare of any offering, tended to by a groundskeeper, whose only job it was to mow the grass in summertime.

The day of Welty's funeral was the first time she or her da had been back. It had been a clear day without wind, and what few clouds were in the sky hung fat and still, their underbellies bruised with coming rain. In the distance was the power station, and Keely remembers seeing the smoke and the fumes pouring out of the chimneys, canted stacks of it collapsing into one another. The world had bigger things on its mind than one little boy who was no longer breathing, who was still and silent in a wooden box that was being lowered into the ground.

IN THE ABSENCE OF her da, who's still refusing to get out of bed, Keely and Gordon spend all day working the coal. They drift away from the others and work alone, without the pressure of feeling they have to talk. Keely knows that if most people in the camp are grieving Welty's death, they're also secretly glad it isn't one of their own, and this gladness makes them guilty. Keely can sense it in them; she can see it scrawled across their drawn and guileless faces, and she's both angry and touched by it. She knows how much they care; she knows that most would do anything in their power to help. But she also knows that they can do nothing, and even though it's terribly unfair, she can't keep herself from resenting them.

Keely and Gordon take turns steering Immy and the cart through the waves, the other one of them with the shovel in their hands, thrusting it into the surf and sliding the glistening black lumps into the cart until it's full and chips start rolling down back into the sea.

They take it back to the camp and empty the cart bags. Immy hauls it over to the truck and they pull open the rear doors and start to load her up. Gordon drives and Keely rides in the passenger seat, and this is how they do the deliveries. She has a list of the addresses in her lap which she reads out for the orders that have been made, and Gordon peers through the grime of the windscreen, turning down the narrow streets of the town, pulling the truck to a stop with a great racket of clinks and clangs and the thunder of the spilling coal chips in the back.

When they're parked, Keely climbs into the back and drags the bags toward Gordon, who waits with a cigarette in his mouth, his face and hands black with dust. He lifts the bags down and places them by the doors of those on the list, and he waits until they answer his sharp knock and hand over the little money they ask for. There are some who can't pay, and Gordon nods and tells them that they'll be expected to add it on to the next delivery. Keely has heard her da say this before and for the most part he doesn't follow up on it. As long as they have enough to get by, then he doesn't want to be making other people's lives a misery.

But soon, she thinks, they won't have enough to get by.

She's already asked about working in the shop full-time and Mr Lister, the owner, has said that he'll consider it. She doesn't want to do it, doesn't want to be trapped inside all day under those dreadful lights that make everyone's faces look so drawn and jaundiced. She doesn't want to be holed up for weeks without feeling even the slightest hint of a breeze. She knows how much she would miss working on the beach. Even with all that happened there, she still loves the whip of the salt air, loves to breathe it in, loves the people of the camp, feels herself to be at home with them even in the difficult times they've been having.

But more and more addresses are being struck off the list. And she remembers her da telling her that the times are changing, that they'll soon be living in a different world, that the people in charge don't care about who they leave behind.

How, just once, she'd like to see him riled up. If her mam was still alive, she wonders if she'd have let him become so spiritless. Somehow, she doesn't think so.

By the last delivery, Keely's muscles ache, as if someone were playing a naked flame over her arms and legs, across the small of her back. Her body retreats into a previous iteration of itself, becoming stringy and hard, as lean as a boy's, a rejection of the gentle curves and swells with which she's been naturally endowed. It makes her feel self-conscious, and even when she has the rare opportunity to dress a little nicer, she sticks to the torn, baggy jumpers and jeans that she wears to work.

She remembers how she used to practise kissing on her shoulder when she was younger and Welty was asleep. The thought makes her smile. The other week, at Sarah's house in town, she'd had her first kiss with a boy, someone she'd never seen before but there he was, a friend of the boy Sarah liked.

She and Sarah have been hanging out more and more often, meeting after Keely has finished work and Sarah has finished school. Keely can no longer bear to spend time trapped in the caravan with her da. The world feels dark and cramped in his presence; he's a black, shapeless weight that she longs to crawl out from under, even if she's pricked by guilt when she returns home late at night and finds him alone and asleep in front of the TV, his face buckled in on itself, slack in the flare of light that flickers across his brow and cheeks.

But Sarah is all charm and laughter. Her company is like a hit of sherbet: everything looks brighter, moves quicker, and it makes Keely feel as if she's been living underwater. Sarah, like everyone else at school, had found out about Welty's death; but she's not once brought it up, which is the way Keely likes it. There are always other things to talk about, other things to do. Sarah is far better versed than Keely in all the trends: she listens to music, buys new clothes, watches films at the cinema – and she can talk about them all. Sarah can talk and talk and talk, but Keely doesn't mind. This is what she so loves about her, because what Keely needs is the relief of being able to sit and listen, the relief of having nothing else on her mind but the words that fly from between Sarah's glossy lips, watching the sweetly innocent, meaningless glow that radiates from her young skin.

The kiss with the boy had happened quickly under a full moon, the wind against the nape of Keely's neck. How different his lips had been to her own skin: their surprising heat, their hardness, and then the tentative dart of his tongue, touching hers, her teeth, frisking the gutter running between her gum and cheek. She'd felt his hand begin to slide up her inner thigh, his thumb moving toward the buttoned crotch of her jeans; but she'd caught him at the wrist and they'd been locked, briefly, in a struggle, their mouths still pressed together but with him trying to lift his hand and her pushing it down, until she'd spun away from him, smiling, her lips moist and plump and feeling almost sore. She'd climbed on her bike and, without saying a word, she'd ridden back home, the taste of his mouth still in hers and the feeling, for the first time in what seemed like years, that she was alive.

THE DAY ARRIVES WHEN her da finally gets back up. A Saturday. In the morning, she finds him in the kitchen, when darkness is still crowding the windows outside. He looks five years older. There are large bags under his eyes. His hair is thinner, and his T-shirt hangs off him. He has his belt in one hand and a knife, pointed down and turning round and round, in the other. He's making another hole in the leather because his jeans don't fit him anymore. She can see them now, like tired bunting below his hips, falling away from the bones of his arse.

You need to eat more, she says.

He turns and smiles at her.

That makes two of us, he says.

She wants to tell him to be serious, to listen properly to what she's saying, but she knows better than to argue with him so soon after he's dragged himself back into the world.

She's spent the past few days thinking of a way to tell him that she might start working at the shop full-time. She thinks he'll be disappointed. She thinks he may construe it as a lack of faith in him and a lack of gratitude for all he's done for her. She knows that he takes pride in seeing her down on the beach, in seeing her work the shovel as well as any man can. The thought hasn't escaped her that with Welty gone, she's taken on two kinds of expectation.

But she can't bear the prospect of making him more miserable than he already is, so she decides against mentioning anything now. She only makes her way over to him and leans into the frail rigging of his side to breathe in the sour, beery, unwashed-sheets smell of him.

You need a shower, she says.

I do, he replies.

He lifts the kettle and pours the steaming water into two mugs. She fetches the milk from the small fridge under the counter and splashes some in both of them. The tea-bags bob about. They both like to drink it with them still in.

The radio plays. They sit at the table and watch as some light creeps into the sky above the camp. Lamps in the other caravans blink on and glow outwards. The dark shapes of bodies move behind the curtains. On the ground, heaps of coal that had been indistinguishable from shadow begin to resolve themselves. There's a scattering of bikes and other toys. The wind blows through the stands of grass, tugs at the dead weeds. There is beauty in all this. They both know it.

They finish their tea.

How about I take that shower? her da says.

She smiles and nods as he stands up.

Come on then, he says.

Her brow furrows as she watches him head over to the door and start pulling his boots on.

What're you doing? she asks.

He bends down to tie his laces and looks up at her, his face red with the rush of blood.

Going for a shower, he says.

He marches through to his bedroom and returns with his towel, then opens the door, breathes in the cold rush of air.

You coming? he asks.

He used to do this sometimes when Welty was alive. It didn't matter what the weather was like. She and Welty would wake to find their da in a good mood. He would be full of winks and smiles and extra sprinklings of sugar on their cereal. And when they'd realize what he was up to, they would race to fetch their towels and come back giggling with excitement.

She goes now and grabs her own towel from her room. The last time they'd done this must have been four or five years ago. Still she feels the pleasant twang and flutter in her stomach. She slips on her boots and finds her da waiting for her outside, his towel thrown over his shoulder, his hands in his pockets, his face lifted to the brightening sky. She thinks his eyes are closed but when he hears her shut the door behind her, he opens them and he smiles, his eyes shining.

Ready? he says.

The wind frisks them, pulls at her da's long and knotted hair. He almost looks as if he's glowing; and the way he's moving, the way he seems to be getting lighter with each step, he has the look of an angel fated to return to heaven.

She thinks she might tell him this. She knows it'll make him laugh. But she doesn't, because there's something between them that she doesn't want to disturb. So they just walk, up into the dunes where they can see the sea stretch out, and both of them pause to look at it, just as every sea-coaler does before heading down to work.

Calm, says her da.

She nods and watches the white surf feather the black

shore. There's a thin seam of custard-coloured sky on the horizon. Above it a layer of lilac and then a vast sheet of softly brooding grey that reaches out toward them, stretching over their heads and carrying on behind them.

They find the track and her da bows slightly, gesturing with the flat of his palm for her to go first, as if they're at some fancy restaurant of the kind she's seen in films. She attempts to curtsy in return, but in her jeans there's no skirt to hold on to, so she bends her knees and pinches the air instead, as if there are two corners of fabric she's gripping. He laughs. Then, with her back excessively straight and her chin thrust haughtily out, she goes down the sloping track toward the low clamour of the sea.

She hears her da's thick-soled boots crunching down on the coal chips behind her. He skids a little and she turns to see him steadying himself with a handful of scrub. He lifts his eyes. They're shining still. She smiles back at him and then she turns and sees it all – the beach, the sea, the sky – and she's visited by the strangest feeling. It's as if she's at the centre of the world, as if the sky were one great peeled eye staring down at just her and no one else. The coal is wet and glistening. Her blood hums in her ears and she closes her eyes. She wants to sink to her knees and offer her thanks, but she's not sure to who or what. She wants to crack herself open and lay herself bare, have whatever is inside her seen and touched and understood by something greater than herself.

She feels the distance between her and Welty closing.

When she turns, she sees that her da is already stripped to the waist; he, too, has his face turned to the sky, his eyes closed. Tears track his cheeks. He opens his eyes and looks at her and she knows that he has the same glimmer trapped inside him, and even though it's ebbing away, second by second, the world returning to how it was, how it is, they both stare at one another and savour it.

Her da hasn't seen her undress since she was a child. But she feels no shame or embarrassment as she takes off her coat and shirt, undoes the laces of her boots and pulls down her jeans so that she stands on the coal with nothing on but her bra and knickers. The wind whips her hair about, frets the skin at the back of her arms until it's pink and raised. But she doesn't fold herself against it; she doesn't feel the cold.

Her da looks even skinnier with only his boxer shorts on. She notices sprigs of greying hair on his chest, around his nipples. His towel is folded over his shoulder. His knees and ankles look hard and misshapen. His feet are already black with the coal, and when she looks down she sees that her own are too.

They walk together toward the water.

Their steps are slow and steady so as not to slip. The roar of the surf gets louder and the wind blows the light across the waves. The water touches their toes first, foams up over their feet and wraps around their ankles. Neither of them realizes it, but they're holding hands.

3

HE'S MANAGED TO FIND A JOB AS A SALESMAN SELLING vacuum cleaners. One of his old friends, he says, a man Keely doesn't know and has never heard of, does the same and tells him it's not a bad life. Plenty of moving around, seeing the sights.

It'll be a breeze compared to lugging around all that coal, he says. And you'll not find yourself stuck at home, trapped inside like a fly banging your head against the window. Always somewhere to be, always somewhere new to go.

Keely can see why the idea appeals to her da, but she doesn't want him to do it. It means he'll be away a lot, and she'll be on her own in the small flat that they've rented in town. The idea of coming back from the shop on the dark, cold evenings that are on their way and finding that there's no one there fills her with dread. She knows she'll want to be back at the camp, will want to be able just to open her door and find Ruth or Evelyn, or see Mick marching over the dunes in the distance in his belted overcoat, tugging on his sideburns.

But she says nothing to him. This is what he wants, and she hopes that maybe by spending time away, by breathing in the air of all these different places, he might find that he wants to come back, and that whatever connection he'd wanted to sever is, in fact, made stronger.

Keely had waited a long time until she'd finally told her da about deciding to work full-time in the shop, fully expecting that he'd be upset. But when she'd done it, he'd looked relieved, almost happy.

We should move, he'd said right away. We should get a place in town.

And it was only then that she realized how much he wanted to be gone himself, how he'd been waiting for an excuse like this to be away from the sea, away from what had been haunting him.

They'd left within the month. Her da had sold the caravan on, and he'd sold the truck to Gordon, who was going to stay on at the camp and keep Immy with him a little longer. He replaced the truck with a small red car, a tired-looking thing with rust around the wheel arches that he immediately started teaching her to drive in.

When she'd said her goodbyes – to Gordon, to Ruth, to Mick and Evelyn and all the rest – she'd not been able to stop crying. For hours and hours, tears had streamed down her face. Even the next day, she'd woken up and her eyes had been damp. These were people that she'd known all her life, and even though they'd not be far away, she knew that it would never be the same again. The camp is a circle, and once you leave it, it will join back up without you, and you'll always be left on the outside.

She'd gone to see Immy in her stable, and she'd made sure to breathe in the sharp, sour pull of the straw and dung that she'd loved since she was a little girl. Leaning over the door and staring into the half-light, Keely watched Immy plod slowly over to greet her; and she faced the slow, quiet shock of how completely this animal seemed to know her – better, she then thought, than any human could claim to. She spent an hour just resting her head against the long, hard plane of Immy's face, feeling the warm jets of air that left her flaring nostrils, letting her tears dampen the silk-smooth muzzle, until finally Keely had turned and walked away, choosing not to look back into the dark eyes that she knew would be watching her go.

Now they're in town, sharing a small flat on a street of narrow, red-brick houses. She settles into working full-time in the shop. She brings with her a book roughly folded in her coat pocket to read on her lunch break, which she takes in a back room, sat on a chair that she likes to push back and lean against the wall on. Her days are largely the same. She talks to the newspaper boys, makes sure they know their routes. She switches on the lights, stands still as they flicker to life. She does everything that's asked of her. She smiles brightly at each and every customer that walks through the door. They know her name and she knows theirs. Even without her telling them, they appear to be privy to certain details about her private life, where she's now living and what her da is up to.

On her lunch, she reads twenty or thirty pages. She doesn't know it but she's a quick reader, can go through two or sometimes three books in a week. She has no one else to compare herself to. No one else she knows reads, and it's treated as an eccentricity. When Mr or Mrs Lister see the book swinging in her pocket, or if they happen to catch her reading at lunch, neither of them can ever help remarking on it. Here she is, reading again. What have you got your nose in now?

She can't imagine her life without books and she thanks Miss Collins every day for dropping that first bag off outside the caravan. She doesn't know how else she would fill her time, or what else could possibly feel as satisfying. She is filled up by words. Whatever pain she suffers in her own life, the characters she reads about set to replenishing her, all of which has led her to treat books with a reverence that she affords nothing else. They are sacred to her, and though in her care they all wind up dog-eared, with pages folded down and spines cracked, she would mourn one if it was ever lost or damaged beyond use.

But even reading can't keep her from loneliness. It comes for her, nudging at her in the same way a fish might swim against the curvature of its bowl; and then, when she least expects it, it will lunge, with something sharp concealed up its sleeve that catches between her ribs and takes her breath away, that makes her long for the warmth and touch and sound of another body.

Though the flat is bigger than the caravan, it can feel more claustrophobic to her. Largely, she thinks, because her da is almost never there. For the first few weeks in his new job, he would come back on the days he was scheduled to. But after a while, she starts to receive phone calls from him on the nights that he's meant to be returning, telling her that he's snowed under with work and that he's having to stay out. His voice sounds strange on these calls, strangled or choked, as if he's suffering from a thick cold.

Keely often puts the phone down and feels herself welling up. Not just her eyes, which do flood with tears, but her whole body, rising from her feet all the way to the crown of her head. It's such a peculiar feeling that she has to sit down for a while for fear she might topple over. Each time he calls to say he's not coming home the sensation is worse, as if she's contracted a kind of degenerative disease.

There are times when he'll come back unexpectedly and surprise her. There'll be a knock at the door and when she opens it he'll be standing there, maybe with a gift in his hands – flowers or a teddy bear or a trashy book that he's picked up from a petrol station – and he'll be smiling in a way that she's never seen him smile before, as if he's forgotten how to do it, as if he's not actually looking at her but through her.

He'll sit down on the sofa and drink his tea and they'll talk for a while, each asking how the other has been. There's a strange formality to it, and after an hour she can already sense that he's restless, that he's fighting the urge to get up and leave again. It stuns and frightens her to consider how different he's become in such a short space of time. She thinks how he used to be back in the caravan, back when Welty had been alive – even if he felt weighed down by work or money problems, he was always there in a way that she knew he was present, available, ready to support her. Even after Welty had died and he'd had his bad days, she'd never felt this distance from him, this expanding separation.

The reality, when it finally hits her, is that these last years have been a gradual vanishing act, and she has the horrible suspicion that this is the final drawing of the curtain. What's still a mystery to her is how he spends his time when he's away, whether he's just the same, just as distant and restless with everyone else as he is with her, or if she's at the centre of it, a problem in his life that he wants rid of.

She finds out by accident.

Six months after leaving the camp, late at night when she's already in bed, Keely receives a phone call. She often falls asleep while reading, so she wakes with the lamp still on and her book awkwardly wedged against her neck. She rubs her eyes, waits for her head to clear. No one normally rings this late. She feels a slight flutter in her stomach, climbs out from beneath the covers, finds the phone in the darkness of the hall and lifts it up.

The plastic is cold against her ear. She hears her da's voice. Immediately she knows he's had a drink. He doesn't wait for her to speak but right away starts talking himself.

It's me, he says. I love you. You're all I want. I want what you want. I want what you talked about the other night.

At first, she thinks he's referring to a conversation that they'd had a week before. Keely had sat down opposite him after tea one night and she'd tried to convey all of her worries about him, about how she feels he's changed and how she wants him to come back more, or at least come back when he says he will. He hadn't said much at the time. He'd done a lot of nodding, but she hadn't been able to see much of his face, because he'd had his forearms resting on the table and he'd kept his eyes lowered.

But when she'd finished, when she'd asked him if he'd understood, he'd looked up and he'd smiled and the blue of his eyes had leapt out at her, and she thought that she'd broken through, that she'd seen a glimpse of the old him, and that everything was salvageable.

Now he's had a while to think about it and he's with her again, he's on her team and they're both after the same things. He's on the phone telling her that he loves her and that he wants everything she does. And even though it's late and she's tired, she's glad that he's decided to ring, that she's hearing his voice, and that there's a measure of the old warmth that used to be in it. She can imagine how he looks on the other end of the line, with his hand running through his hair and the creases at the corners of his eyes. She's sure that he's smiling, and she thinks it's strange that a smile is a thing that you can hear.

She's just about to speak and tell him how glad she is that he's called, when he says something that makes her grow very still.

Angela, he says. Angela, please believe everything I'm saying. It's you I want. It's only you.

At first, Keely thinks he must be so drunk that he's confused her name, and she opens her mouth to let out a strange kind of half-laugh.

But then he continues.

Angela, he says again, please listen to me. Let me come over now. I want to see you. Let me come over.

It dawns on Keely then that he's called the wrong

number. He'd intended to ring someone else, a woman she knows nothing about but who he apparently loves and is all he wants. A woman called Angela.

There are cold runnels down Keely's back. The phone in her hand feels brutally heavy and her wrist cocks under the strain of its weight. She wants to put it down, wants to rip it from the wall; but she holds on to it, and she can hear her da breathing on the other end, waiting for something to be said back to him.

He sniffs, clears his throat. He's crying now. He tries to say something else but sighs. She's heard him sigh like that a thousand times, and she can see the way his hand will be dragging down his face, pulling at his eyes, his nose, his lips.

Go to bed, Da.

She says these words and waits, listens as her da's breathing seems to stop.

Silence.

Only the slight crackle of the line between them. A shuffling noise. He's realized his mistake and she knows his eyes will suddenly be wide, his knuckles white as he grips the phone.

Keely? he says.

But she doesn't reply.

She doesn't slam the phone down but places it very gently back in its cradle. She doesn't walk back to her bedroom but goes to the kitchen where she knows her da keeps a bottle of whiskey, and she pours herself a mug. She sits down and sips at it slowly. She looks at nothing in particular but stares straight ahead at the fridge. She's tacked photos up on it with little coloured magnets. Some are of her mam. A few of Welty in his red windbreaker and her and their da. She knows that her da has seen them but he's never mentioned them. She's watched him whenever he reaches to get some milk out, has seen how he deliberately averts his eyes.

Her arm moves up and down to bring the mug to her lips. She's cold, very cold, but she does nothing to remedy it. Her body feels like it's slowing down, as if she's entering hibernation, a yawning space of warm and scented darkness that's opening up in front of her. She can grasp no single thought; they're all swarming in her head, crawling and lifting and humming with the rote industry of bees in a hive.

She continues like this for an hour, until her body starts to warm with the drink and her thoughts start to unknot themselves. She hears the words of her da again.

I love you. You're all I want. I want what you want. I want what you talked about the other night.

And then she thinks about the person they were intended for. Angela. And some of the shock returns to her, that her da should keep this from her, that he should have found a person to love and who clearly loves him, and not thought to explain any of it, not thought her worthy of being informed.

Slowly her shock starts to thaw into something closer to anger. It's not the fact that her da has found someone. For a long time she's wondered if he might ever find a partner, and even if the idea has made her feel uneasy on occasion, there have been plenty of moments when she's wished for it, has thought that having someone else, someone he could be close to, might bring him back from the isolation she knows he's been living in.

But to hear of it like this? Her anger builds, sharpens. He's been staying away and he's been lying, telling her that he's been working when the whole time he's been in another house, another home, leaving his daughter to spend night after night on her own without anyone to keep her company, to keep her safe. She has needed his love, and she'd thought the only reason he wasn't giving it to her was because of the demands of his job. But he's been keeping his love from her and he's been letting Angela, a perfect stranger to her, have as much of it as she wants.

She stands up, totters over to the sink, leans over and vomits up a thin string of whiskey. She wipes her chin with the sleeve of her pyjama top, sits back down, fills up her mug again. She thinks he might call back, but he doesn't. She tops her mug up again and again. When she next stands up, it's only two hours until she has to be at work. She's wobbly on her feet and she reaches out to steady herself with a palm braced against the table edge. She turns to face the window. Most of the sky is still dark, though there's the faintest bevel of light chinking in the distance.

SHE DOESN'T HEAR FROM him for over a week. She rings his friend, the man who got him the job, but he's of no use. She knows that he's only pretending not to know his whereabouts. She can hear it in his voice, a smugness, as if he knows more about her da's life than she does, and it infuriates her. She tells him to go fuck himself and slams the phone down.

At night, she's started to have a few mugs of whiskey at the table on her own before bed. Not too many, not as many as that first night. But she feels she needs them to soothe her, to round the corners of her thoughts so that they don't dig into her when she's trying to sleep. Otherwise she's up all night, tossing and turning, old memories of her and her da. Simple, ordinary things that must have been lying dormant for years spooling out behind her eyes.

The bottle runs out and she replaces it with tins of lager or cider. Her money is low as she's had to pay the rent using only her own wages. The tins aren't as strong and they don't give her that warm, woozy numbness quite so quickly, but the result is the same, and at the end of the night, she'll lift herself up from the table and her head will feel light, and when she tries to walk back to bed she has to use the wall, her fingers spanned and brushing along the corrugations of the radiator as she pushes herself along, her slippers shuffling across the floorboards.

When she wakes, her mouth is always dry, and there's the same deep throb of pain behind her eyes that she'd felt after their leaving party at the camp. She thinks about going back there after work one evening and telling Ruth, but she feels ashamed. She feels shame that she could love her da so much and yet mean so little to him. She knows Ruth would be furious, that she'd try and take matters into her own hands; Keely needs to feel in control of it herself.

The days pass but still she hears nothing, sees nothing of him. All she wants is to sit at the kitchen table and drink her tins. She has no appetite for anything other than that. It's not as if she has much weight to lose, but she gets thinner, her bones sharpening beneath her skin.

The more she needs people, the more disgusted she feels by the prospect of seeking them out. This is her reality. Time no longer seems to flow in the same way. It feels to her almost identical to grief, only she knows that the person she's missing isn't actually dead.

THE REALIZATION HAS COME so slowly to Keely, drip-fed over the years since Welty's death, that it's now accrued a power that frightens and confuses her: her da has neglected her. For years, he's been no more than a shell, a husk, and it's only now that he's physically started to remove himself from her life that she can see in sharp relief the scars of his absence.

Even when they were living back at the camp in the caravan, he wasn't there. He could be sitting next to her on the sofa, or standing by her side drinking a mug of tea, but he wasn't there, not really. He'd already retreated into himself, refusing to look out at the world, no longer receiving and engaging with it but simply drifting through it, stricken dumb beneath the glare of his own suffering.

At the time, Keely had felt only sympathy for him. Even though she was still a child, after years of looking after Welty, her sense of duty was a keenly honed impulse; it had seemed natural that she minister to her da, that she be the one to rally, to coax, to persevere; and even when she'd been overwhelmed herself, it was she and she alone who'd found the resolve to herd the darkness away and seek the light.

Because Keely knew she was being presented with a choice. What had happened to Welty couldn't ever be forgotten or fixed; it would always be inside her, this terrible, broken half of herself begging and pleading to be put out of its misery. But there was still a choice to be made, a choice between the living and the dead. The dead don't need saving, but the living do. And she had needed saving. Over and over again, she had needed her da to keep her head above the water.

But he never had. And now he's not only disappeared, refusing to face her and their issues, but he's sought out another person into whom he can decant all the love that she'd worked so hard to replenish in him. It's perfectly plausible he might not have even mentioned her to this woman, this woman that she's tried to picture, that she might have walked past a hundred times in the street. Very easily, he could have managed to keep her out of any conversation, even invented an entirely different life for himself, fashioned himself another past.

Angela. She'll be in some other town or village, miles away, with a name she may not even have heard of. Possibly in a house or a charming little cottage with a family of her own, with her da being the one to plug the space that's been left behind by some other man. Because this, she is realizing, is one of the things men are best at: turning their backs on the things they're meant to love and walking in the other direction.

Why could he not have stayed with her? What was it about her that had driven him away?

These questions will not leave her alone. Now it's anger she feels, a fierce, scouring heat that pushes its way around her entire body, that dries out her eyes and makes her skin feel sensitive to even the slightest touch. She wants to break things. She can be making dinner, following one of the recipes Ruth had given her, when she will suddenly pick up the pan and strike it hard enough against the iron grid of the hob for sparks to veer blindly on to the front of her apron. More than once, she's been at the draining board with a tea towel when, without thinking, she's flung a glass across the room, and she's been glad to see it spray and shard across the floor.

It steals upon her so swiftly, this fury, that she grows worried she'll hurt someone. There is no one thing that can set it off. The triggers are so many, and some of them so innocuous, that she can feel an intense rush of loneliness, as if the entire world has been created purely to antagonize her.

IT'S A FRIDAY NIGHT when Keely's da finally returns. Sarah is over. They've been drinking and talking for hours, passing a bottle of gin between them with the radio on, singing snatches of any song that's near the top of the charts. When either of them stands up to go for a piss, they burst into snorting fits of laughter at the feebleness of their own legs, knock-kneed and swaying from wall to wall, groping through the shadows of the hall toward the toilet.

When Keely hears a knock at the door just after nine, she knows it's her da. She can tell by the weight of it, timid and cowardly, barely loud enough to hear over the music.

Sarah looks at her, her eyes rolling slightly, her fringe mussed and lifting free of her pale brow.

Who's that? she slurs.

It's him, says Keely.

Sarah hoists her eyebrows high on to her forehead but says nothing as Keely lifts herself up out of her chair. The room carousels around her. She places her palms flat on the table to steady herself then inhales deeply, closing her eyes and rolling them into the back of her head. When she opens them, she points to the spittled dregs left in the bottle of gin.

Give me that.

Sarah's eyes slide over to the bottle; she stares vacantly at it for a moment and then nudges it toward Keely with the backs of her knuckles. Keely picks it up and takes a swig, sharply throwing back her head so that her hair snaps out of her eyes and her face is flushed white by the shade-less bulb hanging above her.

She moves over toward the door, widening her eyes to try and focus properly. She breathes heavily through her nose. She can taste the gin at the back of her throat, the dry, bitter throb of it. She doesn't feel nervous, and yet she can feel her heart pulsing hard and fast behind her left ear.

As soon as she opens the door, she knows that he's only come back to leave for good. Right away she can see that he's been crying, the rims of his eyes pink and agitated. She knows it, knows it better than anything she's ever known before – he is about to do something terrible.

He says nothing to her, and he refuses to look her in the eye. He doesn't embrace her, doesn't bring her to him like he used to. She simply staggers to one side and gestures for him to enter, then watches as he skulks down the hall to his room without even glancing in Sarah's direction.

Sarah stands up at the table, swaying under the glare of the bulb.

Where's he gone now? she says.

His room, says Keely.

What's he doing in there then?

Keely takes another swig of gin, exposing the blotchy length of her neck.

Let's go have a look, shall we?

The girls link arms and veer down the hall toward Keely's da's room. Like eavesdropping children, they press their ears against the door, half whispering and half giggling to one another. In the pockets of silence that break out, they hear the zip of a bag, drawers opening, old, thick-soled boots moving across the cold wooden floorboards.

Sarah reaches out, steadies her hand theatrically, and then knocks on the door.

Could you hurry up in there? I need to use the bathroom please, she says.

Instantly, she drops to her knees and collapses into hysterics. Her lungs heave as she tries to catch her breath, but when she looks up through the wild curtain of her hair expecting to find Keely in a similar state of disarray, she sees that Keely isn't looking at her. Keely is staring at the door and tears are streaming down her cheeks.

You OK, Kee? Sarah asks, climbing more steadily now to her feet and placing a hand on her shoulder.

But Keely doesn't answer her. Without a word, she begins kicking at the door, the sole of her boot slapping against it, rattling it against the frame, the small brass handle hopping and clucking away. She can feel the thud of her heart trapped at her temples and her shin and thigh simmer with pain but she doesn't stop, connecting now with her heel as the door begins to whine and buckle, the wood splintering at the hinges, until finally it springs open and hangs drunkenly, a hard, glacial wedge of light spilling out the room and on to Keely, making her eyes narrow slightly.

She can't see her da at first, only the rumpled edge of his bed through the motes of dust roiling in the air.

Kee?

Keely turns. It's Sarah. She's at the other end of the hall, her bag on her shoulder, her blue eyes wide and her face stunned into a pale mask of temporary sobriety. She stretches her mouth wide, and with gritted teeth she shrugs and leaves the flat, tiptoeing as she goes, closing the door behind her.

When Keely turns back, she finds that her da is standing in the doorway, his black bag slung over his shoulder. They stare at one another. He's wearing his ripped and faded jeans, his old fleece coat. He looks older to her, the lines of his face grooved deeper, his hair shot through with more bands of white. Everything he needs, she knows, is in that bag. When they'd moved from the camp, he'd not wanted to bring much, had left almost everything behind. Now he's taking himself to another place, away from her, a place he's yet to even tell her about.

He walks by her, close enough that she can smell him, that old mix of sweat and coal and beer. She doesn't want to but she can't keep herself from reaching out and touching him. She is a tiny, helpless girl, clutching at his sleeve as she follows him down the hall.

Please, she begs, please please please.

But he keeps moving until he gets to the kitchen where she has the space to move around in front of him. She places her hand flat against the bones of his chest. She can feel the drum of his heart. His boots point squarely forward. Though just a moment ago she'd thought him aged, there's now something boyish in him, like a naughty child that's been summoned before the headmaster. The hand that grips the strap of his bag bulges white and yellow. Those hands. She stares at them, fascinated by them. How many times have they held hers? How many times have they lifted her up?

The fridge with all of the old photographs pinned to it churns and hums. Cars drive by outside the window, their tyres whispering on roads black with rain. His skin looks as thin as parchment. His hair is on end, made to reach in so many different directions by the hand that she knows he must have been running through it.

Please, says Keely. Talk to me.

He closes his eyes and hangs his head. His free hand, still cracked and dry after years of toil in the sea, reaches up to pinch the bridge of his nose.

I can't stay here, he says.

The words come thickly from his mouth, as if his tongue has grown too big for it.

He still doesn't lift his head when he says, I can't do it anymore.

She sees a tear slip from his face, briefly catch the light, then darken the grain of the floor. She lets her own tears roll down her cheeks, lets her nose run as well, two bright slicks that will dry and that she'll later have to rub away with a rinsed flannel.

Where are you going? she asks.

It comes out as a whisper, but it makes him lift his face up, the blue of his eyes leaping out in the light.

He shakes his head.

She breathes in and out, in and out.

Where are you going?

She means only to whisper it again, but this time it comes out ragged and furious and full of the need that she has for him. She doesn't want to show it. She wants to be strong enough to simply turn away. She wants him to be pleading with her; but all that she's been keeping inside is clamouring to be let loose. Her body feels charged with fury, that same fury she doesn't know how to manage or use.

She looks down and finds that the bottle of gin is still in her hand.

I'll still be paying my half, he says.

She can't believe what she's hearing. Her fist tightens around the neck of the bottle and she feels her scalp prickle, tighten.

I asked where you're going, she says. I couldn't give a fuck about your money.

This isn't true. She knows that she'll need it, but she's boiling over with ways to hurt him, ways to make him feel small. He looks at her now and she's not sorry to see fear in his eyes. He's afraid, and he should be, because she finds that she has the bottle held high above her, ready to come crashing down onto the crown of his skull in a second.

Her da steps back, but he trips and lands on the floor,

his bag sliding away behind him. Her knuckles whiten at their tips. She breathes through her nose, great gusts that sweep from her and that she draws back in. She is full of energy, coursing through every part of her, every muscle and bone, every fibre.

How easy it would be.

Where are you going? she says.

Her voice is low now, flat and hard.

You know where, he says.

Still he doesn't have the courage to tell her; still he would rather just leave, would rather close the door behind him and not have to think about her. But she will make him think about her. She will make him spill it all.

I want you to tell me, she says.

He looks up at her, her face slashed with shadow beneath her raised arm.

Angela's, he says. I'm going to live with her.

He curls on to his side, draws his knees up, scrunches his fists to cover his face. His shoulders start to shake, then his whole body.

I can't be here, he says. I can't do it anymore.

She's furious with him. Furious because Welty's death has stopped him living. Because he's allowed it to take, year by year, a little more of himself away from her, the only one that still needs him and has a use for him.

She could still strike him.

For a moment she thinks she has it in her. She could kill him, and everything would be solved. She could leave him here and no one would find him for days.

But she drops the bottle and hears it roll along the floor.

She takes the keys from the table and she leaves him lying there, sobbing, still shaking.

She walks out the door and steps into the street. The sky is black and the mizzle of the rain shoals down in the orange flare of the streetlights. It feels cool on her face. Down the road she sees the glow of the pub windows, hears the din from inside. She heads there and ducks into the dark doorway, smells the smoke, soaks up the chatter and the laughter.

She sits on a stool and orders. She talks to no one, only stares, lifts her face to the lights and closes her eyes, opens them and throws a look down the length of bar, at the shimmering rings of beer and gin and rum and whiskey. People lean with forearms and palms, feet propped on the brass rail. She knows plenty of faces. They smile and say hello and she wonders if she's smiling back.

When she finally blunders her way back home, she opens the door and finds that he's gone. Everything is as it was before he left. Only she sees something else, a blue and white plastic bag like the ones from the butcher's. She doesn't have to open it to know that he's left his half.

FOR HER, THERE'S NO other real desire. If she is a door, locked and iced shut, then drink is the warm, glowing key that's been pressed into her palm. It's happened quickly, her reliance on it. She never feels like she needs it until she needs it, until the prospect of spending the night alone with her own thoughts hits her, and she reasons that the drink is actually helping her, that it's a contributing factor to her ongoing survival.

She goes down to the shop. Not the shop she works at, but the other shop which is around half a mile walk away. It's a shameful process. She never catches the shopkeeper's eye; she always wears something with a hood, makes sure that her face is mostly shadowed. She skulks and veers to keep out of people's way. She's less likely to be recognized by anyone here, but there are still plenty of times when she's been caught off guard.

It's not that anyone would think it so odd that she's there, but her sense of paranoia sharpens by the day. The more she drinks the less she sleeps, and the more aware she feels of herself, of how she's being perceived by those around her. She feels as if her eyes move too quickly in their sockets. She can't seem to keep her hands still. She imagines that people can see inside her head, can see the great black tangle of fear and pain and anger at work there.

She's late to work on a morning most days now, and Mr and Mrs Lister ask her if everything's all right. They've become cautious around her, inquiring with soft, low voices, their faces lined with worry. She tells them nothing of what's happened. They're kind people and she likes them a great deal, but she has no interest in sharing her private life with them. She can't afford to lose her job – if she talks too much, she fears they might sense the unease in her, the imbalance, and seek someone else.

The money her da has given her is a cushion, no more. She doesn't know if he'll send any more. She hopes he will, hopes it'll be a monthly thing. But she can't be sure. She hasn't heard a word from him, has no idea where he is.

She has no idea what's going to happen.

She still goes into the charity shop to buy books. But whenever she sits down on the sofa and opens one up, she finds that she can't concentrate. Her mind is never still, never empty. That night with her da, with him on the floor and her holding the bottle, comes back to her. She turns a page, and there it is again. Other memories, too. It's like the entire contents of her mind have been unmoored, free to drift in and out of her reality as they please.

At the weekend, the pub, any pub, is where she wants to be. It doesn't matter what time of the day it is, whether it's morning or afternoon or at night. As soon as she steps through the door, as soon as she smells the warm sour pull of the spilled beer, sees the rows and rows of bottles stacked behind the bar, she feels something shift inside her. She is alive again, as if she's been breathing the wrong type of air, as if she's been living underwater.

Within an hour of arriving, she finds that she's laughing or singing or dancing, and she knows there are men looking at her and wanting to touch her, wanting to have their lips against hers and their tongues in her mouth, rooting about as if in search of something she's kept secret from them.

Pressed against a wall or behind the closed door of a cubicle, it's always at this moment that she wants to shrug whoever it is off and away from her. This is her instinct, but she only ever pulls them closer. Grips them around the neck and sometimes bites them, has more than once drawn blood from their lips or cheek; and she'll either cop a slap or punch for it, or she'll find herself tugging at his belt, unbuttoning his jeans, the hard warmth of him inside her mouth as his hand pushes down on the back of her head.

Nothing matters on these days.

When she's with them, these men, the things that have haunted her, the things that in sobriety cling to her and throw their full weight down upon her are suddenly, miraculously lifted. There is space again inside her. Different wants and needs, those connected purely with her body, are stirred back into motion. She can feel the hot thread of her blood in her arms, in her hands, in the very tips of her fingers. Tears sometimes stream from her eyes without her even knowing. People will stop her and ask if she's OK, and she'll look at them, her brow furrowed with confusion, until she reaches up and feels the dampness herself, feels the tears running down her face; and she'll laugh, laugh so hard that she falls down, and sometimes must be carried to a quiet corner to sleep.

As little as ten minutes later, she'll wake with a second wind, and it's as if the night has started all over again. She wants another drink, wants another dance, wants to keep meeting people, must keep laughing.

But there are times when she doesn't wake up, or she wakes hours later, tucked away down an alley and curled behind a dustbin, the wind blowing and her body shaking. She rises stiffly to her feet and rubs her eyes, not knowing where she's been or how she's got there. She sees time jumping forward, leaping back. Flashes of light, colour. Faces: eyes and mouths and teeth and tongues. Sweat patches beneath arms and on backs. A damp curl behind an ear. A gold-link chain nestled in the scuzzy shock of a man's chest. Details that she can't piece together.

She's still not been back to the camp. If Ruth calls her, she tells her that she's too busy to see her. She knows that Mick and Evelyn have moved away, and Gordon too. Immy has gone with him. She doesn't know where they've gone, they've just gone. The camp is slowly closing down, and so is she.

IT'S THE WEEK BEFORE Christmas and Friday rolls around again. There's a buzz around the town. The air is bitingly cold and people are wrapped up in coats, scarves, gloves – all of which Keely wears to work and keeps on through the day to fend the chill that seeps in every time a customer enters or leaves.

The pub is embracing the festive spirit, different coloured lights slung from the guttering and tinsel tacked to the edge of the bar and up along the shelves. Everything shines or winks. Christmas trees in the windows of nearly every house, electric candles lit and shimmering behind muslin curtains, the televisions seeming to flicker more warmly, splashing colour in mirrors, against walls.

She hasn't seen her da in over two months. She's received another sum of money to go toward the rent in the post, but the envelope had no return address on it. No note, nothing. The only way she knew it was him was from his handwriting, the small, cramped letters smudged by the clumsiness of his fist.

She's working only the morning shift today because she's booked the afternoon off to start the festivities early. Sarah has done the same, getting the afternoon off from her work as a receptionist. Their plan is to listen to some music and have a few drinks in Keely's flat and then, at around seven, head to the pub.

As usual, a band have been booked to play. There's a little stage over by the toilets where four people and their instruments can just about squeeze on. Some very strange acts have played over the years. Billy, the old landlord, still plays in a punk band himself. His hair is dyed jet black and both of his ears are hooped and studded with various rings and balls. With his leather trousers and shin-high boots, he's copped a bit of stick from some of the locals since he bought the place, but slowly his eccentricities began to appeal, and the pub's gained something of a reputation for giving acts – comedians, poets, bands – a chance to do their thing.

Keely gets back from her morning shift at the shop. Mrs Lister has taken over behind the till. She knows that Keely's going out and may even see her later in the pub if she and Mr Lister decide to venture out. It's the sort of night when even the tamest people in the town make an appearance and have a drink.

Keely showers, dresses, puts on her makeup. She's started to notice that her skin looks sallower recently. She gives in to the need to put a little more foundation on. Still, she feels attractive, as if most men would want to be with her. It seems strange to her sometimes that this is how she thinks these days. There'd been a time, not so long ago, when she'd barely put a single thought into men or how she might be perceived by them. She'd been aware of them, but not in quite the same way that she is now. Now, there can be times when it's all she's able to think about.

The fridge is stocked with cans and she's bought a bottle of white wine that she and Sarah can share. Neither of them really like it, but it's Christmas and she feels they might as well have something a little different. Plus, wine, when she's drunk it in the past, gives her a slightly different kind of buzz, one she feels keeps her mood higher.

She looks at her watch. It's nearly one thirty. Sarah was meant to be here half an hour ago. She's always late, but she'll likely turn up any minute, bustling down the corridor and throwing the door open, immediately launching into some story or other. So she opens a can and sits at the table. She's in heels and she's wearing a new dress that she found in the charity shop, a little black sequined thing that hugs her slight frame and makes her bum look bigger than it is, which she's pleased about.

When it turns two, Sarah still hasn't arrived.

A minute later, the phone rings. Keely rises to answer it, shimmies her dress down her legs and totters over to the small table where the phone is. It's Sarah. Her boss won't let her leave until she's finished something that's come up, even though she clearly booked it off weeks ago.

I'm not going to get out for another few hours, she says, so you'll just have to start without me. But don't get too fucked, otherwise I might as well not come at all.

They agree to meet at the pub at seven. That gives Keely a good few hours to fill. She's only had one can, so she could pick up a book, maybe even have a nap; but she's tried to read before going out before and she's found it impossible – there's too much energy in her, too much expectation, to keep still.

It's still only just past two and the pub won't shut for another hour. She decides that she might as well go out and have a little drink. See who's there. Get a feel for what the evening might hold, and then she'll come back and decide what to do from there.

She changes her heels for the flats she wears at work, because she doesn't want her feet to be aching. It's bitterly cold outside. The sky is flat and grey and the sun a pale, drifting disc offering no warmth whatsoever. She can smell a hint of salt drifting in from the sea and it briefly takes her back to the camp, to the dunes, to the dark night she'd found Welty.

But she shakes her head and forces herself to think only of now, of the pub coming into view in the distance. Her breath fogs and her nose runs. Even in her coat, she feels the need to fold her arms and tuck her hands beneath her armpits. She can feel her makeup stiffening unpleasantly when the wind blows, and she keeps having to lift the tip of her index finger up to the corners of her eyes to keep them from running.

There's a good crowd in the pub. There must be a few Christmas parties going on. It's warm and stuffy and filled with smoke; the windows are steamed up and most people already look well oiled, their faces red, glistening slightly. Coats are thrown over the backs of chairs. Mistletoe hangs at various points from the ceiling. Music's playing, all the

Christmas songs, the old croony ones and some of the newer ones as well.

She doesn't recognize many people, nods to the few that she does. She squeezes in at the bar and orders herself a drink. She'll have one drink here, maybe two, and when they close at three, she'll head back to hers and put some music on, do her best to keep herself under control until she can head back out to meet Sarah when the pub opens again.

She's been there maybe ten minutes when she sees him.

The old friend of her da's, the man who got him the job working as a salesman. She'd rung him months ago now. He seems to be part of a large group, and for a second she thinks that maybe her da might be here. She looks around, standing on her tiptoes, but he's nowhere to be seen.

The man – she forgets his name – is drunk. He's small, balding, with close, pug-like features and a large barrel chest that strains against the buttons of his shirt. His hair is thin, biscuit coloured, combed over his sweating pate. He's dancing a little with a woman who's much taller than him and who doesn't appear, by the look on her face, to be enjoying whatever he's breathing in her ear.

Keely stays where she is, propped against the bar. Her elbows are damp and tacky with spilled beer, but she doesn't care. She keeps the man fixed in the corner of her eye, making sure not to present the whole of her face to him. It's unlikely that he'll recognize her; he's only met her once, and he'd been in the pub then as well. It had been a couple of weeks after he and her da had started working together. Her da had made out that he was someone worth meeting, a real character, but all she remembers is being bored and moving swiftly away to talk to someone else.

She doesn't know what she's going to do, but she can feel a restlessness building in her, the first spike of unease that she knows can quickly morph into something more boisterous, more dangerous.

She could leave.

She could forget that she's seen him and continue with her day, go home, wait until Sarah arrives, and by the time they return he'll surely be gone, moved on to some other place or passed out in a taxi home.

But she can't leave. She won't allow herself to. It's an opportunity to do something, and even though she has no idea what that something is, she suddenly feels her legs carrying her through the crowd toward him, pressing between the bodies, angling herself so that she can fit through the slight gaps that open up. She can feel sweat prickling her hairline, and she briefly thinks about how difficult it will be this evening to navigate such a crowd in the heels she's planning to wear.

Then she's upon him, tapping his shoulder, and he's turning to her, his bunched face damp and red, his small eyes searching her own in confusion.

What d'you want?

The woman he's been talking to slinks away, glancing back over her shoulder.

Eric's daughter, she says.

The man pauses, searches his brain for an Eric, seems to find it. His features rearrange themselves. He smiles, stretches out both his arms as if to embrace her.

Eric's a top man, he says. One of the best.

The music is louder over here. He draws in his arms, picks up his drink from a table, then turns back to her.

What can I do for you? he asks.

He winks when he says it, loses his balance slightly, then corrects himself with a slight redistribution of his considerable bulk. Now that she's closer to him, Keely can almost feel his weight, and she can smell the sharp, raw scent of him. His neck is a thick stump of bunched flesh and his shoulders slope imperceptibly into his arms, both of which don't so much hang by his sides as remain awkwardly suspended a little, as if he were wearing armbands.

You can give me his address, she says.

He shakes his head, though he's still smiling now, enjoying himself. He's the sort of man who takes every interaction to be a part of his own private game. In his head, he acknowledges that he's the underdog, but if he boxes clever there's a girl who's under half his age that could be nudged in the direction of his bed.

That wouldn't be right, he says. Not my business to be getting involved with you and your daddy. If he's taken himself off, then he must've had his reasons.

He turns away from her slightly as if he's about to leave. But, he says, I might be persuaded.

His porcine eyes roll ceilingward and with one stubby finger he points up at a clutch of mistletoe that happens to be hanging above them.

For a kiss I might be persuaded, he says.

No one has ever looked more revolting to her. This is the man her da works for. She imagines the pair of them drinking together, jawing away, and she feels her fist bunch at her side. She could drive it into his nose before he'd even know what happened. Then she could stomp and kick and scratch at him when he was on the floor. She sees it all in her mind's eye and her palms start to sweat.

All right, she says.

She smiles at him.

Give me the address first.

The man flashes a set of teeth browned by tobacco.

Have it your way, he says. For now.

He turns, finds his coat on the back of a chair and plunges his fat, babyish hand into one of the inner pockets. He retrieves a small black notebook. Keely watches as he feverishly flicks through the pages, and when he finds what he's looking for, he holds it out to her.

Only an hour from here, she hears the man say.

She looks down and reads the few lines under the name Eric. She recognizes the name of the village. She's heard it before, she thinks. There was a boy who Sarah used to see there. How strange, Keely thinks, remembering Sarah's voice complain about the journey. She reads the lines three more times until she knows she has it in her head.

She looks up, still smiling.

Well? he says.

He looks back up at the mistletoe, at the finger-shaped leaves and the small white orbs. He starts to lean in toward her, his fleshy lips slick with beer. But she has her drink still in her hand, and she lifts it up and throws the rest of it in his face. It makes a sound like a single handclap as it's dashed against the flushed skin of his cheeks. The man's hands go up to his face and he staggers back, rubbing at his eyes and crying out a litany of obscenities.

Keely senses that people have turned to look, but she doesn't care. She's already moving through the crowd, repeating over and over and over again the lines of her da's address in her head.

SHE'S ON THE BUS. Strangely, she's never been on one before. They drove in the truck at the camp, and since they moved to town she's had no need to travel anywhere else. She doesn't like the gaudy colours of the seats, and she doesn't like how brightly lit it is. One light flickers on and off, humming like the fridge back in the flat.

She doesn't know what she'll say or what she'll do when she arrives, but she's on her way. She's written the address down on a slip of paper and tucked it away in her pocket. She's brought some of the cans with her. She has one in her hand now, which she periodically lifts to her mouth, sipping away until it starts to lighten in her grip.

It's nearly four o'clock. She'll be back by seven to meet Sarah – she's sure. The sky is already nearly dark. Just a sliver of colour left in it, a shade close to lavender. Cars and their headlights rush by and sweep across her face. She stares out the window: at the houses with their twinkling lights, at the glow of Christmas trees in the windows, at the people together inside.

She's sitting near the front. The bus is almost empty but for three young boys on the back row, the middle one with a football in his lap. They chatter excitedly between themselves.

She remembers when she'd been that age, the Christmases they'd had in the caravan. She and Welty up late on Christmas Eve talking about what might be waiting for them under the little fake tree that their da put up each year. And then waking up early on the day and discussing it some more before they were allowed to get their da up.

When the clock hand finally reached seven, their da would groan and turn over as they leapt on to his bed; and he'd pretend that he wasn't going to get up, that he was going to go back to sleep for another few hours. But they'd keep shaking him and shaking him until finally he'd rise and he'd flick the lights of the tree on and boil the kettle while they tore through their little pile of gifts.

She opens another can. It foams and she lifts it quickly to her mouth. It's cold and slides harshly down her throat. She can feel her mind and her body loosening. Her heart was pounding when she'd walked out of the pub, half expecting to be followed. But no one had come after her.

She hasn't changed – she's still in her dress, though she's put on a warmer coat, an old duffel that she's had for years with horned toggles and a heavy hood, which she decides to pull up now as the bus stops and an old couple walk on together, all grey hair and shrivelled faces, walking sticks and beige cardigans. The driver waits as they shuffle down the aisle and sit down on the two seats directly adjacent to her.

Keely pulls back her hood a little and watches them as they try to make themselves comfortable. The rustle of their coats and bags. The old man's nose is long and red, the wings of his nostrils empurpled by broken capillaries. He sniffs and runs a gloved hand under it. The old woman has her bag in her lap. She's wearing a dark green hat with a loop of little Rudolphs prancing around the trim. She places her hand in his lap and he places his own on top of it. Neither says anything, both just stare ahead at the road and the lights of the cars, heading toward their home.

She's not expecting it, but the sight blurs her vision with tears. It sometimes happens: the shock of stumbling upon an intimacy shared between two strangers. For a second, no more, there forms between them a connective tissue along which entire lifetimes flare and fade before her eyes, so vividly that she believes she's witnessed all that they've been through together, and all that they might yet endure.

And then, as quickly as it arrived, the feeling vanishes and she's back on the bus, passing between villages and stretches of road that aren't lit, so that when she stares out the window she can see only her own face, her skin tinged yellow, her eyes cavernous and black.

This is the furthest she's ever been from the camp and the town. She knows it's sad and ludicrous, but it's the truth. She opens another beer. The old couple glance over at her, look down at the bag by her feet with one of the empty cans sticking out. She shuffles it closer to her with her foot and slouches lower in her seat. She adjusts the hood of her duffel so that she can no longer see either side of her. She has to keep swapping hands to hold the can because it's cold. She plunges the one that's not being used into her pocket and bunches it up until it warms a little, then swaps it again.

The bus pulls over and the three boys at the back get off, still jabbering away between themselves. The ball rolls down the aisle, is trapped under a heel and then picked up.

They're a few years older than Welty was. Or still is. Strange to think that time has moved on, the years have passed, but he's no older. She doesn't believe in heaven or hell and never has; but she knows with little doubt that the dead exist in a realm of their own, one that's governed by different rules, rules that'll never be clear to the living.

At the next stop, the old couple get off. It is the man who turns to her and offers her a small smile. She'd like to return it, but she can only look back to the window and stare beyond her reflection where a graffitied bench glows beneath a streetlight, looking for all the world as if it's been jilted, waiting for someone who will never show.

She knows that she is close and she feels a flutter of nerves. They pass through another village. More houses with lights glowing out, more cars parked on kerbs. A pub, brightly lit, with a painted sign. A crowd of men are singing something out the front. She catches a tiny bit of it over the engine of the bus as it drives past, a Christmas song that she's heard on the radio in the shop.

The bus leaves the village and pushes back into the darkness again. She's the only passenger left. She can't see the driver, can't even remember what they look like. The engine shifts, clunks loudly, roars on. The lights fizz above her and when the tyres hit a divot or some other inconsistency in the road, they flicker off until the wheels strike something else and then they flicker back on.

She begins to imagine that no one is driving, that the bus is moving independently of human agency and has no destination. It will simply continue, powered by a force that will remain a mystery to her. It could be that she's dead, she thinks, and that this is her conveyance from the land of the living to where Welty could be waiting for her, standing pale and silent at an unnamed stop. He'll climb on board and sit next to her, and the pair of them will ride around for eternity, letting some passengers on, letting other passengers off.

The bus has stopped and she hasn't even realized it. It's only when she hears two girls climb on and pay the driver that she sees the sign of the village out the window, the same one that's written on the slip of paper in her pocket. She rises quickly, picks up the bag, and hurries down the aisle and off the bus.

She doesn't know which direction to walk in, so she just stands and watches as the doors hiss closed and the bus moves away on to the road, watches the glow of its red taillights until they disappear over the brow of a hill.

She's on a slope, so that she has to stand with one leg jammed straight and the other cocked to keep from teetering over. There's a cluster of houses on the other side of the road slightly further up, lamps nestled in a row of prettily framed windows. Fields stretch out behind her into a darkness punctuated by little trinkets of light stitched across a rise of distant blue hills. The smell of manure rushes her nose, almost sweet in the chill air, the white shadows of her breath lifting and then vanishing, lifting and then vanishing.

A shiver darts up her spine and the bag rustles in her hand. She picks out the empties and drops them into a bin with a hollow, tinny cackle. She lifts out the last full one, opens it, and feels her upper lip sting with the punch of the cold as she drinks.

She holds herself very still.

Her da is somewhere near. The thought, if she lets it, will be enough to paralyse her. She hasn't seen him in so long. He's lived only in her mind, in imagined meetings and imagined conversations. There's no scenario she hasn't considered, no bitter argument or tender embrace she hasn't screened and dissected a thousand times.

But now that she can just go and see him in the flesh, she feels afraid. The fact of his existence, of his face and body appearing before her eyes, brings the hairs up on the nape of her neck.

She thinks of crossing the road and getting the next bus back.

She can meet Sarah in the pub and never mention this little episode again. She doesn't have to see her da. She's been doing fine without him. Surely it's him that should be coming to her, not the other way around. Why, in fact, is she even here? Why has she decided to track him down when she was the one left to fend for herself?

Her breath is a silvery, smoky trickle from her nostrils. Perhaps she doesn't need to see him to say what she wants to say; maybe what she wants to say can be done much more effectively without words.

She steps off the kerb and makes her way across the road toward the houses. She brings the sleeve of her coat across her nose. Not a single car has passed by since she was dropped off. No pubs, no parties, no singing or carrying on like in town. A silence flavoured by the cold, as hard and brittle as ice, waiting to be cracked.

On the bus, she hadn't been able to feel the effects of the cans she's had; but now her head is light and her thoughts fizz behind the jittery scan of her eyes. She sees a stone and then another two, all of them a good size. She stoops down, picks them up, and drops them into the pockets of her coat.

They click in her pocket like dice as she walks up the slope, the tops of her thighs burning with the effort. She stops, takes out the slip of paper. She reads the street name, the number of the house, and then carries on.

There's no real sprawl of streets here but a close weave of homes, all dotted near one another. She nears the first street. It has a curve to it, so that she can't see all the way along it. Just the closest three or four of these queerly low houses, lights blazing, Christmas trees twinkling.

She wasn't expecting this first road to be the one he lives on, but it is. She moves along it. She finishes the can, her last, and places it on the wall that edges the front garden she's passing.

She reaches into her pocket and takes out one of the stones. The chill of it stings the mottled pink of her palm. She runs the length of her thumb across its chapped surface and is reminded of those very rare days when the sea had been flat at the camp, and her da would always take a moment to show her and Welty the particular flick of the wrist needed to skim a stone, hopping and jumping across the surface.

This is what she'll do now.

She'll throw this one, the one she feels will do the most damage, just as her da taught her to. A kaleidoscopic reel of violence brightens behind her eyes: a cracked window, a mouth twisted in pain, the spray and mist of blood.

She doesn't hear the car coming, it's just suddenly on

her, rounding the bend with its headlights sweeping over her. She has to stop herself from running. Her hood is still up, shadowing her features. She keeps walking, but she turns her face away and puts her hand with the stone back in her pocket.

It could be her da.

The car slows behind her. She hears the register of the engine change, then feels it draw up alongside her. The window rolls down with a shuddery whine. Her heart is going. She has to get away; she has to turn and run and not stop until she's out of sight.

Then again, if this is the moment she has to face her da, then this is the moment. She'll do or say whatever must be done right here on the street. But the voice that speaks to her from the darkness of the car is not her da's. It's a woman talking to her: a pale, owlish face with red lipstick peering out. She's on her way to a Christmas party and she's got herself lost. Could she have some help at all with directions?

Keely says nothing. She only shakes her head and stares at the woman, who stares back at her with a smile that slowly straightens into a look of worry until it vanishes, and her eyes start to shift back to the road. The car idles for a moment longer, and then the woman starts to wind up her window and the car moves on, turns hastily in a drive-way, and then speeds back past her again.

The number of the house – 80 – is in her head. It is all she can see when she blinks, pinned to the backs of her eyelids.

On one of the doors – 76. The lights from a wreath catch it and it shines out at her.

Only two away.

She keeps walking.

She takes the stone back out from her pocket.

The closer she gets to the number that's flashing in her mind – 80, 80, 80 – the more she feels that she has nothing to say, that she's had every conversation with her da before now in her head. She knows every way it might turn out, and she wants none of them.

What she wants is to see him hurt. She wants to leave him with the feeling that he left her with, with emptiness and worthlessness. She wants him to feel loveless. That's what she wants him to be: loveless. To be alone like her. To have nothing. To have no one but himself.

She arrives at the right number.

The lights are on in the house. She moves on to the soft, dark lawn. The stone throbs in her grip. She edges closer toward the window, through which she can now see a sofa and two people sitting on it. One is a woman, still young and slight with dark hair and a pretty face. And the other is her da. He's sitting next to the woman and his arm is around her shoulder. Their faces are lit by the TV. They're smiling. She watches the woman's hand as it strokes her da's knee. And beyond them, or before them, she can see herself, can see her arm raised and the stone locked in her fist, poised to throw.

PART TWO
SPURDOG

1

A DARK RUN OF WATER BETWEEN THE COBBLES. IT leaks from his boots as he stands looking down into his palm at what he's gathered. Amongst the silt and grit, the green fray of weed and algae, there sits a pale, horned object.

He steps out from beneath the strutted shadows of the bridge. The noise of the traffic shifts from a dull, thunderous roar to a sharper, leaner clamour. It almost hisses now, tyres running slickly on the rain-dark road, carrying people away from their homes or back to them, where they'll sit and sleep and think and dream, lives passing just as his does.

The water laps at his feet. He turns the object in his fingers, then holds it up to the pearlescent light of the sky. One end is flat and smooth, but from the other prongs a single horn, its edge now rounded but must once, he thinks, have been sharp. Strangely, it appears darker to his eye here, seamed with hues of brown and yellow that remind him of the pages of old books. He brings it up to his nose, inhales sharply but smells nothing other than the water, deep notes of rust and earth, but also something sweet, as if the river were just on the turn, on the cusp of going to rot.

He looks up and out across the dark span of the water, fascinated as he always is by it and what it coughs up for him. At a glance, it looks the same, as if a pattern is repeating itself, over and over again. But look more closely and he knows that it's always different. Each second it forms something it hasn't before, twisting and braiding itself into a state of constant newness. And the thought of it – even if he's at home in bed and can only see it in his mind – makes the skin on his arms pimple, and the knot that has lived in his stomach for as long as he can remember slacken, allowing him to breathe a little easier.

He likes to think that he's the same as the river. He might look to other people as he always has done, but really he's changing all the time, and there's a new version of himself with each passing second. Depending on how crowded his thoughts are, this feeling might unsettle him, might make him long to be still, so that he climbs into his bed and lies in the darkness beneath his blankets for hours on end. Or it will fill him with a kind of joyous emptiness, and his vision will glitter at the edges, the world somehow ceasing to terrify him.

He comes here, down to the bank, as often as he can. His nan and grandad don't know that this is where he goes. The sodden boots he's wearing are not his, otherwise he would have been found out long ago. His own trainers are further up the bank, hidden beneath a covering of grass and several large stones. He'd found the boots strewn on the pavement on his way to school. He'd looked up at the windows of the nearest house and, seeing that the curtains were still drawn, he'd picked them up and carried them straight back home, where he'd pretended to his nan that he'd forgotten something and slipped upstairs to place the boots beneath his bed.

They're at least three sizes too big for him, but without them he'd have to go into the river in his own trainers. He can't go in barefoot. He's tried once before, but he cut the sole of his foot on a piece of glass, and had to spend a week trying not to limp when near his nan, so she'd not fuss over him and ask him what happened.

When he looks down again at his palm, he sees that the ends of his fingers have started to shrivel; but the object, now that it's dried, has changed again. Very fine cracks score its surface, and when he turns it upside down, he finds that he can see through it, through a small hole to the other side of the river, where the weeds grow tall and bits of rubbish – bags and cans and wrappers – are snagged on the rusty barbs of an old chain-link fence.

He slips it into his pocket and heads back under the shadows of the bridge. He takes off the sodden boots and tucks them neatly away, hoping, as he always does, that they'll be waiting for him the next time he's back. His nose wrinkles as the smell of them drifts up from his hands. It wasn't long before they'd started to stink. One time, he'd slipped his foot into the right boot, only to find that a rat or mouse had made a nest of it and, when he lifted it up and shook it, five or six pink, hairless bodies fell out and groped blindly on the ground. For several minutes he'd panicked and, crouched low by them, he'd desperately tried to corral them with a stick to a place of safety. But the little bodies squirmed and writhed without response to his efforts, so he'd had no option but to leave and hope that the mother would return to take care of them. When he returned, they were gone, and he'd spent weeks afterward worrying he'd caused them harm.

He steps back out from under the bridge and climbs up the bank in his bare feet, doing his best to hop from stone to stone and dodge the thistles that spring up in dense little crowns. There is such pleasure in being here, in this place that can feel like his and his alone. He stands and looks back out across the river, at the slow, measured run of it, the keeper of so much he is yet to find out.

IT'S THE END OF September. The sky is low and grey, and there's already a chill in the air. Clouds scud above him as he walks with his eyes lowered and his hands thrust deep in his pockets. He doesn't take the object out, but allows his fingers to turn it over, growing more and more familiar with it with each passing second.

His street. The name of it tacked high on the red bricks of the first house. Windows with their netted curtains. Some of the doors propped wide open. A cat, yellow-eyed and sharp-eared, stares out at him through a pane of dusted glass. He knows everyone's name here, even the adults, but he's never said a word to most of them. It's the place he knows best in the world; he can conjure it in his mind in every detail, and yet still he feels the knot in his stomach tighten to be here, feels himself to be on the outside of something that's not quite his.

There are other kids out playing, kicking balls or racing from one end of the street to the other, dodging the cars parked up on the kerb. Their cries echo cleanly, slapping against the brick. Most of the kids are younger than him. No one turns to stare at him. No one calls out or raises a hand in greeting.

He's never lived anywhere else. He has no memory of either of his parents and knows almost nothing about them. He's been told that they're still alive, but that's about the measure of it. Both went their separate ways when he was too small to remember them, but neither, apparently, had deemed him worthy of bringing with them.

He lives with his mam's parents, his nan and grandad. They've made it clear that they don't like to talk about their daughter. There are no pictures of her anywhere in plain sight, but he's seen one, the time he'd quietly, guiltily searched the drawers of his nan's prized mahogany chiffonier when they were out at a funeral a few years ago. He'd held it for a long time and he'd known it was his mam just by the look of her: they shared the same dark hair, the same wide-set green eyes.

He's not felt the need to see it again since. His memory is like this: sometimes he has only to glance at something and he can capture it vividly in his mind, can revisit it months, even years down the line, and it won't have dimmed.

As for his da, he's seen nothing, not even a single picture. There's been almost no mention of him, and he hasn't yet felt the need to ask. To ask would be to set something in motion, something that he might not want. He's very conscious of words and their power, and he fears them. He's not sure where this fear comes from, why he's so reluctant to speak. Better to stay quiet. Better yet, say nothing at all. Around his brain he imagines there to be a trench so deep and wide that no bridge can span it. It's beyond this trench that he hides. No one can reach him; he is safe, secure. He's all alone but he is in control, and it's this that matters to him most.

All he really knows is that he loves his nan and grandad. They say they'll tell him anything he needs to know in time, when he's ready. They've always cared for him and looked after him. This is enough, at least for the time being.

THE DOOR OF HIS home, number 21, is unlocked. He slips inside, pulling down the handle as quietly as possible so as not to disturb anyone. His grandad is too absorbed by the TV to notice him, and his nan's in the kitchen. The radio is on and she's frying pork medallions, the butter hissing and spitting, the smell reaching his nostrils and making his mouth water a little. He takes off his trainers, arranges them neatly at the bottom of the stairs, then takes the treads two at a time up on to the tiny landing.

There'd once been only two rooms, but the room that had been his mam's when she was a girl has been split into two so that there's now a bathroom in the house rather than outside. Still, his room is big enough to fit his bed and a chest of drawers, and there's a thin strip of faded grey carpet where he can sit and study his belongings. His walls are painted yellow and blue, and he likes how the roof slants down above his bed, so he can reach up and touch it when he's lying awake at night.

He knows that he and his mam must have touched the same things in this room. Their feet must have padded across the same stretches of floor, or their knuckles grazed the same patch of wall. The thought can sometimes give him a sharp rush of feeling: a pulse or flare that burns brightly behind his eyes, and then disappears. It's almost as if, for a split second, he can picture the place she is now, the life she's living without him, possibly thousands of miles away. It's a connection that sometimes unnerves him, but he is for the most part pleased when it happens. He wonders why feelings must always be like this: never one, definite entity, but forever branching and splintering into rivalrous factions, all of them forced to bunk with one another in the cluttered dark of his mind.

He likes small spaces and always has. Any room he enters that's too big and he feels himself to be exposed; immediately he wants to fold in on himself and shy away. In the canteen at school, he chooses to sit with his back to the wall on the far side, so that there's no one behind him. Sometimes, he finds that his seat has been taken, and he's forced to sit in plain view of all the others, and he can barely swallow his food down for the worry of being stared at and – in some vitally intimate way he doesn't have control of – noticed.

He keeps the box of everything he finds in the river under his bed, pushed up against the wall and wrapped in a dark plastic bag. He knows the chances of either his nan or grandad getting down on their knees to have a look under here are very slim, but he has to be cautious. He doesn't think they'd want to take anything away from him, but they'd ask him questions that he wouldn't have the answers for, and he knows already that his quietness troubles them. The last thing he wants is to trouble them any more than he already does.

He lies flat on his stomach and reaches under the bed. He pulls out the box, then stays very still, listening to make sure that no one is coming up the stairs. He can only hear the TV. The racing his grandad watches is on, the commentator barking out names and positions, the voice becoming more and more enthused as the seconds go by.

When he's sure that he's in no danger of being discovered, he removes the dark plastic bag. His name – Finn – is scrawled on the lid in faded red ink. He doesn't remember where the box came from. It's too small to be a shoebox and too large to have held anything as delicate as jewellery. He opens it up and looks down at his treasures. If the box were any bigger, then the collection might look less impressive; but in here, they have to jostle for space, and when he reaches his hand in and sifts through them all, he gets the same feeling every time: not elation, not pride, but a form of peace, a glorious distillation of his thoughts into one single beat of pleasure.

He reaches into his pocket and takes out what he found today. He holds it up to the light that comes in through the small window set into the slanting roof. It's not like any-thing he's found before, and though it doesn't matter to him what it is, he thinks it's starting to resemble a tooth. He places it amongst his other finds. Like all of them, it'll give him its own particular kind of satisfaction when he holds it. No thing, he knows, is ever the same.

Drifting under his door, he can smell the waft of the butter and pork. This is what his nan does every Saturday morning. His grandad sits himself by the TV in the living room and she cooks him up his breakfast. He likes to have it late because he'll soon be going to the pub, and he doesn't like to leave the house with the feeling of an empty stom-ach. He'll have a glass of milk to wash it down, and then he'll be away, pulling the peak of his hat low over his eyes and whistling his own meandering tune.

Finn moves down the stairs, quietly. He looks at the clock that hangs from the patterned wallpaper in the hall-way beside the mirror. It ticks away, never stopping. It's later than he thought. He knows that Ronan's da is picking him up at eleven. He only has a few minutes to get himself ready, though when he thinks about it, he doesn't really know how he's meant to be preparing himself.

He's been invited to a party that he doesn't want to go to. The boy who's invited him, Ronan, isn't really a friend. There'd been a time, when Finn was much younger, that he'd had friends at school, and he'd fitted in far better amongst the other children. But that was before he – and they – had sensed that there was something different about him, something he'd have to protect. He'd had a small group who he could talk to and share his thoughts with without fear of being ridiculed. Some of them had liked the same things he did: digging around in the muck and bringing up anything that was buried down there. Like him, they kept little bits and bobs in their pockets: stones, dead insects, leaves, sticks that they could sharpen into arrows or spears.

But around four or five years ago, they'd all seemed to grow out of those habits. He'd watched as slowly they began to drift away from him to talk about things that he didn't understand, or didn't interest him. Eventually, he stopped talking to them altogether. So now, at breaktimes, he walks around the perimeter of the playground on his own. His hands reach out from the cuffs of his coat like pale little leaves, and he thrusts them down into the dirt to lift up anything he can find: old bottle caps, ring pulls, coins, wrappers, scraps of metal that he takes home to rinse under the tap and inspect.

He knows the only reason that he's been invited today is because Ronan's mam sometimes works with his nan in the bakery in town. They do the occasional shift together, and she knows that his nan worries about him. She worries that he doesn't have any friends, that he spends so much time on his own, that he so rarely talks. He knows all this because he likes to sit on the stairs when he can't sleep, his face pressed between the same two spindles of the banister, and he listens to his nan fretting endlessly about him to his grandad.

Last week he'd heard them again.

What's wrong with him? his nan asked.

Nothing's bloody wrong with him, said his grandad. He's a boy. He's growing up.

But he's so quiet, she said. He'd not say a word if he had

it his way. He'd be up in his room or out doing God knows what.

The news started, and Finn could hear the familiar theme tune building to a crescendo. There'd be more stories that would have his grandad in a foul mood the next morning, muttering to himself over his breakfast of tea and eggs.

Leave him be, said his grandad. He doesn't need you breathing down his neck.

Maybe he doesn't need me breathing down his neck, but he could do with his mother. Don't you think? Don't you think we could—

That's enough, his grandad said. That's enough.

Finn had heard his nan getting up from the sofa then, so he'd stood without making the stairs creak and returned to his bed. But he'd not been able to sleep. He'd stayed up long enough to hear his nan and grandad's footsteps on the stairs, and then the snoring coming from across the hall. When he'd finally drifted off, he'd dreamt of his mam in the photograph, and when he woke in the morning with the light sluicing down through the window, he could still see, somehow feel, the green of her eyes on him.

The ticking of the clock in the hall. He stands, watching his nan in the kitchen, the handle of the pan in one hand, a spatula in the other. Finely glinting hairs on the carpet tiles of the kitchen floor. Beyond her, he can see the brightly coloured pegs on the washing line bouncing in the wind outside. Her glasses are perched on the end of her nose, her lips gently puckering. She turns and sees him standing there, and immediately she shouts over the spit of the butter and the noise of the TV.

Where've you been?

But she doesn't wait for an answer. She shifts the pan off the heat and comes bustling toward him, her apron tied around her thick waist, her worn slippers whispering on the green carpet.

She doesn't look like some people's nans do. Her hair isn't grey but dyed a dark, almost ruddy brown, and though her face is slightly wrinkled around the nose and mouth, she still has a youthful quality to her, a brightness that lives in the pale blue of her eyes.

She goes upstairs with her apron still on. She seems to do most things with it on. Even when she sits down at night to watch TV, she still sometimes wears it. He used to wonder when he was younger if she wore it to sleep in, because she'd have it on in the morning when he woke up, stirring his porridge over the blue flame of the gas ring.

She comes back down a couple of minutes later with a heap of T-shirts and jumpers and a cagoule that he hasn't seen in many years but knows is hers.

You'll need these, she says.

She thrusts them at him and he sifts through them.

Do I need all of them? he asks. He speaks quietly, not much above a whisper.

You do, she says. Now put them on.

By the time he's put everything on, he feels about a stone heavier. He's yet to have his growth spurt, so his nan's cagoule reaches down to his knees. It's purple and green, and there are two toggles that swing pendulously and clack together whenever he turns his head. Even his smallest movements make the fabric rustle and crackle unpleasantly.

He has sense enough to know he looks stupid. He wants to tell her that he doesn't want to wear it, that he'll be fine without; but he simply zips it up and stands there, his hands lost in the long, dangling sleeves.

His grandad has put some money down on a horse, so he's leaning forward in his favourite chair, his fists clenched and resting on his knees. The faded tattoos on his forearms shift slightly as the muscles cinch and slacken beneath the skin. There's a half-full ashtray resting on the arm of his chair, a thin spiral of smoke lifting from it. Sometimes, if the horse he's put money on wins, he jumps up and knocks the ashtray over, so his nan has to come and suck up all the ash with the little hand-held hoover she keeps in the kitchen to get rid of crumbs.

A horn sounds from outside.

That'll be them, says his nan.

He feels a flutter of nerves in his stomach and he can't keep from wincing. His nan sees his face, places the papery skin of her palm on his dark head of hair. He can smell the sweetness of the perfume that she dabs on her wrists.

You'll be fine, she says.

She opens the door and pulls him with her out on to the street. He wants to say goodbye to his grandad, but he's already outside, his cagoule rustling like a steeple of kindling catching alight.

There's a blue car parked over the road, two wheels up on the kerb. His nan marches him toward it. He knows that she'll want to talk with Ronan's da. The window rolls down as they near. A large face with a dark beard and very light blue eyes appears, hair greying at the temples. Ronan is sitting beside his da in the front, and there are two other boys in the back. Finn can see that their faces are turned toward him, can make out the paleness of their cheeks and chins; but the sun is just out from behind a cloud and smears itself across the glass so that their eyes are obscured; and he can't put a name to either of them.

I want you to take good care of this boy, he hears his nan say.

She's standing behind him, her hands clamped on his shoulders. Her fingers rustle the cagoule, and he sees Ronan's da's eyes drift down to look at the length of it, the way it hangs by his knees.

He's in good hands, he says.

Will they be wearing a life jacket? she asks.

Every last one of them, he says. I'll have him back to you. Now hop in the car, lad. We need to be on our way.

INSIDE THE CAR, THE air is close and briny. Finn is pressed against a boy he knows is new at school. His name is Evan and Finn feels a clammy heat rise up his neck and into his cheeks to be so close to another body, to be able to feel each miniscule shift of this other boy's leg and shoulder against his own whenever the car changes direction slightly.

No one's spoken yet. Ronan is yet to turn around. He's slumped in his seat, his arms folded over his chest. He looks displeased, irritated – he's been forced to do something he doesn't want to do. Finn knows that Ronan has a temper on him, a surliness that always seems to be on the brink of boiling over into something more menacing. Even the back of his neck, smooth and stiff and pale beneath the arrowed finish of his light hair, gives off an air of distaste for what's behind him in the backseat.

Ronan's da's eyes appear in the rear-view mirror, vanish, reappear, then vanish again. He lights a cigarette with something from the dash of the car, a small, thumb-sized stick that glows bright with heat. He rolls down the window. Finn is sitting directly behind him, so the wind chops at his brow and cheeks, whips the smoke and flecks of ash from the cigarette into his face.

Finn brings the balls of his fists up to his eyes, rubs at them, and by the time he opens them again, they've left the town behind, and the road has opened up. Lanes of cars speed by, their tyres spuming last night's rain. The windscreen wipers shudder and moan as they drag themselves across the glass. Ronan's da winds the window back up, then flicks a lever by the steering wheel so that a sudsy stream of water runs back up the pane and is swept from side to side until only thin, jittery runnels remain.

Finn keeps his face close to the window, close enough for his breath to mist the glass. They pass the great drums and scaffolds and chimneys of the factory his grandad works at. Smoke billows darkly into the sky, threads itself into the passage of grey-nosed clouds. On the verge is a mattress, folded over as if it's just been punched; winking dully from stands of sickly, wilting grass are alloys that have spun away from wheels worn down by years of rust.

Evan sits with his hands clasped in his lap. Finn hasn't looked at him directly yet, but he has a picture of him in his head from seeing him in the corridor at school: his features are sharp, elfin, with ears that poke through his hair and redden easily. He's small, even smaller than Finn, though there's something more robust in his bearing, a quiet strength that Finn knows is lacking in himself.

Beside Evan sits a boy called Mark. Finn's been at school with him since they were very small, but they've never spoken, not properly. Mark is large for his age, nearly a whole foot taller than any of his peers. Finn's noticed during PE lessons that he has dark, wiry hair on his legs. The sight of it makes him uneasy. He's studied his own legs for signs of such growth, but he can only ever find small, pale hairs that disappear when he's away from the light. Exactly what these differences between them mean, he isn't sure; but he has sense enough to glean that a change is on the cusp of happening, happening somewhere inside of him, one that he'd like to arrest and study for signs of its intentions with him, but knows full well to be beyond his control.

It's not clear to Finn why or how it's come to be that these four boys should be here together. Ronan has managed to achieve some popularity at school, mainly through the brusqueness of his attitude with teachers, but Finn's seen no evidence of him having made friends with Evan or Mark. Parental interference is the only answer that carries any plausibility.

The eyes appear in the mirror again, and Finn feels his own lift to meet them. He stares into the reflected blue gaze and feels the knot in his stomach tighten, the blood-warm rush of heat brighten his cheeks. He wants to look away but he can't, can't bring himself to do so even when the blue eyes move on to Evan and Mark, narrowing and flicking between the three of them.

Looking forward to being out on the boat? he asks.

Ronan's da lives and works on the coast as a fisherman. He goes out on the sea most mornings and comes back with lobsters and crabs and fish to sell. His nan has told Finn all this as if he should be impressed or excited by it, but he doesn't understand why such a thing should be the focus of a party, why it should be chosen as an activity to take part in and enjoy.

His grandad, once in the Navy, has said that Finn will love going on the boat, that there's nothing like it, being out there, surrounded by all that water, by all that mystery.

Mystery – the word had sounded strange coming out of his grandad's mouth, and the way his eyes had gathered light in their corners. Finn had never heard him speak about anything in such a way before, and it had made his grandad look like a different person altogether.

But now they're all on their way, and the question is still hanging in the air. No one is sure who it's directed at, if they're looking forward to being out on the boat or not. For the first time, Finn turns to glance at Evan and Mark. Both faces look vaguely panicked; but then Mark says yes and Evan follows, and Finn opens his mouth, but no sound comes out. His throat does this – closes up on him in the presence of people he doesn't know well, tightening so that he has the need to reach up and swat at the air beneath his chin, as if trying to slap away an invisible pair of hands that are throttling him. So he just nods his head up and down, and hopes that he's been seen.

Ronan's da's hairy, red-knuckled hand reaches to switch the radio on. It hisses and crackles, then snatches of a melody and a man's voice come through. Mark and Evan start to sing along under their breath. Ronan hears them and leans over to turn the volume up. They all seem to know the words apart from Finn and he feels himself tense up, folds himself toward the window.

Over the years, he's come to be an expert in recognizing moments that might result in his being humiliated. He knows when he's at his most visible, when he ought to hide himself away, and this is one of them.

But here there is nowhere to hide. He's trapped, and all he can do is keep his head down and stay as still as possible, hoping that no one will ask him anything else.

You not much of a singer? says Ronan's da, his eyes in the mirror again, looking directly at Finn.

Ronan twists in his seat to stare back now. It's the first time Finn has seen his face, the freckles across his cheeks and the bridge of his nose, the wings of his nostrils flaring slightly, like an animal that's picked up the scent of spilled blood.

Finn can feel Mark and Evan's eyes on him, as well. His cagoule rustles as he shifts in his seat and his palms begin to sweat. He doesn't know what to say. His throat is so tight that he can only shake his head and lower his eyes as he feels the knot in his stomach twist and strain.

He stays like this for what seems like an hour, his chin digging so hard into his chest that it will leave a small, heart-shaped mark he'll discover later before bed. He screws his eyes shut so tight that colours – psychedelic bands of green and yellow and red – swirl dizzyingly across his eyelids and then break apart, drifting like embers from the last kernel of heat in a dying blaze.

When he finally lifts his head and opens his eyes, he finds that no one is looking at him anymore. Evan is talking to Mark about the song that's now just finished. It turns out they've both been to the music shop in town with the money that they'd saved to buy it. Finn doesn't know where either of them have managed to get this money, or what it's been saved from. The only money he ever receives is when he's told to go and get his nan and grandad cigarettes from the shop, and to buy himself some sweets or chocolate with the change.

It's not that he's been completely unaware that boys of his own age live very different lives to the one he lives, but something about this music and the way they're talking about it makes him freshly, painfully certain of his own strangeness.

Evan reveals that he has a guitar. He's been learning to play the song that everyone's just been singing along to. He has the chords figured out but the only problem, he says, is that he can't sing. He shakes his head and lets out a small, sad laugh.

Finn wants to be a part of what Evan's talking about. There's a new, urgent need in him to be involved, to be liked. It's like looking down and finding that he's grown another limb. Where has it come from? Why now? The oddness of it is so complete, so total, that he mistakes the sound of the exhaust scraping over a speed bump for something breaking apart in himself, the cleaving of one version of himself from another.

He feels the tightening knot in his stomach start to climb through his innards, pushing up, up, up until it reaches the very back of his throat, where it squats and pulses expectantly, secreting a bitter oiliness that films his tongue, his teeth, his cheeks.

It wants him to open his mouth and speak.

But he shakes his head.

He keeps his lips so firmly pressed together that they turn pale. He doesn't know where it's come from, this awful compulsion to have his voice be heard, but it's like trying not to be sick. He gags and brings his hand up to his mouth, then turns to the window and pleads with himself to keep quiet, to return to his hiding place as he's always, always done.

But he can hear the words in his head: I can sing. Surely he won't actually say them – they are ludicrous, not his own, as if they've winged their way into his consciousness from some stranger's head; and yet he can feel them trying to work their way out, prising open his jaw, wanting to be released into the world.

He opens his mouth.

He feels the dryness of his throat.

It's happening now, he is about to speak.

But it's Ronan's da who saves him.

Look, he says, pointing out the window to their right, and all heads turn to see the sea, a blue slab of it stretching out into the distance, glittering beneath the flat grey sky.

THE MINUTES THAT LEAD up to them being out in the boat pass in a blur. The horseshoe-shaped bay, the pale slopes and cliffs with the small white houses stacked like a poorly shuffled deck of cards; the pub with the gulls screeching from the black fire escape that climbs up its white, sooty exterior; the boats covered in blue twists of frayed, knotted rope, their sides flaking paintwork and their swollen under-bellies slicked green with seaweed, humped with shells.

It's a different world to him, filled with things that he's never seen before, never even been aware of. And now they're actually out on the water, surrounded by the dark chop and slap of the sea, the curve of the bay a distant smudge. There are boats as small as a thumbnail tacking across the horizon, their chimneys pluming smoke. He wonders who's aboard them, what they could possibly be doing all the way out there.

Finn and the other boys are sitting on thin, uncomfortable slats of wood. The wind is strong and cold and Finn is glad for the first time of his nan's cagoule, even if it still rustles with every gust. The focus is now all on Ronan's da, who's holding the rod with his large, square hands, purpling at the knuckle in the wind. The boys have all already taken a turn and none of them have felt a single thing, have seen nothing but the endless swell of the waves.

There's a tension in the air, a level of expectation that's rising by the second. Up until this point, Ronan's da has been full of nothing but jokes, his smile peering through the dark swatch of his beard. But suddenly he's changed. His body is alert. His eyes are wide and his tongue probes at the air as he manoeuvres the rod around, pulling the line up and winding, then letting it dip back down into the swell of the water.

Something is about to happen.

Finn knows it. He turns to look at Evan, at Mark, at Ronan. They're all huddled together, their hands tucked up their sleeves. Ronan, who'd claimed just before climbing aboard to be impervious to seasickness, has turned a limpid shade of green and holds himself as still as he possibly can.

All their eyes are trained on the bulk of Ronan's da, and a moment later they see the line go taut and Ronan's da lets out a small grunt as his body feels the impact of something deep below the surface, something large enough to cause him to stagger forward a bit.

Fuck me, he says.

Finn turns to look at the other boys. The three of them beside him on the bench share a nervous giggle. But Finn doesn't feel afraid. He feels a rush of emotion, but it's not fear – or maybe it is fear, but it's divorced from him, from any concern for his own safety; what he feels is a kind of extension of himself toward whatever is on the other end of the line, whatever is on its way to meet him.

There's sweat on Ronan's da's brow and his teeth are biting into his lower lip. His beard bristles against the collar of his coat and his waders stream the drops of spray that lift up onto him.

Finn gets to his feet.

The other boys look at him. They exchange glances between one another, then stand and follow. They stare over the edge of the boat, down into the water that's starting to boil and froth. A long patch of foam stretches out and almost shimmers, like the wedding dress of a drowned bride.

Then the darkness returns.

Keep yourselves away from me, says Ronan's da.

His stance is wide now. He's connected to whatever is down there, but not in the same way Finn feels connected to it. His eyes have stopped blinking. Finn stares beyond the dark face of the surface. He sees a pale flash of movement cut across his vision, then disappear again. Whatever's down there is unhappy, in pain. He can feel it.

He hears the wind and click of the rod next to him.

Here we go, says Ronan's da.

It's coming toward them now, the water spraying them as the pale creature thrashes around, but it can do nothing but succumb to the strength of Ronan's da as it's lifted clear of the water.

Finn stays very still. He's too amazed by it, by the slick grey length of it, by the pointed snout, the rows of white spots along its flanks, by the underbelly, yellowed slightly in parts, that flashes up at them each time it twists and writhes onto its back on the deck of the boat. But what really holds him are its eyes, set into the side of its head and staring out, the vast black pupil that seems to take in him and everything else.

Evan and Ronan and Mark are all cowering on the far side of the boat.

Spurdog, says Ronan's da, who has it trapped now beneath his large hands. He pinches it at the tail and under its heaving gills, then lifts it up, clutching it to himself. Don't see too many of these around anymore, he says.

Spurdog. The word chases itself around in Finn's mind. He's never seen anything like it; he wasn't even aware that such otherworldly animals could exist so near him, in these cold, bruised waters. It's all muscle, a taut length of writhing energy, the mouth working, opening and closing, wrestling with the air it's being forced to swallow.

Want to touch it? asks Ronan's da.

Evan, Ronan and Mark all simultaneously shrink away, their pale lips turned down in disgust, but Finn feels himself nod.

Come on then, says Ronan's da.

The boat is still swaying with the slurp and suck of the waves as Finn makes his way toward Ronan's da, his arms outstretched to keep his balance, the sleeves of his cagoule snapping in the wind. Finn can see the creature is still visited by small jolts, but it's slowed now, its flanks steadily rising and falling.

Ronan's da inclines his head toward the nearest wooden slat.

Sit yourself down there and I'll let you have a hold of him.

Finn takes his seat and holds out his arms; his palms, upturned as if in supplication, are bright with the flat sheen of the sky overhead. He can smell the spurdog now, is alert to the scent of its very aliveness, and he feels that when he touches it, when his fingers can palpate its flesh, he'll be able to map the journey of its life in his mind: from the dark drift of the egg to its ghostly knifing through the water to this moment, with its round, prehistoric eye staring at him, a black moon Finn feels he could fall into and disappear, leaving this world for another one, safe in the still, silent darkness of his own private cosmos.

Ronan's da crouches slightly.

He'll likely kick up a fuss, so make sure you get a strong hold.

Then the spurdog's weight is in Finn's arms: the slick, corded strength of it, its deep-sea slime leaving tracks like a snail's across his nan's cagoule. One of its fins pushes awkwardly, unyieldingly into his midriff. He feels his own heart at the base of his throat, though it's not hammering but pumping deep, luxurious beats through his body that make his vision brighten and his head feel light.

His body has never felt more still and yet he feels brutally, almost painfully alive. He's braced for the spurdog to fight his grip and free itself, but it remains still, so still that Finn worries it might have died. But when he cranes his neck to look along the length of its snout, he can see its mouth still opening and closing, and the small, slanted blades of its teeth set into the rubbery trim of its jaw.

Finn can feel Ronan's eyes on him, and Mark and Evan's too, and he can hear Ronan's da saying something to the three of them, something about taking the spurdog back and showing off what they've caught.

But Finn already knows this won't happen. Tears well in his eyes at the thought of being partly responsible for the extinction of this strange, alien life he's holding. He feels love for it – that is the only word for it he can muster – a love that is purer, more intuitive than any kind he has ever felt, even for his nan and grandad.

He's never prayed before, even in school assemblies when everyone's asked to bow their heads. But now he feels an urge to commune with this creature, to thread some of himself into it, to offer it whatever he can. So he places his brow against the cold, hard plane of the spurdog's back, then he closes his eyes and begins to slowly graze his nose along the shark's skin, back and forth, nuzzling it like a mother would her baby's scalp.

What's he doing?

He hears Ronan say these words, but Finn doesn't look up. It is only him and the spurdog as he presses his lips to it, tastes the salt of the sea and something else, something primal that he knows he'll never taste again.

When he opens his eyes, he finds that he's standing. The other boys and Ronan's da are all looking at him. He's never felt more in control, more sure of the dimensions of himself and his place in the world. He is at the very centre of it, at the centre of time, and as he walks to the edge of the boat, stooping slightly, he lets the spurdog push from his arms and dart back down into the deep.

2

HE STILL GOES DOWN TO THE RIVER. HE STILL HIDES his trainers beneath a small cairn made up of stones and weeds, then slips beneath the shadows of the bridge and finds the boots in the same place he's always kept them. They fit him now, but they're starting to fall apart. The laces have frayed and snapped off, and the leather has shrivelled up in places, has become creased and layered so that strips of it sometimes fall away when he's wading through the water.

The texture of them reminds him of the faces of people he's recently seen in a book kept in the school library. Bog People, they're called. Bodies that lived years and years ago, that were sacrificed, throats slit or heads sawn off, then dumped and folded back into the earth. They ought to be no more than bones by now, but the special qualities of the land they've been resting in all this time – what Finn understands to be called peat – has preserved some of them in ways he still finds difficult to believe.

Some are still whole. Their skin has gone hard and dark as leather, but every part of them is intact. Their eyes, noses, ears, lips. Faces that had once moved just like his own; faces that looked out at the world and heard it, heard the wind and the birds and stared up to find them wheeling through cloud or in acres of sharp blue sky. Limbs that had lifted them up so they could walk just like he does, so they could sit themselves down at a table to eat, so they could lay themselves back down to dream. Hair and clothes and possessions still gathered around them, clutched in their fingers.

He can't describe the feeling it gives him to look at these pictures. When he closes his eyes at night, he sees the figures curled up in the earth, sees every detail of their faces. He can't help imagining who they were, what lives they lived, what they would make of him, a fifteen-year-old boy poring over them, with his hair now reaching down to his shoulders and hanging over his eyes.

These thoughts he has of the Bog People don't depress him. They're a solace. It's not that he would wish to be found in such a way. When he dies, he hopes that he's left undisturbed, that he's been buried so deep that he can never be discovered and dredged back up to the light. He likes the idea that, after a certain point, a life no longer stands for anything. He likes that it can become as blank and nameless as a stone.

But he's also aware that there's a contradiction in his behaviour. He's felt the occasional pang of guilt when unearthing the small fragments from the river, claiming these fragments of lives lived long ago, or perhaps yet still living, for his own. Because he's appalled by the prospect of his life ever coming under the scrutiny of some snooping stranger. He feels protective of his body. It's his, and everything that it will experience should remain so, if only out of a peculiar fear that something of his sadness and loneliness might still be able to be detected. He wants to keep this to himself. The whole point of his own life, at least to him, isn't to leave something of himself behind, but to pass through time without leaving a single trace.

THE LAST SUMMER OF school passes. He leaves with few qualifications, his results far worse than his teachers had predicted. There were some who had seemed genuinely invested in him, who had hoped he might achieve something out of the ordinary, and go on to study at university.

But by the end of it, he'd been too tired to care, and so he'd just stopped. It feels to him as if the past few years have hollowed him out, have sucked something vital from his bones. All he wants to do is sleep. He wants to close his eyes and sleep for year after year after year and hope that when he opens them, he'll find himself somewhere other than here.

It might not have ended up like this, but everything changed that weekend three years previously, when he went out on the boat with Ronan and Mark and Evan. That day has come back to haunt him in ways he couldn't possibly have imagined. It has been responsible for so much misery, more than seems reasonable or fair to him.

There was a time when his invisibility had been his

greatest asset. There had been something about him, something that had allowed him to pursue his business without ever being bothered, without being asked what he was doing or where he was going. There were some boys that he knew didn't have this privilege. Something about them seemed to attract attention, seemed to excite a kind of urge in other people to intercept them and disrupt their lives.

But not him. He'd been able to go down to the river. He'd been able to walk meaninglessly through the town, down the streets, in and out of shops; and not once would he be stopped. Not once would he feel a hand on his shoulder or a voice in his ear. It was a skill, a gift, a blessing.

But the world, he's come to understand, is a cruel and chaotic place. This is the conclusion he's reached, and he can't see himself shifting away from it. He's always been fearful of it, the world, but that day taught him to resent it.

It had happened so quickly. The Monday after Ronan's party, it had spread like wildfire. At first, he hadn't known the precise reason why he was being called it. Of course, he knew the word; it was still very fresh in his mind. But he'd presumed it was just that the story had been passed around, that he'd touched the shark, thrown it overboard, and he'd supposed that there was some sort of shame in having done this, that it had revealed something in himself that he should have kept hidden, a kind of sensitivity or cowardice that boys weren't supposed to have and which naturally deserved to be mocked.

But soon he'd found out the name was only partially to do with this. Because when certain boys and girls passed by him in the corridor, or when they were out on the field at breaktime, they didn't simply just shout the name at him. There were gestures that accompanied the word: they would run up to him, stretch open their eyes using their thumbs and forefingers, and they would shout: Spurdog! Spurdog! Spurdog! then run away, laughing and barking manically, and he'd understood, then, that some resemblance between him and the animal had been drawn.

It was Ronan who'd started it. He wasn't so popular that anything he normally said could hold much sway, but the story he'd told was so unique, and the name so strange and funny, that it was latched on to immediately.

He'd thought it would stop, that it would exhaust itself, but it didn't. Every day, every time someone saw him, without fail – Spurdog! Spurdog! Spurdog! Younger kids, older kids, kids in his own year. Boys and girls and even one teacher. Inside of school and outside of school. It spread to people that he didn't know, that lived on the estates miles away from his own street. They somehow came to know him, came to be able to point him out in passing.

Perhaps he could have dealt with the name alone, but the fact that he was rushed every time, that people would cross roads or turn their bikes around to come and leer at him, to laugh and prise their eyes wide open and start barking – it frightened him, and he couldn't ever get used to it. He was always on edge, always waiting for the next skirmish. Now, after all this time, he's still known everywhere as Spurdog. He can't even guess at how many times he's heard it over the past three years. Not only shouted at him but in his own head, echoing around day after day, night after night.

Neither his nan or grandad has noticed anything different about him. They complain about his hair and plead with him to get it cut. His nan remarks every day on the height of him, how long his legs have grown, and how thin he now seems. But all of his pain over these last years has been of the kind that can't be seen, that lives inside his head, that torments him out of sight of those who might choose to protect him. He's looked at himself in the mirror and he's seen what everyone else must see: the deep, unsettling strangeness of his own face, the wide-set eyes allegedly similar to those of the spurdog. The name has, in some fundamental way, become him, so that when he tries to picture himself at night, his face is his own for only a second before it begins to morph slowly into the long snout of the shark, and he finds that he's staring into the dark eyes of the spurdog, its mouth not gasping for air but barking madly.

Over the years, he's learned to understand that people where he's from can't change. They can't change their circumstances, can't change who they are or what they've done or what they'll become. Only the most astonishing interventions can alter the trajectory of a life. Money has this power but nothing else he can think of does. He knows that his nan and grandad don't have money, and he knows that it's more than likely that he'll not have any. So he'll be as he's always been. People are born here and they stay here, and the same will happen to him.

HE SPENDS THE FIRST week after leaving school at home. He gets up late and eats at irregular hours. His nan has had an operation on her hip, so she's not as mobile as she once was. She uses a cane to hobble from room to room, but she still fusses over him and his grandad, and she tries to encourage him to go outside and get some fresh air.

It'll do you good, she says, looking at him and worrying the strings of her apron.

He thinks that maybe this will be his life. He won't move out. He'll stay here with his nan and grandad. Eventually, they'll die, and then he'll be left alone. He'll rattle around the rooms, will sit in his grandad's old chair, will start smoking and heap cigarettes in the ashtray the same way his grandad does now. Time will pass and he'll get older, day by day by day, until one morning he'll wake to find that he's an old man, and his life is mercifully nearing its end.

It doesn't seem so bad. Like with the book of the Bog People that he had to leave behind in the school library, there's something comforting about these thoughts, that removes him from the pain and uselessness of his current existence.

But these morbid ruminations come to an abrupt end when his grandad announces one Friday night that he's taking him with him to the pub. He tells him to wash and dress himself as smartly as he can, and to maybe run a comb through his hair, at least keep it out of his eyes.

People will want to be able to see your face, he says. They won't want to be talking to your bloody hair.

He does as his grandad says.

He finds a shirt that his nan bought him. It's plain black, which he doesn't mind; then he puts on his jeans and his trainers and he finds a comb and does his best to run it through the kinks and knots of his hair. It snags and pulls at his scalp, but he manages to push it away from his eyes, then fingers some water through it to try and fix it in place.

He's been to the pub with his grandad before, but only when he was much younger, when he would sit on a stool beside him with a glass of pop and some crisps and stare out the window while his grandad chatted away to some other old men. He hadn't ever minded going. People would greet him but then quickly forget about him, and he'd be allowed to sit and daydream in a way that would've seen him told off at school.

This time is different.

The invitation and the instructions have an unfamiliar whiff of formality to them. He and his grandad almost never spend time alone together. It's his nan that serves as the bridge between them, that holds everything together. If she weren't there, Finn has the feeling that he and his grandad would simply stop talking to each other, only passing in the kitchen or on their way to the toilet at night, never exchanging a single word.

His grandad has been going to the same pub for years. Every Friday night, and on Saturday and Sunday as well. His nan might join him on the Sunday, but otherwise she'll spend her evening at the bingo, or sipping a small glass of something in front of the TV while doing her knitting. The pub has always belonged to his grandad. It's his time, time that he's entitled to, that he's worked hard for, to meet and talk with his friends, to drink until he's had his fill and can wend his way home, the collar of his shirt sour with beer and sweet with smoke.

His grandad's waiting for him at the bottom of the stairs. He looks Finn up and down, sighs and shakes his head.

It'll do, he says.

His grandad's wearing a white shirt and his brown suede jacket. The elbows are faded, but other than that it doesn't look much different from when Finn was small. His grey trousers are neatly pressed, his black brogues polished. He likes to take care of his appearance. He believes it to be one of the most important things in life, to make a good first impression.

Never give anyone a reason to think less of you, he says, always with the same look on his face, his dark eyes narrowed and his lips drawn thin and straight.

They walk along the pavement side by side. It's still light but the sun is nowhere to be seen, the sky busy with the drift of grey clouds. There's a chill in the air, enough for them both to put their hands in their pockets.

Finn glances at his grandad. He's significantly taller than him now. He doesn't often think about his grandad, at least not in terms of what might be going on behind his eyes. There's always been something impenetrable about him, with his stringy arms and his faded tattoos. He's a man – this seems to be the principal part of his identity, and no man that Finn has ever seen looks as if they want themselves to be known. It's in a man's nature to keep nearly everything locked away. To invite prying eyes would be to expose a weakness, and weaknesses can be exploited. So the truth is, he loves his grandad but he doesn't know him, and he has a feeling that his grandad feels the same about Finn, that he has no idea of what or who he really is.

They hear the pub before they see it. Men's muffled voices, talking and laughing. They can smell the vinegar and the salt from the chippy over the road, the neon sign of a fish leaping up and down and flashing red. The sky above them has nearly emptied. It's blue and green and wisped through with scribbles of dirty cloud. A pocked sliver of the moon shows itself, staring blindly down.

They round the corner and there it is: a low, squat building with a flat roof and large dark windows. There's movement inside but it's difficult to discern. The frames of the windows are painted white but they're chipped and flaking. The brickwork is even and ruddy but there's also a horizontal patch, about the size of a door, that's been pebble-dashed. The actual door is blue with a panel of frosted glass and chicken wire set into it, and there's a scrawl of graffiti in yellow to one side of it, the writing illegible. There used to be a sign but it's gone now, blown away in the wind or ripped down by vandals.

Finn's never been here on an evening. It feels different now. There's an energy, an excitement, a buzz he feels in his temples and in his chest. He doesn't know whether there will be anyone he knows inside, anyone who might shout Spurdog! at him. He may be forced to explain it to his grandad, who might well be ashamed to learn that his grandson has been the victim of such bullying all these years without ever defending himself.

His grandad opens the door and they both walk in. The

noise and the smell slaps Finn across both cheeks, nearly lifts him off his feet. Smoke hangs and slowly creeps beneath the ceiling. Voices – what feels like hundreds of them – rush his ears. The carpet beneath his feet sticks slightly to his trainers as he weaves after his grandad, pressing against bodies that all smell different: old leather and cologne and beer and nicotine-stained fingers.

People know who his grandad is. They nod at him or shake his hand, then their eyes drift to Finn and linger for a moment to take in his height, his hair, then move away again. His grandad makes his way to the bar. He props his elbows on the dark gleam of wood and waits until he's served by a woman with blonde hair and dark makeup around her eyes. She's heavy-set but pretty, and as she pours two pints of beer she talks to his grandad about something Finn can't quite catch, something about another man who's been causing her grief. She smiles and takes the money and his grandad heads away from the bar toward a corner with a small round table and a bench of chapped red leather, the yellow stuffing showing in places.

He has never tasted beer before. He knows that plenty of people in school have been drinking it for years. They would buy cans from the shop and find somewhere – a park, a wall, a bench – and stand around and drink. His understanding of drunkenness is limited. He knows only that people lose their balance, or that they find things funnier than they might normally do. He's seen his grandad come back through the door and totter to his chair, and he's heard him bellow with laughter in a way he wouldn't normally.

When his grandad lifts his pint and holds it out to him,

he hesitates for a moment, then lifts his own and tilts it until they touch. He watches his grandad bring the glass up to his lips and he does the same. It's not much above room temperature, and it tastes both sweet and bitter at the same time. The fizz of it makes his eyes water a little. He can't help but wrinkle his nose. He's aware that his grandad is watching him, so right away he goes back for a second sip, a larger one this time, and he wipes the back of his hand across his mouth, drying the fine down on his upper lip.

His grandad nods at him, and his lips threaten to curl slightly into a smile. That's all that passes between them. They sit in silence and they look around, sipping away at their drinks, listening to the tidal rush and retreat of voices and laughter. Finn keeps an eye on his grandad's pint, and he makes sure that he keeps abreast of his progress.

He knows that his grandad doesn't really care about the results of his school exams. It's not that he sees no value in education, but he's far from convinced that it's the only route to be travelled, which is what some people are starting to suggest. That's not the way he sees it. Finn knows that his grandad is proud of himself. He's proud of the work he's done in a job that he's excelled in. He would've liked a bit more money, and he would've liked to have been able to provide more for his family; but there's no shame in the life he's led, not as he sees it.

He's no less intelligent than any man who wears a suit every day and sits in an office. Just because he hasn't had as much schooling, doesn't mean he ought to start bowing down to anyone who happens to have read more books than he has. Because that's not life. What a life adds up to is more than any of that; it's more than filling your head with information, with words and numbers that in the end all add up to the same thing. What he has are facts, and he has them neatly squared away in his own mind, there to stay until the day he dies.

Finn watches as his grandad holds his drink in one hand and rests the other flat on the dark wood of the table. His wedding band gleams dimly, makes a little tapping noise when he rolls his fingers. The noise of the pub continues around them, a ceaseless roll and pitch of voices, of other lives being lived.

It can overwhelm Finn at times, this feeling. Not the voices or what's being said, exactly – all of this he can block out – it's what he knows must be hidden, what must be kept inside of heads that are tired by the lifting of simple, ordinary problems. The kind of problems that never leave. He doesn't know whether other people feel this weight, not only of their own thoughts and fears but those of others, those of complete strangers.

He focuses now on his grandad. His eyes are dark, his nose ruddy, and the skin around the corners of his thin lips slightly red from the closeness of his shave. His hair has been combed back in very fine bands. It's not yet fully grey but shot through with black. Finn has seen only the one picture of him when he was young, on a ship with his shirt off and a cigarette in his mouth, a hand resting rakishly on his hip. It's from his Navy days, and there's a playfulness in his face that Finn's never seen in real life, a lightness to his features that's no longer in the face he's looking at now.

His grandad coughs into his fist. Finn becomes aware

that he's preparing to say something. He sits still and feels himself tense up, feels the knot in his stomach tighten.

You're older now, his grandad says.

He pauses, looks down at the table. Finn thinks that this might be it, that these words are meant to convey something that he should understand. But then his grandad lifts his eyes again to continue.

And you'll not hear a word from your nan or me about how you spend your life, he says. That's for you to choose and for you to live by.

He takes a sip of his pint, then clears his throat again.

But if you're to keep with us, under our roof, then you'll need some money of your own. You'll need to find your feet in a job that'll keep you busy. Because a life that isn't busy is a life that'll be wasted. A life that'll turn bad.

His grandad nods his head, sure of the words that have left his mouth. He lifts his pint again, sips from it, places it on the table, then stares down at the faded ink on his forearms: a dagger on his right, a serpent on his left.

You understand me? his grandad asks him then.

Finn nods. For once, his mind feels pleasingly unburdened, though of what he can't quite be sure. He will do this for his nan and grandad, because they deserve it. Because he knows how much they have sacrificed for him.

His grandad finishes his drink and rises, then heads back toward the bar. Finn turns and watches him shake more hands. He thinks he glimpses some of that playfulness captured in the old photo come alive in his features, the smile and the short, even teeth gritted together.

He comes back with two more pints. Neither of them talk. They simply sit together, though it's not awkward or tense. They have one more pint each, and then his grandad sends him home.

I promised your nan I'd have you back for nine, he says.

Finn doesn't want to go. The drink has made him want to stay. He is thawing out, an unfamiliar willingness to talk and to attempt, against all the odds, to try and have himself be understood. He might even consider asking about his mam and da, seeing if his grandad will tell him some more about them. This could be a turning point in both their lives. Here, now, amidst the hum of all these other words being passed and pushed and shunted around, they could have their own quiet discussion. So many of the things that have remained a mystery to Finn could be revealed to him; his grandad would talk and with each new detail he divulged there would begin to hatch, improbably, from all the shadows and all the silences that have dogged them both over the years, a story, and it would be Finn's story, that he could tell himself and anyone else who wanted to hear it, and maybe, just maybe, he would start to feel like he imagined other people did: whole and true and bright with the knowledge of which direction he should point his life in next.

But Finn knows deep down that this hour they've shared between them is over. So he asks nothing. He nods his head, gets up from the bench, sways a little and then steadies himself.

Take your time on the way back, his grandad tells him.

Thanks, Finn says, and he holds his grandad's eyes longer than he's ever held them before.

OUTSIDE, THE AIR IS colder, the sky dark and faintly studded with stars. There's no sign of the moon. He walks away from the noise, away from the warmth and the glow of the windows.

He feels light on his feet. He veers slightly and starts to laugh. He can't remember ever really hearing himself laugh. It strikes the pavement, the walls of the houses that he passes, finds him again. It sounds like someone else is with him, which makes him laugh all the harder.

The chippy is over the road. People are queuing inside, staring into the glass cases steamed with the heat of fish and battered sausages. Outside, the flashing neon fish leaps and brightens a huddle of young men leaning back against the window, eating from greasy newspaper pages. They're dressed differently to Finn, in jeans and boots laced up to their calves, jackets unzipped. Most of their heads are shaved. Only one has hair, coiffed and fixed into a single dark track of spikes.

Finn's still laughing on the other side of the street as he looks over at them. They lift their eyes from their food, drawn to the noise. He wants to stop laughing, but finds that he can't, that he's stuck in an inescapable loop. There's no one near him, no one he could claim to be talking to.

They are looking at him, all of them.

He can feel it. He glances up, laughs again, laughs harder from the nerves that are now firing through his body, that have his whole body tingling. He knows he must stop; he sees them out of the corner of his eye start to stir. One drops his newspaper to the floor and wipes his hands on his jeans. Another shouts something that he doesn't catch. They're going to come for him. They believe that he's laughing at them, mocking them, and he knows that they won't wait to hear any excuse, that they'll only want to punish him.

He's going to have to run. He keeps looking out the corner of his eye. The flashing red of the fish. The customers still queuing inside in the glow of the light. A car passes, then another, their engines rattling and tyres crunching. Then he sees them push off from the wall and they're running across the road toward him, and he's running too, tearing off down the street.

Blood and booze course through him. His whole body is bright, shining with fear. He can hear them shouting behind him. Their boots thundering on the flags. An army, a herd.

Fucking stop, he hears one of them shout. Stop where you fucking are.

But he doesn't stop.

He pumps his arms and his legs. He's never been good at sport, but he's not slow. His stride is long since he's grown, and his lungs are strong. Hours and hours of wading through the river, of walking through the town. He's covered as many as eight or nine miles in a day before.

He whirs past an old woman walking her dog, nearly knocks her to the pavement. She cries out, brings her little terrier close to her and stoops to lift it into her arms. The streetlights blur by, winking orange stars above him. The cool air rushes through his long hair, throws it back onto his shoulders.

He knows that the playing fields are coming up on his left. He decides that he's going to turn. As soon as he sees the grass open out in front of him and the pale skeletal goal posts in the distance, he's going to head for the copse of trees on the other side.

His chest starts to heave. He chances a look over his shoulder. Some of them have dropped away, but two are still in pursuit, only a couple of metres behind. One of them, the one with the spiked hair, has his teeth gritted together and he's snorting like a Rottweiler. With every breath out he spits the word fuck.

Their boots look heavy, the way they slap against the pavement, and he imagines how they'll feel when they slam into his ribs, into the side of his head. But he has his trainers on and he knows this is an advantage. Once he gets to the grass, he will surely be able to outrun them.

He reaches the playing fields, veers left on to them, leaping the small black railing that runs around their perimeter. His feet hit the grass. It hasn't been cut and his trainers tear through it with a ripping noise that almost sounds like Velcro. The fields stretch out blue in front of him. He can see the dark stand of the trees on the other side. He's been there before, he knows that there are plenty of places to hide.

He turns, throws his jaw over his shoulder and sees that the two are still chasing him. Now that they're away from the streetlights and the cars, they're as black and featureless as shadows. Moving over the grass, their boots meeting the earth with dulled, rhythmic blows, like a fist striking the thick meat of a palm.

Grunting and spitting and cursing.

Fuck you, cunt.

The words reach his ears and he accelerates a little more. Moving quicker and quicker, his legs feeling weightless, blood roaring in his ears. They want him badly, want to hurt him, want to break his teeth and his ribs.

He passes the goalposts, the nets long since stripped. The vague paintwork of the pitch. The six-yard box and the penalty spot all churned-up mud, footprints going in every direction that have dried in the wind.

He looks over his shoulder again and can no longer see them. He tunes out the ragged lurching of his own breath and finds that he can't hear them either. They must have given up and fallen back out of sight. Then he can hear their voices in the distance, shouting after him, threatening him, telling him that they'll find him again, that they know what he looks like.

He allows himself to slow to a walk, folding his hands on the back of his head, the night air cooling him. On the other side of the copse he'll find another road that will take him back home.

Beneath the trees, he breathes in the darkness: damp earth and bark, leaf mould, the vaguely acidic whiff of nettles. His feet crunch down on fallen twigs. His heart is still motoring. He hears the handclap of wings from above him somewhere, a nodding branch that slowly stills itself.

His vision is filled with bright, bursting pinpricks of light. His heart butts against his ribs. He feels as if his legs might give way beneath him, and when he looks down at his hands, he finds that they're shaking, his long fingers vibrating with a current that travels the entire length of his body, coursing up and down, up and down. If the sky were to open above him and he were to be beamed up, he wouldn't be surprised. He feels as if anything could happen, as if some permanent order has been temporarily rewired. For a moment, he stands still and closes his eyes. He wants to savour the last of this feeling, which he can already sense is ebbing away.

He emerges out the other side into the amber glow of streetlight. A quiet road, one of the nicer ones. It's only fifteen minutes from his grandparents' house, and yet it feels alien to him. The houses have gardens with lawns and flowers and ornaments. The windows are bigger, cleaner. The brickwork isn't as dirty or scarred. All the roofs have a complete set of tiles. There are cars that have been recently washed, with doors that don't look in danger of rusting shut. Even the air seems to smell different, no tired, sour edge to it.

He walks slowly along the pavement. He keeps looking over his shoulder just in case he's about to be ambushed. He knows that he can't switch off, that he can't let his guard down just yet.

Down the road there's another patch of grass with a small building set on it. It had been an electrical sub-station with one of those huge, menacing fences around it and a sign: KEEP OUT DANGER OF DEATH. Now it's no longer in use. The fence has been ripped away and the building left to stand. Smaller kids tend to sit on the flat roof in summer, because it's low enough for most to jump up or to dig the toe-ends of their trainers into the brick-work and scramble on to the sun-warmed tar.

He hasn't been for a long time. Back when he was young, he would only have gone near it if no one else was around. Then he might have climbed up and sat and let his legs dangle, doing nothing in particular, just looking out and thinking. It was a good spot to think, set back far enough from the road that the noise wasn't too loud, but close enough to watch the cars go by and look at the faces peer-ing through the windows. Men and women, children belted in the backseat. He'd liked to imagine the places they might be going, to the cinema or the pet store or church. And he could stay there for hours and think of nothing else besides this.

He should be back home.

His nan will be worried about him. But he's not ready to go back, not just yet. The drinks he's had with his grandad have worn off slightly from all the running, but he feels now a kind of dreaminess, a yearning for some unspecified thing that he wants to cling on to, so he thinks he'll go to the old electrical station and climb up on the roof, maybe just lie down and look up at the stars.

He keeps checking over his shoulder as he walks along past the nice houses. Lights are on in the windows, though they're not the harsh pale lights he's used to but soft and warm, with a glow that turns the walls an alluring shade of orange. He thinks that he'd like to be in one of those rooms, just for a moment, just to see what it feels like. He's never had any friends to invite him round to theirs.

He feels the urge to knock on a door and ask if he might just stand in the hallway, or have a look around if they didn't mind. He imagines himself walking from room to room, his hands behind his back, nodding and admiring things, raising his eyebrows every now and then. The thought doesn't frighten him. He thinks that he might even be quite charming. He could push his hair away from his face, sweep it back behind his ears. All smiles and compliments.

The houses come to an end and the square of grass appears with the old station on it. There's a scrawl of fresh graffiti on the brickwork, the word WOMP written in red. He has no idea what it means, and he briefly wonders about the person who has done it, whether it means anything to them or if it's just nonsense and, if so, what pleasure they might derive from seeing it written there.

The building looks smaller to him in this moment than it did the last time he'd seen it. The edge of the roof is beginning to peel, just above head height. He places his palms flat on it, cocks his elbows and pushes off the ground until he's holding himself up, his arms shaking slightly. Then he lifts one trainer and scrambles up. He crouches and looks all round him. He would have thought there would be some kids still here, even though it's completely dark now. He knows it must be well past nine.

He makes sure all the buttons of his coat are done up and then he lies down. He thrusts his legs over the edge of the roof. The stars wheel above him. He closes his eyes and folds his arms across his chest, tucks his hands into the warmth of his armpits.

He doesn't feel tired. His mind still feels very active, but when he tries to open his eyes, he finds that he doesn't want to. He's enjoying the darkness. The cars driving by whisper to him. He yawns, and he feels the dryness of his mouth. He belches out a sour gust of beer, and something about the taste seems to lift him up and out of his body and into one of the Bog People's bodies.

He's suddenly one of them, curled up deep in the ground, buried alone in the damp darkness. The pressure of all that earth on top of him. Holding him perfectly still. But he's not dead. None of them are dead. He's still breathing and they're all still breathing. What they're doing, he discovers, is waiting, though he doesn't know what for. All he knows is that they're waiting for something and that in time it will reveal itself. He must keep still and he must wait.

This is all he has to do.

But something has reached in, through the dirt and the peat, to start pulling on his leg. He can feel it tugging him by the ankle, grasping at him, trying to drag him up and out of the darkness. He's happy in the darkness. He doesn't want to go. He wants to stay here for ever, waiting in the stillness, with the sweet promise of something moving inexorably toward him.

He sits up sharply.

His chin is slick with drool. He stares about and finds himself still on the roof of the old station. Nothing is wrong. He must have dozed off and started dreaming. But then he can feel something, something that has a hold of his foot, that's trying to loosen his trainer, pulling down hard on the heel.

He kicks out and leaps to his feet, but his trainer comes off in the process and he's left standing on the roof with one trainer on and the other foot in just a white sock, the toes black with dirt.

He can't see anyone. He thinks it must be the boys from the chippy come back for him, come to finish what they started, and he's about to spring off the roof and start running again, when a face appears that he recognizes.

He knows the face, even through the gloom: the shape of the nose and the slightly pointed ears, the brightness in the eyes. It's Evan, the boy he'd sat next to in the car on the way to the coast all those years ago at Ronan's birthday. He's smiling, laughing almost, pushing little jets of air out through his nose and swaying slightly. He has a can of something in his hand and he's holding Finn's trainer in the other. He lifts it up, waggles it in the air.

All right, Finn.

3

HE WRITES EVERY DAY, SCRATCHES IT ALL DOWN IN his cramped, slanting hand: the way an old woman takes her seat on a bench; a spider abseiling down a wall; the violent smear of ketchup as it falls from the tines of his fork. In the little black chapbook that he keeps in his coat pocket, he notes what he sees. His entries rarely depict anything extraordinary; he's happy just to catch a moment and record it, to still time and keep it pressed between the pages. He has faith in words. He knows that they'll always add up to something, that none are ever wasted.

The feel of the book in his pocket has become vital to him. Pressed against his ribs, its solid weight. He has flashes of pure panic where his palms sweat and the skin on the nape of his neck tightens if he's left the house without it. For so long, he's been yearning for a way of dealing with the world, of trying to exercise control over it, and now that he's found it, now that he no longer feels so helpless, he refuses to let it go.

How his notes wind up as lyrics is an altogether more peculiar thing; but he doesn't want it explaining, and anyone who does ought to simply listen to the songs harder. He's become almost militant in his views on the creative process. After gigs, in the pubs and clubs in town, he can be heard asserting his opinions with a quiet dogmatism, receiving any contesting argument with a slow, sad shake of his head.

He's still getting used to hearing the sound of his own voice in conversation with people. For so many years, his thoughts existed only in his head, chained there by the fear and panic that he'd be launched down a series of doomed pathways. Now, even if he can still be shy and awkward, words move through and out of him with ease, so much so that, when he's talking, a small, astonished portion of his brain is able to look on in wonder at the miraculous transformation.

He's done as his grandad told him and found a job in a large store in town; he contributes a decent sum of money to the house every week in return, and he can consider himself a living, breathing, functioning member of society.

But neither his nan nor his grandad can quite reconcile the small, insular boy he was with this tall, languorous figure that eats at the kitchen table each morning, and returns home late smelling of smoke and alcohol, his hair now well past his shoulders, his long coat darkly billowing behind him. It's not that he talks a great deal more, or that he's become boisterous or obnoxious in any way. It's how he carries himself, the way he seems to be – not always, but sometimes – at ease in his own skin.

They've never seen the band he's in perform, but they know enough to understand that he's found the strength and courage to stand on a stage in front of an audience and sing. Who knew he could sing? Where has he got this confidence from? They ask these questions frequently, and then sit in stunned silence, the lights of the TV flickering over their ageing faces.

HE'S NOT SAID IT out loud to Evan, but joining the band has saved his life. It sounds dramatic, mawkish, but he feels it to be true. He's found what he is meant to be doing with his life. He couldn't have imagined that it would be this. He would never have thought that he could write lyrics, could stand up in front of an audience and, with his whole body pulsing with music, sing for hours at a time about all that he's gone through.

But this is what he's done now for the past two and a bit years. He's walked out on to dozens and dozens of stages, in all the pubs and the clubs in town, and in front of as many as a hundred people, he's opened his mouth, and he's sent words, sounds, flying toward a sea of strange faces, all of them turned to look at him, the boy who was once so terrified of words that he wouldn't talk, the boy other people had chosen to laugh at and torment, the boy who hadn't thought himself worthy of leaving any kind of impression on anybody.

His first few performances, he was sick with nerves. They'd only ever practised in Evan's garage. For a long and terrifying two minutes on that first night, he'd gone literally blind with panic, stumbling around the small, cluttered room in the back of the pub that they'd been told to wait in.

The knot in his stomach had tightened to nausea, and he'd wanted to escape, to run back to the river and the bridge where'd he'd gone as a boy, to spend those quiet hours sifting with his fingers through the silt and the stones.

But it was Evan who'd calmed him down and told him that everything was going to be all right. Once he was out there, he'd enjoy himself. He'd feel the sense of freedom that they'd spent so many nights talking about between themselves. There'd be, he said, a place where Finn could create who he wanted to be, could control how others saw him, rather than sit and wait and let everyone else decide who he was.

It was talks like this that had bonded them so swiftly after that night they'd met again on the roof of the old substation. They'd spent almost every day together since then. They each spoke of how lost and alone and afraid they'd felt as boys, of having a space inside them, an emptiness that they both had a terrible desperation to fill.

So he'd mentioned the box beneath his bed; he'd told Evan he didn't have a mam or a da. Sometimes Evan would simply nod. This was one of the things Finn appreciated most about Evan: it seemed to have been inculcated in him – by who or what, Finn didn't know – the simple, often misunderstood practice of listening, of when to say something and when to remain silent.

Evan had suffered in his own ways, too. He'd not been targeted with the same persistence and aggression that Finn had, but he said he still had no real friends, and those that had been like-minded and willing to talk to him were often quick to put him down. He felt that his enthusiasm was often misconstrued as arrogance, so his ideas or theories, though he knew they were more sophisticated than most others, were dismissed as attempts to assert his authority. He had been searching, just as Finn had, for a place that he could be himself, without feeling as if he was going to be jeered at.

What so often struck Finn about Evan was the strength of his relationship with himself, with his own thoughts and feelings. Where Finn could only look upon himself from a great distance, never knowing how to build the bridge between what he felt and how it might be expressed, Evan had established a vocabulary with which to feel. He spoke about himself as if he were another person, who he'd been following around, observing his every move. That's what music had given him, he said, a way of searching his own heart and conveying what he found there.

Evan explained to Finn that music could be a part of solving their problems. That's why he'd formed a band. A band, he claimed, could be a kind of family. He'd put up a recruitment notice on every noticeboard he could find: Lead guitarist looking for singer, drummer, bassist. He'd found two brothers: Allan to play drums, and Jake – whose sweeping fringe was the envy of both boys and girls – to play bass. They were nice, decent lads. They liked good stuff, and they were serious about their craft.

Three months later, Finn was backstage in the pub waiting to go on stage, and then he was out there, thrust into the strobes of light and the scented pockets of darkness, sweat and beer and urine lifting from the floor, the walls, the jostling bodies. He'd closed his eyes for most of it, and he'd imagined that he was up there alone, that there was no audience, that the words he was uttering were a kind of prayer, a conversation between him and something bigger than himself, not a god or any other kind of higher power, but maybe the space that he and Evan had talked about: the emptiness that they'd each recognized in the other.

He'd closed his eyes and imagined that he was filling it with words.

WHEN THEY WRITE THEIR songs, they usually sit together in the same room, and while Evan starts playing around on his guitar, Finn can hitch his mind to the plucked strings or strummed chords, and without knowing what he's going to write, he simply puts his pen to paper and sees what comes out.

For Finn, these moments feel very much separate from their friendship. He can almost feel himself to be alone. They rarely talk, and sometimes don't even look at one another for hours on end. All of Finn's focus is on himself, on the words that start to stir and then offer themselves out for him to pick and handle.

He feels as if he's working, though not in the same way as when he was studying at school, or when he's stacking shelves in the store. Writing with Evan feels like an active investigation, not only of himself, but of what's around him. Where normally he does his best to keep the world at bay, here he invites it in, allows himself to be touched and affected by it, even if that risks his being made to feel hurt or afraid. He doesn't find it easy. He can become anxious and have to go for long walks up and down the avenue of trees in the park down the road from Evan's house; or he can grow frustrated when he feels he's not giving himself over to the process fully enough, in which case he has a habit of pressing the heels of his hands hard into his eyes until colours flare and fade.

At the end of a session, he and Evan will discuss what they've done. More often than not, it's Evan who will do most of the talking. He'll play the riff or melody that he's come up with in full, and then explain to Finn how he's achieved the particular sound, which people or bands he suspects have influenced it, what arrangements of bass and drums he thinks could accompany it.

Only then will Finn read over the lyrics he's set down. He'll never sing it straight away to Evan's music. This comes later, after Evan has exhausted his excitement in his own creation. Only then will Evan allow Finn's words to make a space for themselves.

Then there are other times when they'll work independently for a week, and by the end of it, there'll always be something new to show and discuss. Once the songs are finished, Finn tends to step back; he's content for Evan to take control when they're introducing what they've made to Allan and Jake. Finn doesn't feel the proprietorship of the song that he knows Evan does. Music is only ever fleetingly his. Once he starts performing it, it ceases to make sense to him in any one way, but shifts its meaning so he can't be sure of what it was he'd felt at its inception.

In every other context of his life, he's found strangers to be frightening, potentially dangerous; he is forever anticipating their desire to humiliate him in ways he's now come to find he's impervious to when performing. The knot's still there in his stomach when he performs, the same as it always has been, but it's morphed into something he wants, something he can manipulate for good. It creates a tension in his voice, a bristling energy that rises up to the surface of his body so that the audience knows his anguish, can recognize his truth and soak it up for themselves. Very quickly, performing has come to feel like an extension of his vulnerability, rather than the attempted suffocation or destruction of it. He doesn't feel exposed, but rather that the audience are being exposed to him.

Because it's him that they're seeing, and yet it's not. He can speak and move in ways that would be impossible off stage. Off stage, he's still locked in himself; he still has too much time, too much room to conjure up all his insecurities and have them play out in his head. Off stage, his wounds are there for all to see, and they can be made to bleed with only a glance.

But when he's singing, he's tending to these wounds, and he's bringing things – feelings and thoughts and doubts and worries that have always mystified or hurt him or made him feel insignificant – closer. He wants them so close that he can touch them, hear them, smell them. Because only then can he begin to understand them. In this way, performing has taken on a kind of sacred quality in his life. He feels that without it, he'd be in danger somehow, that he'd turn on himself again and he'd have no weapons to fight back.

He has no instrument to hide behind, only his long black trench coat that he sometimes likes to draw close to him or, as a song is reaching its final moments, span out around him like wings. Evan is always to his left on lead guitar, screeching and yowling, and the other two band-mates, Allan on the drums and Jake on bass, keeping a steady, crashing, industrial rhythm.

It's Finn's voice, a flat, solid baritone that stretches and wraps around his words, that drives the songs. Some words he spits out, others he has to drag up from deep inside him. Each one feels different in his mouth, and sometimes even leaves its own particular taste in its wake. He's in com-mand. He has both the questions and the answers; he can challenge the audience to come closer, and then with the flick of his long fingers he can push them away.

After a show, sometimes the band will just walk straight off the stage into the audience. Some people buy them drinks, and Finn often gets collared. They lavish him with praise, and immediately the attention feels different to the kind he can feel on stage. His old wariness creeps back in. His shield is gone. He's thinking, thinking, thinking. He is back amongst people, and more than once he's had to try and brush aside the unwelcome suspicion that singing and performing isn't the complete remedy he continues to hope it might be, and that whatever good it does for him will never achieve the permanence he so desires.

The band have cultivated something of a cult following in the town. The same people turn up at their gigs week in, week out. From time to time, he's recognized in the store where he and now Evan both work, when he's at the till or stacking shelves. Evan jokes about him becoming famous, and Finn's thought about what it would be like to be known beyond the confines of the town, to be recognized on the same scale as some of his heroes, fills him with dread.

It's not what he wants. What he likes about performing in the small, familiar, intimate spaces that they do, is that he feels heard and understood, as if it's under his control.

One of the local papers has reviewed their act favourably; they're the cream of the crop among all the local bands. They have a swagger and a confidence, and Finn, with his hair and his height, has a natural presence that people seem to gravitate toward. Whenever there are conversations about which band is most likely to make it, theirs comes out on top.

What Finn truly doesn't like about the band is their name.

Spurdog.

It was a week after he'd joined that Evan had suggested it. Think about it, Evan had said. Think how you could take something that's caused you so much shit, and you can turn it into something else, something that's yours. It can mean what you want it to mean, or it can mean fuck all. It's in your hands now.

Even hearing Evan say it had made him flinch. Since he'd grown, no one really threw that name at him anymore. That phase of his life had come to an end, and he was starting a new one. He felt like associating this new joy with his troubled, painful past would be foolish. He didn't want to have to think when he heard it about every time he'd ever been tormented.

But Evan had pushed and pushed, and finally Finn had

given in. Maybe he was right. Maybe it could mean what he wanted it to mean, that was all in his hands now.

AS THE SUMMER PROGRESSES, they try to play at least two gigs a week. They have a kind of residency in one club on the far side of town, which gives them the opportunity to play new material, because Finn is always writing, and so is Evan.

In Finn's eyes, things couldn't be going better. The people he meets at the gigs have started to seem like friends to him. It's a community, a space that's opened itself up to him, that wants him to be a part of it.

He's lost his virginity with a girl called Amy. She's training to be a nurse in the local hospital. She's much shorter than him, with a pale face, crow-black hair and dark makeup around her eyes that he finds incredibly alluring. She comes to every gig, and he normally ends up back at the small flat she shares with another nursing student.

It's taken some time for him to relax in Amy's company, to undress and climb into bed and let himself be touched. At first, it had made him so nervous that he could barely move. His limbs had felt like they needed to be oiled, and each of his movements carried with it a tension and an awkwardness that he knew must make him seem cold, unyielding. But Amy is gentle and patient, and he's come to savour the moment that their limbs lock together, that he can feel the arch of her back and smell the sweetness of her throat as he comes inside her.

It's the luxurious sense of stillness and peace he feels in these hours with Amy that bring into sharp relief Evan's increasing restlessness. It's only recently that he's started to complain, pacing around the garage of his parents' place after practice and lamenting their position. He lives on one of the nice streets Finn had walked past that night he'd run from the chippy. His parents don't mind them practising there, seem to like it, only interrupting to bring in drinks or snacks.

The band has become too comfortable, Evan says. If we're going to progress, then we need a new challenge. We can't just stay where we are. The industry isn't kind to those who wait for something to happen. We've got to make it happen. We've got to go out there and grab every opportunity we can.

So when Allan and Jake's da, a bricklayer, needs an operation on his back and offers to sell them his old white van, Evan suggests a tour. They could all pool their money and buy the van. He wants to travel down South and play some of the clubs that they've heard about.

That's where we'll get spotted, he says. That's where all the big bands get their foot in the door.

The idea seems to appeal to the rest of the band much more than it does to Finn. Finn feels happy playing the pubs and clubs around the town. He has his platform here and it feels enough to him. He likes the number of people that turn up; he likes that he knows most of them now, that he can call some of them his friends; he likes Amy, and he likes thinking about the months, maybe even years, that they could have together. Everything that he needs from performing is right here on his doorstep.

But Evan disagrees, and he snaps at Finn one night after practice when the two of them are alone. They're sitting beside one another on the old, lumpy sofa in the corner of the garage drinking from a can when Finn suggests that he's not so keen on the idea of going on tour.

What are you going to do? Evan spits. Keep picking up shit out of the river and hiding it under your bed?

Finn looks down at the black boots with the zips that he recently bought. He doesn't know how to reply. This is the first time that Evan's ever been angry with him. He feels ashamed: that he's shown Evan this private part of himself, that Evan knows about the river and the box under his bed.

Things have just been going well here, he says.

Evan slaps the flat of his palm against the arm of the sofa. Dust swirls in the hard light.

And they can go even better somewhere else, he says. This place is dead. There's nothing here for us. You can fuck around all you like here, but not me. I've got better things to do than waste my time up here.

And then he stands up and storms from the room, leaving Finn alone in the garage, sitting on the sofa and staring down at the zip on his left boot until he eventually gets up and leaves.

The next day, Evan calls round. Finn's nan answers the door and calls Finn downstairs. He finds Evan out on the street, his hands tucked in his pockets, pacing around, his sharp nose slightly sunburned after a very hot last day of September.

Finn steps out and shuts the door behind him.

I shouldn't have said some of the stuff I said last night, Evan says.

Finn says nothing, only nods.

Evan continues pacing, his eyes occasionally lifting to meet Finn's.

But the tour's an opportunity, he says. That's all I'm saying. Why not try it and see what happens? If it goes tits up, then that's fine. We can come back and carry on here.

He stops and claps Finn hard on the top of his arm. He smiles.

Think about it, he says, and then he turns and walks away down the street, his head lowered, his steps short and quick.

The next day, Finn agrees and they buy the van. It would be more sensible to wait until next summer to set off, since they'll be sleeping in the back of it, and the winter nights will surely freeze them half to death. But Evan doesn't want to wait. So it's decided that come the beginning of December, they'll set off for three weeks and be back before Christmas.

THE MONTHS PASS AND they practise more and more, honing their set until it's as slick as it's ever been. Finn and Evan write two new songs, both of which they try out at the pub they play at every week, and which get a good response. There's one in particular that's slightly different from all of their other stuff. There's a little less distortion in the guitars and Allan's drumming is less erratic, which gives Finn's voice and lyrics some more room to breathe. And it's the first time that he's written a proper chorus, one that he looks forward to slipping back into, and that he quickly becomes aware people are eager to join in on.

We're moving in the right direction, Evan says.

They all quit their jobs on the same day. Finn and Evan walk out of the store into the cold December sunshine. Evan reaches up, grabs the collar of Finn's coat and rags it around.

This is it, he says. This is the beginning of it all. Tomorrow we'll be off. Tomorrow we start writing our own script.

Finn has told his nan and grandad about the tour. His nan isn't happy about it, but it's his grandad who urges her to keep calm.

If it's what he wants to do, then it's what he wants to do, he says.

Finn can tell that he's disappointed that he's left his job in such a cavalier fashion. His grandad has respect for the workplace, and Finn knows that his quitting so brazenly will have upset him. And yet still he seems to want to support him. It surprises Finn, who still struggles to see beyond his grandad's gruff exterior. He wonders if there'll ever come a time when the two of them will do their best to explain who they really feel themselves to be, or the distance between them now will be the distance between them for evermore.

The van is packed with their equipment, with their bags of clothes and great heaps of blankets and duvets and pillows, tins of food and bottles of drink. Evan's already managed to organize a few gigs along the way, one or two in the cities where some of the biggest bands have come from. When they arrive down South, it'll be up to them to hustle around and make an impression. They'll be gone for nearly a month, so they're going to have to rely on people they meet to offer the use of showers and sofas once in a while.

Finn is waiting in the dark of the morning for the van to pick him up, his breath fogging in front of him. His hands are buried deep into his pockets and he stamps the soles of his boots against the flags to warm his numbing toes.

The street – the street that he's lived on his entire life – is quiet. Now that he's leaving it behind, he feels a swell of fondness for it. He remembers how he'd slink back here from the river, his feet still cold and damp in his trainers from the water. It'd been busy with kids then, with its own small dramas playing out every day. Now it's silent but for his heels on the scuffed, gummed flags. One or two lights are on, but mostly the windows are dark. Some are boarded up. In recent years, houses have been abandoned, some with the furniture still in them. He's looked through the windows and it has unnerved him, as if the family hasn't moved away but has simply vanished, dropped off the face of the earth.

He imagines Amy still sleeping in bed, the tousled nest of her dark hair spilling across the pillow, and he feels a pang to be by her side, pressing his body against her and hearing her moan softly in her sleep. When he comes back, he wonders if things might become more serious. They've been talking about it, the idea of becoming an item, the kind that walks around holding hands, that makes dinner together on an evening and curls up on the sofa to watch TV. He thinks he could ring her up and tell her now that this is what he wants, but he knows she'll have to get up for work soon, so he promises himself that she'll be the first person he sees when he gets back.

The van roars around the corner then, and the horn blares once, twice, three times. A second after it pulls up, Evan slides the door open, hops out and snatches Finn's bag from his hand.

Time to go, he says.

He barely looks Finn in the face before he's back in the van, and a chant goes up from Allan and Jake, hands clapping and their voices echoing down the street.

THE FOUR GIGS THEY play on the way are nearly empty. The venues are unfamiliar, and the sound is nowhere near as good as back home. They arrange themselves on stage to a light, almost imperceptible smattering of applause on each occasion. Heads nod along, but they can hear chatter at some points, and Evan leaves the stage furious after the final song, complaining that the further south they go, the ruder people become.

Allan and Jake are the only ones who can drive, and they both complain that their arms feel tired when they're on stage. None of them have slept properly in the back of the van. Twice they've stopped in a lay-by for the night, and every time a car speeds by the van shakes and the suspension lets out a haunting groan, waking all of them up. Even with the heaps of duvets and pillows, the cold seeps through the interstices in the metalwork, and they wake shivering. None of them have showered in days and the smell is potent: sweat and sour breath, the stale, back-of-the-cupboard smell of unwashed clothes.

There's an intimacy to the whole experience that Finn – so accustomed to being alone with himself and his body – has never experienced before. He can't seem to move without touching somebody else or one of their belongings. He's always crouched beneath the low ceiling, his long limbs tucked and folded into himself like an ironing board. When he tries to move and find purchase to haul himself through the van toward the back doors, his hands touch jeans and sweat-soaked T-shirts, socks stiff and crusted with spilled beer, underwear twisted and strewn in a way he's only ever seen his own at the foot of Amy's bed on a morning.

At one point, disoriented in the middle of the night and reaching out for his bottle of water, his fingers grope blindly in the chill dark, and find something slick and warm, and it's only when it begins to move and he feels a short blast of warm air that he realizes he's had the tips of his fingers in one of his bandmates' mouths.

The constant closeness makes him retreat into himself. He has been quiet, distant, never quite present. His performances, for the first ever time, become lacklustre. He's not got sufficient energy, and he's struggled to work his way into the songs. The words, for reasons that he hasn't been able to fathom, haven't felt like his but somebody else's. Though Evan hasn't mentioned anything, Finn can tell that he's noticed; and he knows that he'll not address it immediately but will keep it safely stowed away until he thinks it the right time to strike.

They arrive. The capital city – they had all been excited about it in their own different ways, having only ever seen it in pictures and in films or read about it in books. But they don't see any of the fancy or historic buildings around them, none of the wide streets and the expensive stores, no bridge swooping over the glistening roll of the river. Not even the faintest whiff of glamour.

What they find is a place that looks even more run-down than where they're from. Rain-grey streets with bruised, scarred buildings. The houses all have a different colour of brick – sickly pale, almost yellow. People trudge about with a strange kind of wariness, keeping themselves to themselves, as if holding back a secret.

They find a cafe on a corner with red lacquer seats and chipped plywood tables. They sit down and order tea and some sausage sandwiches. They handle what little money they have with great care, picking out coins and dropping them into the outstretched palm of the woman behind the till.

Darkness is closing in outside. Finn can feel the knot in his stomach tightening by the minute. They're all tired, worn out. They need to have a shower and a good night's sleep, but they all know that's not possible. It's only Evan who talks, telling them all to get ready for what's coming up, the biggest opportunity of their lives.

This is it, he says. This is what we've come here for. To be in amongst it all. To start living our lives.

But Allan and Jake both sulk beneath their fringes,

sipping at their tea and prodding disconsolately at the crusts on their plates. And Finn can only smile at Evan, though he can't be sure what his lips are doing, and that they haven't turned down into more of a grimace.

It goes on like this.

Some nights they find a slot to play, and others they find nothing and have to entertain themselves. They drive around from borough to borough, sometimes catching sight of a famous landmark, but only fleetingly. The grey quilt of clouds seems permanently pinned above them. Even the Christmas lights that hang from lamp posts do little to add any cheer.

Some of the gigs they manage to find and play are bouncing, and they come off the stage drenched in sweat, exhilarated. Finn finds it in himself to forget whatever seems to be troubling him, and he gets back into his old groove, feeling his words pouring out of him, faces in the audience turned toward him, eyes wide and cheeks glistening, hair plastered down on foreheads.

But there are other venues in which all he can do is half-heartedly run through the songs, the words alien to him, until they're done and they can leave – or, if they're lucky, find someone there whose house or flat they can go back to for a shower.

After one show where Finn could sense his performance to be particularly dispirited, Evan corners him in a narrow corridor at the back of the venue that smells of damp and urine. The light above them is about to blow, sputtering on and off, and splashing the dripping, flaking walls with a sickly yellow light.

What the fuck was that? Evan says.

He is close to Finn, his body low and his fists clenched, like a boxer about to give his ribs a working over.

What was what? Finn says.

You know fucking well what, snaps Evan. We come all this way and you churn out shit like that. Like you've just got out of fucking bed.

Finn stammers but says nothing. He can hear Evan's breath gusting out through his flaring nostrils. He can feel the heat coming off him. He wants to tell Evan that something doesn't feel right about the whole thing. He's not happy; he feels uncomfortable. None of this is what he wants.

But as soon as he opens his mouth again, he sees Evan raise up his hand as if to strike him. He closes his eyes, expecting the sing or thud of a blow, but feels only three light slaps on his cheek.

Turn it up next time, Evan says, and Finn opens his eyes to see him walking away down the flickering corridor.

The nights in the van become increasingly unpleasant. They do their best to find quiet streets to park on, but one night Finn hears movement outside. The rest of them are sleeping, Allan curled in one corner snoring, and Evan and Jake side by side, sharing two duvets. Their equipment towers over them, the amps stacked on top of one another, the two guitars propped and crossed at the neck in the opposite corner to Allan, like some new-fangled coat of arms. The only light they have is a battery-powered torch that they pass around to find their bearings.

Finn flicks the torch on.

He listens again and hears nothing. He thinks that maybe

he was just dreaming. But a moment later the van starts to shake, and there are shouts and manic laughter coming through the rusting panels. The rest of them wake up, but they're all too stunned to say or do anything. Finn directs the torchlight from face to face, each one looking paler and more shocked than the last. They listen as they hear glass smashing and more laughter, then they hear someone climb up on to the roof above them, the metal warping and popping under the weight. One of the amps falls and both guitars slide awkwardly to the floor, their strings twanging tunelessly.

They do nothing but wait until the person climbs down, and the shouts and laughter slowly recede. When it's been silent for a good five minutes, they gingerly open the back doors and step out into the frigid night air. They find that both wing mirrors have been smashed clean off, and there are dents in the bonnet and on the roof. Fortunately, the windscreen is still intact. They have no spare money to get the wing mirrors replaced, so they'll just have to drive home without.

TWO WEEKS INTO THE tour and a general torpor settles over the group. Only Evan remains optimistic. Though it's true he's also been unnerved by the attack, he tries to convince the others that the whole experience will serve as the kind of gritty anecdote that they'll be able to churn out for people when they get back. Or, maybe one day, they'll be able to tell it to journalists, who'll be impressed by the rawness of their origins and drive to succeed.

For the first time, Finn begins to doubt Evan. For all he

admires Evan's drive and optimism, he can't help but feel his vision for the band is becoming increasingly misguided. Their altercation in the corridor after the gig has very nearly severed the connection between them. Finn loves the band, and he loves creating and singing the songs – but he doesn't want to make himself miserable doing it. It's exactly what he feared before they came: it feels like they're trying to change something that ought to stay as it is.

Jake is the first to suggest they go home a week early. Allan immediately agrees. It's obvious they have been discussing it between themselves for a while. They're in the corner of a low-ceilinged pub when they bring it up. Christmas lights and tinsel are strung about.

Evan receives the news in stunned silence. His eyes dart between both of them.

You can't be serious, he says.

Jake nods, his blonde fringe falling over his eyes.

We are, he says. We're sick of sleeping in the van. We want to get back. We've had enough.

Despite their occasional petty arguments, it's always been clear to Finn how loyal the brothers are to one another. They have talked in passing with Finn about a younger sister at home with some kind of disability, and it had been apparent in the way they talked about her, with their mouths set straight and their heads nodding slowly, how protective they are of her, and how they already know there are more important things in life than playing in a successful band.

Evan shakes his head, sips his pint, and then wipes his lips with a bunched fist.

Fine, he snarls. You two take the van, and me and Finn will stay. We can run through a few songs without you, and we'll earn enough money to get the bus back.

He turns to Finn. Finn stays very still. He doesn't want to disappoint his best friend, the one person who knows so much about him, who saved him with this band. He owes him so much, but he also knows that the two of them carrying on without Jake and Allan is a terrible idea.

Where will we stay? he asks.

We'll find places, Evan says.

Finn shakes his head and lowers his eyes to the table.

I think we should go back, he says.

What? says Evan.

It doesn't make sense to stay. We're all tired. You're tired.

Being fucking tired is part of the job, Evan says. We came here to work, not sleep.

They argue about it for an hour until Evan eventually storms off. They don't find him back at the van, so they spend another two hours walking around the cold streets looking for him. Eventually, they come across him on a corner, propped against a letter box. He's drunk the best part of a bottle of rum, and he's been sick down himself, a pulp of regurgitated crisps smeared across one shoulder. They pick him up and carry him back to the van, where they watch him fall asleep.

In the morning, it's Evan who wakes them.

If we're going to go, he says, then we'd best get started.

His face is pale and drawn, and there's the tang of vomit coming off his clothes. Finn tries to make eye contact with him, but Evan keeps his eyes lowered. At one point, while they're making sure everything is secure in the back, Finn puts a hand on his shoulder, but Evan immediately shrugs it off.

They're around halfway home, when Evan comes back from the service station, his face looking a little brighter. He tells them he's been in the payphone to a friend of his. There's a slot become available to play tonight in a pub. It's up in a town they've all heard of, but none of them have ever been to.

But that's past ours, says Allan. It's right up on the coast.

It is, says Evan. But we're already coming back early, what difference would one extra night make? He claps his hands together and rubs them. Come on! he pleads. Why don't we go out with a bit of a bang?

Finn's the first to agree to it. He feels sorry for Evan, the way his face looks so open and vulnerable, and he also likes the idea of playing in the North – further north even than their town. Evan's been almost silent up until this point; if doing this will go some way to repairing what he feels will be a terrible rift in their relationship, then he wants to do it.

Jake and Allan are less enthusiastic. They both look exhausted and fed up.

It'll add at least an hour on to the drive, Jake says. We're already looking tight for petrol, and we still don't have any wing mirrors.

The brothers have spent the entire journey having to stick their heads out the window into the freezing wind, checking if they can move lanes without causing an accident.

We've made it this far, Evan says. And this gig pays a little bit more. Don't worry about petrol.

The brothers look at each other, shrug, and then smile. They look most alike when they're smiling, the way their lips lift to reveal pale, hard-looking gums and their heavily lashed eyes narrow to slits.

OK, let's do it, Allan says. One more show.

The hours pass and darkness starts to settle outside. They drive past the turn-off for their own town, the van rattling under the orange blur of the streetlights. They'll not have long to set up when they get there, but Evan is back to his old self, claiming that this pub, though in the arse end of nowhere, has a bit of a reputation for getting some decent bands going.

When they arrive, they know that they're near the sea, but it's too dark to see anything much, other than the little row of shops and the narrow streets, and then the pub with its Christmas lights strung raggedly from the guttering.

Inside, it's more spacious than they'd first thought. There's a small stage in the corner and a decent little space for people to watch or dance. Christmas decorations are up, an artificial tree in the corner, and mistletoe hanging from the ceiling. The carpet is red and clammy underfoot.

The landlord – an old punk named Billy, with a shock of spiked black hair and one eye that rolls queasily from side to side as he speaks – greets them just inside the door. His voice is softer than Finn had anticipated, though his accent is so strong that some of the words that leave his mouth might as well be in another language. They're told that they have a forty-five-minute slot. The pub reopens at seven and they'll not come on until ten, but they ought to start setting up now.

Evan is pretty much back to his old self. He wants to mix up the setlist. He can't be sure what kind of an audience they're going to have, but he reckons they need to keep it as lively as possible.

They'll be wanting a dance tonight, I reckon, he says with his hands on his hips, his eyes narrowed and taking in every feature of their venue.

The pub has only been open for around twenty minutes before it's packed. Most of the revellers look like they've already put away a good few drinks. The atmosphere is rowdy, and there's a lovely mix of people here: young and old, men and women his nan and grandad's age, and also boys and girls their own age.

They linger by the bar, sip at their drinks and talk. Finn says little, preferring to save his voice for the performance. Around an hour before they go on, he sees two girls come through the door. It looks as if they've been here for a while already. One has dark hair and plain features, but there's something about the other that attracts Finn's attention. She's blonde, her face pale and thin. He sees that her eyes are large and blue, and that he can still discern the slightly darkened discs of skin beneath the makeup she's applied. She, too, looks like she's had more than her fair share of drinks, the way she half stumbles and laughs, then commences sliding past people to get to the bar.

He watches them for a minute, maybe more, before they disappear from view. Before they know it, Billy is barking into the mic to introduce them.

The lights go down to applause and jeers.

*

THE BAND FINISH PLAYING just before eleven. Finn is sweating, his hair damp, wild. He can tell that Evan is pleased with how it's gone. They embrace, and when Jake and Allan join them, there's the feeling that something has been healed, that the fractures of their tour might be put behind them, and the possibility of their continuing on together opens up.

The plan was to leave immediately after they've packed all the equipment back in the van, but they find that on returning to get their pay, they're swept along with the surge of people toward the bar, and suddenly Evan is accosted by a girl that had been right up by the stage watching him all gig. Finn watches him and can see that he's relishing the attention.

When Finn turns around, he sees that Allan and Jake are also engaged with two different girls. They've managed to secure themselves a table in a corner. Smoke hangs near the ceiling, thin tendrils of it snaking up from ashtrays. All the lights are back blazing, and three or four men are playing darts, taking it in turns to line themselves up, the dart moving back and forth with their cocked wrists, then releasing it through the air as it strikes the board to either cheers or whistles of derision.

Finn stays at the bar and drinks the pint that he's ordered and is sloshed his way. Some people come up to him and slap him on the back. He can barely hear what they're saying, whether they're praising him or insulting him. He does little but stare around him. It sometimes happens after a gig that he slips into dreaminess, where time passes by without his knowing, and all his interactions seem like he's communing with figments of his imagination.

Evan finds him an hour later. He's wild-eyed, his pupils large and dark. He tells Finn that he's going back to the girl's place, and that she has a sofa if he wants to crash there. Finn shakes his head. He senses Evan doesn't really want him there, that he needs his own time, so he says he'll stay and finish his drink, and he'll probably just sleep in the van. Evan nods, claps him on his shoulder, spins around to find the girl and sees her waiting by the door for him. Finn watches Evan leave, his arm around her waist.

A few moments later, Allan and Jake appear, just as last orders are being called. The blinds are being drawn and those that are known, those men and women who've been coming here for years and years, take their seats for the lock-in, and the rest are told to leave by Billy the landlord. Billy slips Finn the small wad of money for the gig, and thanks him for their performance.

You're not a bad little unit, he says. Some interesting stuff you played.

Finn thanks him and pockets the money, then finds himself outside in the cold, his breath clouding up in front of him, his hands shaking as he tries to roll a cigarette.

Outside, Allan and Jake are on the corner, both kissing the two girls they've been talking to. They look up at Finn and smile, their mouths smeared red with lipstick, and call him over. Almost word for word, they say the same as Evan, that they're going back to a flat and that he can come along if he wants, there's a sofa available for him to sleep on, then they'll all drive back in the morning. But Finn shakes his head again. He asks for the keys for the van from Jake, and says that he'll see them tomorrow.

The brothers nod and turn, then slope off down the street that's still loud with chatter. Finn watches them and he feels, not for the first time, a pang of jealousy. How different life must be, when one has been born into a relationship like theirs.

He lights his cigarette, hears the end crackle as it glows to life. He inhales and feels the tight pull of the smoke at the back of his throat, breathes it out and watches it drift up beneath the amber glow of the streetlight and disappear. The van's parked around the corner, pulled up on the kerb across the road from a row of shops, but he doesn't want to go back yet, so he starts walking in the opposite direction.

He doesn't know where he's going, but he has his little black chapbook and pen in his pocket, and he might find something that's worth jotting down. The heels of his boots click on the pavement. Over the course of the tour, a hole in the crotch of his black jeans has opened up, and he can feel a chill there, a single point of cold on his left inner thigh.

He turns left on to a street.

It doesn't seem to have any name, and there are no streetlamps down here, but he can see that most of the houses still have one or two lights on, and he decides to walk down it. He looks through some of the people's windows. In the first one, he sees two small children, a boy and a girl, curled up on a sofa, their heads inclined toward each other, almost touching. The blue and white light of the TV flashes over their sleeping faces. Through another, he sees an old man simply sitting on his own in a chair. There's no TV, just a bare bulb glowing above him, washing him in pale, almost white light.

He knows nothing of these lives, and yet he feels envious of them in some way. There's nothing to say that they have anything he doesn't, or that he should covet them in any particular way. Perhaps, he thinks, it's only that they're different to his own, and he wonders if this is the problem that everyone on earth must learn to deal with one way or another: that being trapped for years and years in the same body feels like a curse as much as it does a blessing.

He should have gone back with Evan. He wouldn't be thinking such morbid, existential thoughts if he had. At least he'd have some company, even if he was a third wheel; and at least he'd be warm, because the cold is starting to get to him now, seeping into his bones. He should just return to the van and bury himself beneath the heap of old duvets for one last night. Even after the buzz of the gig, he knows that he's tired enough to drift off, having not slept properly for two weeks straight. He turns the corner at the end of the street.

Across the road, he sees that there's a patch of grass and a large fir tree, surrounded by a small black railing no taller than waist height. The whole thing looks incongruous, almost fake, as if it's part of a film set. He studies it a moment, then feels himself drawn to it in a way that he's learned to pay attention to. That wonderful darkness of the Bog People that he still so frequently conjures up for himself. Perhaps it's this that he's now seeking, that he hopes he might be able to feel something of.

The moon appears from behind a cloud, shines down and silvers the streets, the rooftops, the wagging fronds of the tree. He wants to be near it, wants to touch it, smell it. He climbs over the small black railing. He looks around to see if anyone's watching him. He can't make out any faces at the windows, can hear only music playing somewhere, and then a distant shout followed by the barking of a dog. The heels of his boots sink into the grass. He approaches the tree as if it were sleeping, as if it might be roused and made angry by his presence, then smells the pepperiness of the fronds as he parts them and enters the darkness.

PART THREE

SNOW

1

SHE TURNS THE FAUCET AND WAITS FOR THE WATER
to gush. It runs brown for a minute before it clears, then
she fills her cupped palms and splashes her face until her
cheeks feel numb. Her breath mists beneath the bare bulb,
drifts and hangs above her like a sulphurous fog. She balls
her fists and rubs her eyes. She looks at herself in the mirror.
Her face is the colour of mustard beneath the ugly glow of
the light, and there are dark smudges where her makeup
has run. Her throat feels raw and the muscles in her stomach tender, which normally means that she's been sick at
some point.

It's only when she dries her hand on the towel that she
sees the blood. There's a cut across her knuckles on her
right hand, deep enough that she has to grab a handful of
sheets of toilet paper and staunch the flow. She hadn't felt
any pain before, but now it stings and she winces as she
reaches up into the cupboard above the sink and fetches
down a plaster, which she sticks clumsily over the wound.

She remembers nothing of the night before.

It's a mosaic of images that she has no wish to piece together. She intends to leave it like this, a fractured, broken mess, and if some of it happens to resolve itself into a whole, then she'll pay it no attention. She's learned that nothing can be gained from such things. It's all better left forgotten.

She can recall very well what happened during the day: the afternoon in the pub with her da's old friend, the address, the bus journey, then seeing him through the window with that woman, the smile on their faces, the weight of the stone in her hand that she'd so wanted to hurl with all her might. She'd stayed there looking for what could have been an hour, but finally she'd dropped the stone and turned round, then got the bus back and met Sarah at some point. There's little more she can recall after arriving at the pub.

Tears smart in her eyes; she doesn't blink but holds them there, still looking in the mirror, then wipes them harshly away before they have a chance to fall. She doesn't want to think about her da or any of it, and so she decides there and then that she isn't going to. It's happened, but she's strong enough to pretend that it hasn't. She trusts that she can leave her da behind her now; she knows she's getting good at it, this little trick of altering her past, deleting certain memories and protecting others, imposing herself on life rather than letting life impose itself on her.

When she gets back to her room, she can see only one of her shoes on the floor by her bed. She looks for the other one, lifts the duvet and pulls the bed away from the wall, but can't find it and realizes that she must've lost it somewhere and walked home without it. It isn't the first time it's happened, and she's feeling too fragile to care about it right now. What she needs is to be outside. She needs to take a walk and breathe in some fresh air. Only then will she start to feel more like herself.

She showers and dresses, slips on her trainers at the door. Letters addressed to her are heaped on the stiff bristles of the doormat. She finds nothing from her da and kicks through the rest of them like dead leaves. Outside it's bitterly cold, the sky high and blue and the sun silvery in colour. All the Christmas lights have been switched off, now strung dully from behind the windows of the houses she passes. She buttons her coat up to her chin. Her jeans feel chill and tight, nipping at the sensitive skin on her inner thighs, grating along the lengths of her shins.

She heads in the direction of the high street, toward the cafe. There, she'll sit and do her best to stomach some tea and toast, and she'll wait for an hour or so until she deems it fair to call at Sarah's and rouse her from her slumber. The two of them can chat away, and at some point, if they've sufficiently recovered, they might move on to the pub again to start making the first plans for tonight.

She's only a matter of minutes from the cafe when she sees him. She doesn't know who he is. She can't put a name to him, but there's something she recognizes about his hair, about the dark length of it that reaches down to his shoulders. She slows her pace and keeps her eye on him. The back doors of a van on the other side of the road are flung open and he's sitting at the rear of it, his legs cocked and the toes of his boots planted flat on the road. He's wearing a black coat that bunches around his narrow shoulders, and his jeans have ridden up to reveal the cold gleam of the zips that track his leather boots. Even from here, she can see that there's a hole near the crotch of his jeans, a coin-sized circle of pale flesh on show.

She can't see his face, because he's looking at something in his lap, staring down intently, his hair curtaining his features. She turns her gaze away and carries on walking. She doesn't want to attract any attention from him. She just wants to get to the cafe and sit down. The last thing she needs is some bloke thinking she's taking an interest and following her down the street.

But she can't keep herself from looking again when she draws level with the van, and it's then that she thinks she can make out what it is he's holding in his lap. Something dark and oddly shaped. He's turning it still in his hands, and as she follows it in his fingers, it starts to resolve itself, the strange angles and appendages coming together to form a whole, a whole that she suddenly knows to be her shoe.

She feels her blood start to simmer. She's sick of men. Sick of how they think everything is theirs to take. She waits for a car to belch past, then she heads straight for him, hoping to catch him off guard, hoping maybe to snatch it right out of his hands and give him a clip around the ear with it.

As she approaches he lifts his head, and she sees the colour of his wide-set green eyes, a lucent green, staring out at her from his high, pale cheeks. Something in his look stops her in her tracks – but she's not quite made it all the way across the road, so that another car has to slow and sound its horn until she's stirred back into herself, and hurries the final few paces to his van.

He's on his feet, standing awkwardly with her shoe held slightly aloft. She plants herself firmly in front of him. She jabs her finger through the air.

That's my shoe, she says.

He stares at her and nods, then holds it out for her to take.

I know, he says.

His voice is quiet, almost a whisper. He smiles and she sees his top lip is cut and slightly swollen, and there's a chip in his front tooth, large enough that she can see a crooked little window of darkness beyond it. She takes the shoe from him but does so gently. She stares at him, at the way he seems to be wincing with pain.

What happened to your mouth? she says.

You did, he replies.

THEY SPEND THE DAY together in the cafe, ordering endless cups of tea and talking. He feels more nervous to be indoors with her. When he sits down, he chooses not to sit opposite her but beside her, so that when she asks him questions he occasionally twists in his seat to look at her, but for the most part he looks straight ahead through the window on to the road, as if addressing some invisible presence outside.

He tells her the story.

He starts with how he's in the band that was playing in the pub the previous night. He tells her that he'd seen her in there, but that she'd disappeared. After the pub had closed, he'd gone for a walk, and he'd found her asleep beneath a tree, just along one of the streets near the pub. He'd thought that she needed help, but when he'd shaken her, she'd been so spooked that she'd struck him and stumbled away, leaving one of her shoes behind. He would've given it back, but she'd made it abundantly clear that she didn't want him following her.

She listens carefully to him. She doesn't interrupt and shows no sign that she recalls anything of what he's saying. Her features seem to close in on themselves, as if she's used to hiding anything that might threaten to give away what she's thinking. He watches her look down at her fist, at the plaster that's there.

Does it hurt? he asks.

She nods.

A little, she says, and for the first time her cheeks colour slightly.

She apologizes to him for the tooth and he apologizes for ending up with her shoe. He hadn't meant to take it. The whole thing was a mess. He waits, prepares himself for her to contest this point, thinking that her suspicions might be fanned into something like anger. But she shakes her head and she tells him that she understands.

I'd had a bit to drink yesterday, she says.

You remember any of it? he asks.

She shrugs and looks down into her empty mug. She smiles a little, the corners of her dry lips lifting.

It's starting to come back to me, she says.

He likes her accent, the gentle musicality of it; and he

notices now that her features are sharper than they'd seemed in the dark of the previous night when he'd found her. The moment he'd parted the fronds of the tree, she'd been there, slumped against the trunk. He'd not known what to do. Her coat had no fastening, so he'd tried his best to pinch the two halves and hold them together and stop her shivering. He'd held her wrist to check her pulse, and he'd felt it come quick and light, as nervous and darting as a captured bird's. He'd thought that he'd have to lay her down and cover her with his own coat, then go and knock on one of the doors across the way and ask if he could use their phone. He'd have to explain that he needed to call the police or maybe an ambulance, because there was a girl who'd passed out, over there under the tree, who was unwell and in need of help.

But as soon as he'd put a hand on her shoulder, she'd sprung to life, and before he could say anything, she'd driven her fist hard into his face, catching his front tooth. He swallowed something hard and gritty that left a chalkiness on his tongue in its wake. He could taste blood, and when he ran his tongue over his front teeth, he'd found a jagged edge, and his upper lip had started to pulse with pain.

He'd seen the shoe and he'd carried it out after her, but she was already weaving her way down the moonstruck street, past the blue glow of the windows in the houses, then around the corner out of his sight. He could have thrown it back down, but that seemed somehow wrong or dirty, so he'd kept it and taken it back to the van with him.

He looks at her now: there's a light that's crept into her skin as the day's progressed, a glow so pure that there are times he has to stop himself from reaching out and touching her. And her eyes: soft, delicate whorls of blue. They sit deep in their two hollows, leaping out at him every now and then, almost causing him to flinch.

They order toast and more cups of tea. He's watching her empty a sachet of sugar into her mug, taking note of the length and fineness of her fingers, when she suddenly looks up at him.

I don't even know your name, she says.

He laughs and winces slightly with the pain of his lip, then offers his hand for her to shake.

He tells her his name and she tells him hers: Keely.

Now that he's done his best to explain the events of the previous night, he feels himself relax a little. He makes her laugh just by the way he blows on the steaming surface of his tea, with the involuntary lift of his little finger as he brings it up to his mouth.

She starts to ask him about his life: where he grew up, his family, what he does for a living, about the band and what kind of stuff they play. He's better at talking about himself these days, though he still feels slightly on edge when he reveals anything about his past, even the most banal details of which some part of him still considers to be private. But her blue eyes are so intent that he tells her, and as he does he finds that he's enjoying himself, that there's pleasure in offering this person – this stranger who'd punched him only hours before – a taste of those things he's kept guarded for so long.

It's nearly dark by the time she asks if he'd like to come back to her flat. He's surprised by the offer, and for the first time he thinks about Evan and Jake and Allan. He's left the keys of the van under the rear left wheel, which is what they've always agreed to do in case of a change of plan. He presumes they will have waited for him. After all, he spent the night in the van waiting for them.

He tells her that he should probably get back, that the other members of the band will be waiting for him and wanting to be going.

She nods.

Well, I wish I could remember seeing you play, she says.

Maybe it's best that you don't, he says. You might not be sat here now if you had.

They leave the cafe and walk back toward the van, and he's careful to do his best to shorten his stride and match her pace. But when they get to where the van had been parked, they find that it's nowhere to be seen.

He stays still, just looking at the empty space.

What now? she asks him.

He turns to her and shrugs, half smiling.

I guess we go back to yours, he says.

They pass the pub they were in last night, the lights on the guttering still dead, and a few minutes later they come to a narrow house that she tells him has been split into two flats. She opens the door and immediately begins to busy herself. She's embarrassed by the state it's in: the blinds are drawn against what's left of the day; the air feels cold and smells stale, sour like old alcohol, as if the window hasn't been opened in a long while. When the light's switched on, he sees clothes lying on the sofa, unwashed plates and glasses scattered all about.

There are also books. Lots and lots of books. She has no shelves up on the wall, so they're mostly arranged on the floor around the room in teetering piles, some of which look ready to come crashing down. He wants to ask about them, but she looks so flustered that he doesn't, and he just lets her go about her business. She flicks the electric fire on. She tells him to sit down and make himself comfortable until she's got the place looking a bit more decent.

He doesn't sit but walks around aimlessly as she carries on cleaning, looking at things, peering down the hall toward the two closed doors. The only other girl's flat that he's been in is Amy's, though she shares hers. He wonders if Keely lives with anyone else. This space exudes an intimacy, which seems to show Keely's every touch, her every movement.

Amy's face – the pale skin and the dark eyes – briefly flares in his mind. He'd rung her when they'd decided to head home to say that he'd be back the next day, that he was looking forward to seeing her, and that he'd come over to her flat as soon as he could. He'd meant everything he'd said, had even felt himself longing for her over the past couple of weeks. And yet now, in the presence of Keely, Amy feels like a distant memory, someone he hasn't seen for years, not just a matter of weeks.

He stops at the fridge and looks at the photographs pinned there. He lifts up the magnet and takes one in his hands. He holds it up to study closer. Keely's in it, with the same wisps of blonde hair, the same large blue eyes, the same slightly angular, awkward frame. Beside her is a small boy wearing a red windbreaker, with a dark fringe cut un-evenly across his brow, and a thin wrist reaching up to rest, cocked, on her shoulder. He puts the photo back and picks up another of a man, tall and broad with hard, rugged features, and a head of wiry hair that sprigs out in all directions. His eyes are kind, the same shade as Keely's.

Keely has her back to him at the sink, the water steaming in the chill air, scrubbing at the plates and glasses that she's collected. Through the fabric of her jumper, he can see the sharp angles of her shoulder blades; her legs are long, her knees and feet turned slightly inward. There's a window directly in front of her that he can see her reflection in.

He holds up the photo.

Your family? he asks.

WEDNESDAY IS CHRISTMAS EVE, and Keely agrees to travel with Finn to his nan and grandad's to have lunch, and for him to fetch what he wants of his belongings to bring back to her flat.

They've only known each other five days, but they've decided Finn should move in with her. It was Keely who'd suggested it, and he'd answered right away without a moment's hesitation. The idea of them being apart, even after so little time, had struck them both as an impossibility; already, they've begun to laugh at how difficult it is to recall what their lives were like before meeting one another; and the past, which has had them both in its grip for so long, is quickly receding, its power dwindling, and only the future, deliciously unspoiled, stretches out before them.

Both, in their own way, consider themselves to have undergone a radical change. Adulthood – previously a distant and unwelcome prospect – has arrived to claim them; but rather than feel the grief they've so often heard accompanies the abandoning of youth, they feel euphoric, liberated, gifted a sense of command over their own lives that it seems suddenly absurd they were ever without. It's an addictive rush, this new-found control, and both of them feel high on it, their eyes bright and their skins glowing, even after sleepless nights next to one another, talking and waking and drifting in and out of dreams, each unused to the feeling of another body beside them.

By the third day of Finn's stay, a rhythm had established itself between them – the getting up together, the eating together, the watching TV and fucking and brushing their teeth together – that didn't seem so far removed, in their minds, from the rituals of a marriage; and they walked through the flat unable to stop smiling, more sure in their bodies, moving around one another in the kitchen with the practised ease of a couple, a proper couple, the kind that might one day buy a house together, that might one day have children and live out a safe, happy, normal life.

They need to get two buses back to Finn's town. Finn still has the money from the gig he'd played, some of which they use to pay. The rest, he says, can go toward fixing his tooth. He says this absentmindedly while looking into the fogged mirror in the bathroom, and he's surprised when Keely places her hands on his cheeks and asks him to smile for her. He does so, and she studies the broken tooth with all the seriousness she imagines a dentist might, her brow knitted darkly and the tip of her tongue poking out from between her lips.

I think I like what I've done, she says. It suits you.

You like it?

She nods.

It can be a reminder.

Of how you can hurt me? he says.

She smiles but shakes her head.

Of how you can love me, she says.

He looks down at her, then stoops to swiftly kiss her, just long enough for her to be able to taste the sweetness of his saliva.

So you'll leave it as it is? she says. For me?

He smiles and shrugs, then takes her hand.

For you, he says.

The journey will take at least two hours, so they set off early in the morning when it's still dark. Mr and Mrs Lister always take this shift themselves and let Keely have it off, so she won't be back to work until Boxing Day.

Even though they'd not mentioned anything about getting a gift for one another, on the morning Finn had presented her with a scarf that he'd found in the charity shop on the high street. It's blue and long and closely knitted and Keely's wearing it now, coiled lumpily around her throat, even if the musty smell of it wafts up her nostrils every time she moves her head.

They sit side by side on the hard, worn seats of the bus. Finn falls asleep quickly, the length of him tucked and folded to fit himself in, his head jarring against the scratched and dirty window. The sky slowly brightens outside to reveal fields and hills and bare, black trees, then the grey stretch of the road and the blur of the white lines passing beneath them. The road isn't empty but it's quiet, and those that Keely sees driving are mostly families, parents and children travelling to a relative's house, though there are some men and women on their own, staring blankly ahead of them, perhaps with nowhere to go.

When they'd lived at the camp, Christmas had been her favourite time of year. People were in and out of each other's caravans all day long, constantly eating and drinking, laughing and joking. All the kids would be comparing their new toys, playing, and the adults would be dancing, every radio turned up full blast, swaying with glasses of wine and sherry and whiskey in their hands.

This year, her first with her da gone, she'd been planning to go to Ruth's. She's one of the only ones left in the camp now; even her partner, Harvo, has upped and gone. Keely had felt terrible doing it, but she'd rang Ruth yesterday to say that she wasn't going to be coming anymore. She'd explained that she'd met a boy, and that he was moving in with her, and that she was now going to his nan and grandad's house on the bus to have dinner with them.

She spoke quickly, wanting to get it all out, and at first Ruth had thought she was joking. There'd been a long pause, and then she'd burst out laughing, but Keely had had to tell her that she was serious, and after a minute Ruth had slowly realized that what she was hearing was true, and she'd struggled to string any words together other than Fuck me.

She looks at Finn sleeping beside her, and there's an intensity and depth of feeling she has for him that she doesn't understand, and that she almost can't bear. She can feel it in the pit of her stomach, an electrical jolt that scales the knuckles of her spine and feathers the back of her neck, causing her to shiver and writhe. What is it he possesses that can make her feel such a way? Not since Welty died, in those weeks and months afterward, has she felt so acutely aware of her own body, of the fact that she's a living, breathing organism moving through the world.

The first night, when she'd turned around to see him pointing at the photos of her mam and her da and Welty, and he'd asked if they were her family, she'd not been able to answer him. In that moment, Keely had had the strangest feeling that her mam and her da and Welty were all in the room with her, staring at her, expecting her to say something. But she hadn't known what they were expecting her to say, and before she knew it she'd starting weeping, at first just a little, but then uncontrollably, her shoulders shaking and her chest heaving.

Through the shimmer of her tears, she could see him standing there, watching her, her sudsy hands hanging by her side and dripping on the floor. She'd felt her nose start to run, and she'd felt angry then, furiously angry and embarrassed to be doing this in front of a near perfect stranger, and also angry with him, this tall, gawking boy who was next to her fridge and doing nothing but observing her weakness.

She'd felt like she'd lost control. Life was imposing itself on her in exactly the way she'd told herself she wouldn't let it. So she had to do something, something to break whatever this moment was, whatever was threatening to unfold between them, and so she'd reached for the drying rack, picked up a plate, and flung it at the wall.

The sound of it cleaved the air. Out of the corner of her eye, she saw him duck and cower as shards of it sprayed like a whip of sea foam through the air. Then silence. Both of them staring down at the myriad shards and chips that were on the floor. She'd looked at him and seen the pale sprinkling of dust across the shoulders of his black coat, clinging to the strands of his dark hair. She'd wanted him out of her flat. She'd wanted never to see him again, wanted nothing more than to be left alone.

But that was when he'd moved quietly over to her. He hadn't held her or even touched her, not even just to lay a hand on her shoulder; but he'd stayed close to her, and she could feel that he cared, that she meant something to him, that being there in that very moment hadn't frightened him but had opened something up in him too.

And that night her life poured out of her in a way it never had before, wave after wave of words. She told him about growing up on the camp, about her mam, about Welty, about moving to the flat with her da, about his leaving, about the bus ride out to confront him and the stone gripped in her hand.

Keely looks at him, still sleeping on the bus, and she thinks that she loves him. She's aware how mad it sounds – how could she not be aware? Surely, she can't love him; she's not sure she knows what love is, not to mention that so much of him is still unknown to her – and yet it presents itself to her as fact, this love she has for him, because that's the only word that comes to her mind, and it feels so vital to her now, with the drone of passing cars rattling the window, that she can barely keep still. It's inside of her, flooding her every sense, her every movement, both making her whole and trying to tear her apart.

Now, here, on this journey, she wants to wake Finn and ask if he's feeling the same way. She wants to ask if he understands what she's talking about, or if she has, in fact, lost her mind. But she can't bring herself to do it. She lets him sleep on, and he wakes up of his own accord half an hour later at the service station where they're getting the next bus to the town he's from.

When they're travelling again, there's a part of her that wishes she were with Ruth, but by the time they get there, just before midday, the sun is shining, and she can see a bridge and a river, a strip of golden water that curves off into the distance.

She turns to him and finds him looking at it, squinting slightly through the window.

Is this your river? she asks.

He nods and smiles.

This is my river, he says.

HE TOLD HER SO much about himself that first night. The plate that she'd flung against the wall – he would've thought that he'd be terrified by such a thing. Any violence or confrontation normally shuts him down, the knot in his stomach tightening unbearably, so much so that he can do nothing but allow himself to be sucked into an airless, impenetrable silence.

But looking down at all those pieces on the floor, something had given way in him, a tension inside his chest had been sundered so thoroughly that he'd felt a rush of freedom, the likes of which he'd only ever experienced as a boy when he'd been in the river, sifting through the silt, watching the patterns of the water, that constant state of newness that had always so fascinated him.

He'd felt that same newness in himself then, and he'd moved toward her and he'd kept himself close, offering himself to her, not touching her, but somehow knowing that soon enough she'd reach out and touch him.

And she did touch him: the tips of his fingers with her own, and moments later, they'd found themselves quietly undressing in the frigid air of her bedroom, their pale bodies shivering, then climbing under the covers to clutch at each other, to lock and press and then fall away, their hearts thudding against the mattress.

Afterward, they lay awake until dawn, with their limbs tangled and the duvet pulled up to their throats so that their heads turned and lolled as if independent of their bodies.

That space that had opened up inside him remained, and he'd felt no limits to what he could tell her. He wanted to be known. A flurry of opaque, arrow-headed feelings suddenly gathered into a single desperate need: to have her see him, have her understand him, have her insinuate herself under his skin.

On the phone with his nan, when he'd rung from Keely's flat to tell her that he'd been left behind by the van and that he was staying with a friend, his hands had been sweating with nerves. Not because he thought that his nan would kick up a fuss to hear such vague information regarding his safety, but because he could hear the strength of feeling for this girl gradually building, a pressure that he'd never felt before in his life.

And now they're walking up his street, the street that he can call his old street. He feels as if he's been away from it for years, as if he's looking at it through Keely's eyes, taking in everything he's known, the things he's looked at nearly every day of his life. And it makes him feel old and proud, as if his life has only just now discovered its meaning, has finally, after all these years, begun.

He stops outside number 21. In the window his nan's put the little ceramic Nativity set on display, the one with the donkey that had to have its head glued back on after he'd dropped it down the stairs as a small boy. He could open the door and walk straight in, just as he always has done, but something about doing that doesn't feel right now. He knocks and steps back to wait. He looks at Keely, the scarf that he bought her wrapped around her neck. She looks at him and does a nervous little dance, hopping from foot to foot, which makes him smile.

He hears his nan approaching from the other side of the door. The knot in his stomach tightens. The single person he's introduced to them before is Evan. Not once has he ever even mentioned girls in front of either his nan or grandad, let alone brought one back to the house. His nan had been surprised when he'd asked her on the phone if he could bring someone with him.

Who? she'd said.

Keely, he'd said. A girl I've met.

A long silence had ensued, and then a volley of questions, most of which he'd had to parry and say that he'd explain on Christmas Eve.

When his nan opens the door, she's in her old apron. The

sight of her nearly makes him cry. She's recently had her hair dyed, and she's wearing her fanciest earrings, the fluted green and gold ones his grandad had bought her for their anniversary a few years ago. There's a slackness to the skin beneath her chin that Finn can't recall seeing before, but her cheeks still look round and firm, so that she still manages to look, from some angles, like a much younger woman.

Why're you knocking? she cries.

She hurries them both in out of the cold and into the lounge where his grandad is sitting in his chair with the TV on, a cigarette smoking idly between his fingers. He's wearing a red knitted jumper, the same one that he's worn every Christmas since Finn was a boy. He stands up to greet them. He shakes Finn by the hand, and then he shakes Keely's hand as well. He says nothing, but does a great deal of nodding, and tries his best to stretch his thin lips into a smile.

After they've had drinks standing on the carpet tiles in the kitchen, and Keely has answered the first barrage of his nan's questions, he takes Keely upstairs to his room. His nan has changed the sheets of his bed and hoovered the floor for his return. He knows that she thinks he'll be staying, that he's come back for good. He hasn't yet told her that he's moving in with Keely.

He gets down on his knees. The smell of gravy wafts up the stairs and under the door. He reaches under his bed and pulls out the bag with his box in it. Keely kneels down beside him and watches as he takes off the lid, his name scrawled on the top. He's missed looking inside here. He puts his hand in and picks up as many different things as he can. He lets them fall slowly through his fingers and then looks at her, suddenly fearing that her face will show some confusion, that she'll think him strange; but she's smiling, and she plunges her own hand into the box to do the same as him.

He has a roll of bin liners in his coat pocket. Quietly, they start to pack the things he wants. Some books, his box, the clothes that aren't already in the bag that he took on tour. The truth is, he doesn't own much. He has a small stack of notebooks that he's hidden away from prying eyes at the very back of his bottom drawer, but he doesn't want them. He's barely thought about the band since he was left behind, and when he has he's been filled with a quiet anger that he knows is directed toward Evan. Not just for the van having taken off without him, but for the whole tour, for turning something he'd loved into something he now felt glad to be away from.

They eat shepherd's pie, Finn's favourite, which his nan had insisted she cook for them all. His nan and grandad sit at opposite ends of the table, and he and Keely sit in the middle facing one another. The mince is grainy, but the mash and the veg and the gravy are all piping hot and full of flavour. They pull crackers and wear the coloured party hats made of tissue paper. His grandad drinks stout. Finn declines one and so does Keely, though he catches her more than once looking over as his grandad lifts the bottle to his lips before carefully placing it back down, the foam washing down the fat glass sides.

His nan tells him that Evan has been ringing a lot, and that he sounds very eager to talk to him. He tells her that he's already got in contact with him and that everything's been sorted out. This isn't true. He feels no desire to speak to Evan whatsoever; he feels happy to leave the band behind him; already, he feels as if there was something childish about it that he ought to distance himself from.

His grandad stays mostly silent, but his nan asks Keely questions. Keely answers nervously, her voice quiet, never alluding to the true state of her family, but reporting that they're all well, that they live further north in the same place she'd grown up. She talks about her job in the shop, how she basically runs the place, opening it up and closing it down. None of her answers surprise Finn. She'd told him on the bus before they arrived that she wasn't going to tell the truth about her circumstances, and he'd told her that she should only say what she felt comfortable with. As long as she's happy, then he is too.

They finish dinner and retire to the sofa. His grandad flicks the TV on while his nan gives him some presents, all neatly wrapped in paper with a motif of a snowman wearing a top hat and holding a candy cane. He gets socks and underwear and a new pair of black jeans, along with a new comb.

If you're going to have your hair that long, she says, then you might as well do your best to keep it neat.

His grandad falls asleep with his party hat on. It slips down over his face, so that it rustles and crackles slightly when he breathes out. The noise reminds Finn of something, and it takes him a while to figure out that it's the cagoule that he'd worn all those years before in Ronan's da's car. The sound makes him want to leave. He can feel himself being sucked back into his childhood, and he wants to be away from it, wants be starting his life again with Keely.

At six o'clock, he stands up. If he's going to tell his nan that he's leaving, then he wants to make it as swift as possible. He wants to avoid any kind of questioning. He must be as blunt and terse as possible, even if it does hurt her feelings. The bin bags are packed and waiting in his room. All he needs to do is fetch them down and say his goodbyes, and then they can be on their way.

We'll have to be heading back now, he says.

His nan looks up at him, her eyes wide with confusion, her chin dimpling slightly.

You're going back? she says.

He sees the pain in her face, the surprise. Out of the corner of his eye he sees his grandad is awake and looking at him, though he can't quite gauge his expression, whether it's filled with sorrow or with indifference.

Where are you going? his nan asks.

With me, says Keely.

He feels her hand in his as he explains to his nan that he'll be living with Keely from now on. His nan stays sitting down on the sofa. The cigarette she's been smoking is still between the V of her fingers, burning so that the ash reaches out like a crooked twig.

When will you be back? she asks as he leans down to kiss her on her cheek, breathing in the same sweet perfume that she's always worn.

As much as I can, he says.

His nan stays sitting and staring up at them both as his grandad stands to shake his hand and then Keely's after.

Good luck, he says.

Finn looks into his eyes and wishes he knew more about this man. He'd like to hug him and feel his body pressed against his own. But he doesn't. Instead, he quickly runs upstairs to grab the bags, leaving Keely standing awkwardly by the door. When he comes down, his nan is in the hallway. She looks at the bags he's carrying and she shakes her head.

She looks frail and very old suddenly. He wants to hold her, but they're out the door and waving goodbye, walking down the street. His old street. They pass beneath the globes of orange streetlight – Keely's hand warm in his – the darkness of the night stretched like a tarp above all that he's ever known.

They're about to round the corner when Finn hears someone call out his name. He turns and sees his nan: she's still wearing her apron, her slippers, and she's walking, waving both of her hands, threatening every few steps to break into an awkward, flat-footed jog. Finn can see her earrings, her favourites, glinting in the streetlight.

When she finally reaches where they're standing, she's out of breath and she leans a hand against the nearest lamp post.

Can I speak with you, Finn? she asks. Alone.

As much as he loves this woman, Finn can't help but feel his temper begin to fray.

He shakes his head. You can say it here, he says.

His nan swallows audibly, shifts her feet slightly. Her hand drops from the lamp post.

It'll only take a min, she says. Just a few words.

But Finn shakes his head again. Whatever it is, he's sure that it's of absolutely no importance. And she needs to learn that things are different now. She needs to learn that he's a man, and now that he's a man she'll no longer be able to fuss over him, to treat him like a child.

His nan says nothing. She nods. Then she smiles weakly and, standing on her tiptoes, she places a clumsy, glancing kiss on Finn's jaw.

Safe journey, she says. To you both.

Finn watches her turn and walk back to the house. He hears her close the door behind her, and he wonders if she'll speak to his grandad of what's just happened, or if she'll go straight through to the kitchen, where she'll flick the radio on and start doing the dishes.

Everything OK? asks Keely.

He nods, squeezes her hand.

Almost as soon as they're on the bus, Keely falls asleep beside him. She rests her head against the window. Her skin alternates between the blue of shadow and the blush of the streetlights. He can't take his eyes away from her, from the light and dark, the light and dark, the light and dark.

BILLY THE LANDLORD SETS off a handful of small, unspectacular fireworks outside the pub to bring in the New Year. Keely and Finn are there, their gloved fingers linked, looking up as the whine and crack of colour – purple, red, white – blooms and fades over their upturned faces. People cheer and hug as children carve at the air with sparklers, trying to etch their names on to the darkness. There's a group of men, all of them bald, with their arms linked and their chests thrust out, turning in drunken circles as they sing echoingly down the streets.

Sarah is with them, standing a little awkwardly to one side, so that Keely and Finn only kiss glancingly, as opposed to some of the other couples scattered through the crowd, who lean hungrily into one another, hands frisking beneath coats and jumpers, thin snares of bone-white breath escaping the corners of their searching lips.

It's already apparent to Keely, by Sarah's folded arms and the sullen flourish of her lips, that she's taken a dislike to Finn. Sarah's never been one to conceal her thoughts, and it's clear she has no idea what Keely could possibly see in Finn, with his eyes the size of saucers and the sickly, vampiric sheen of his skin. Keely had warned her that he was shy, hoping she might see beyond his reticence; but it's not difficult to recall how often their drunken conversations would meander back to Sarah's notion of the ideal man: bigger, stronger, more assertive; ready to make every situation bend to his will.

Keely sees Finn flinch at the final explosion above; he smiles and turns to look at her, still hunched into himself, as if expecting a volley of shrapnel to come raining down. Sarah catches her eye and makes a face, a face that Keely's seen a thousand times before – the frown, the widening of the eyes, the thrusting out of the chin – that she knows is meant to unite them in a derisory spirit against Finn, as if she'll suddenly cast him aside and flounce off to the pub with Sarah to drink herself into oblivion.

But she huddles next to him and squeezes his hand, and she can't help but feel already that her friendship with Sarah, which has never been based on any foundation greater than a love of gossip and drinking, won't survive much longer. For all that she likes about her – her laugh, her energy, her bolshiness – she also knows that without Keely's full attention Sarah will grow bitter and jealous, and their nights out will collapse into a ruin of petty arguments and absurd rivalries.

Rather than go back in the pub, Keely and Finn decide to take a walk. They each say goodbye to Sarah, who does nothing to disguise her disgust at being left alone.

So you're just leaving? she says, shaking her head, her gloved hands outstretched.

Keely nods. She has no appetite for confrontation, and so she just takes Finn's hand – who's all too happy to be led anywhere Keely wants to go – and pulls him away.

There's a pleasant tiredness in their limbs that speaks more of a desire to be alone with one another than it does the need to rest or sleep. It's a feeling both have come to familiarize themselves with over the past week since they got back from Finn's nan and grandad's, of being connected to one another in ways that seem to transcend the natural order of their lives up until that point. Thoughts, feelings, sensations, infinitesimal shifts of mood and humour – all are startlingly clear in the other without having to ask. The world they share needs no explaining. Everything just is.

Does everyone, at some point, feel the way that they feel about each other now? Of course, there are hundreds of songs and books about love, but why do the people they know not talk about it? Why did Keely's da never speak about her mam in such terms? Why did Finn's nan and grandad never have the look of being the happy victims of such intoxication? It strikes them as strange, almost sinister, this conspiracy of silence to keep secret the most joyous and transformative of experiences, as if there should be a terrible price to pay for having revealed it.

They walk, hand in hand, neither of them saying anything. The silences they've both been used to, before their meeting, have always marked the advent of shame or grief; there was something darkly ceremonial about its arrival in their lives, like the raising of a black flag casting its shadow over them, until one day, often without explanation, it would suddenly lift and all would return to normal. Silence was the territory of adults, a weapon they had at their disposal, one they could abuse without ever truly incriminating themselves.

Keely remembers the meals with her da after Welty had died: only the chilling scrape of the tines of a fork across a plate, or a dog barking, or the scythe of the wind coming in off the sea. And Finn can still feel the way his legs would lock when he watched TV at night with his grandad; how he could never quite relax, knowing their lack of exchange ran deeper than the fact that their attention was directed elsewhere, that it sprang from a deep well of unexpressed emotion and embarrassment, both having lived with shame for much of their lives.

But this silence, the one between themselves, is different. It's not freighted with any significance beyond the intimacy of the moment itself, which passes and is immediately reborn, time moving like a golden thread of honey from a spoon. Finn likes to imagine what Keely is thinking, and he sneaks glances at her, smiling at the seriousness of her expression, at the way she looks down her nose and her fringe falls over her eyes.

The voices of the crowd fade behind them until the only sounds are the scuff and click of their own footsteps on the pavement. The stone flags glitter with settling frost.

Where d'you want to go? asks Finn.

Keely shrugs. The tip of her nose looks blue with cold in the blocks of shadow between streetlamps. She brings up her balled fist to dab at it, her eyes never lifting from the ground.

Maybe the sea, she says.

She hadn't been expecting to say this. She and Finn are yet to visit it together. She's explained to him her troubled relationship with it, the longing she still feels for the spray of it against her cheek, and the nauseous quiver that will climb her throat at the thought of it pushing and pulling and plunging her brother beneath its surface until he could no longer breathe.

But Finn only nods, and they continue on until they reach the edge of the town, leaving the streetlights behind them. The moon slips from behind a convoy of cloud and silvers the black arrow of road, the crowns of their heads, the long grass at the verge they tromp over, darkening the cuffs of their jeans with dew. Not a single car passes them. The wind is cold enough to make the tips of their ears burn, their jaws ache.

They hear them before they see it: the waves against the shore, quiet and occasionally malevolent, their rasping hush like an intermittent leak of gas from a damaged valve. They top the brow of the hill and come to a halt. Their hands feel as hot and dry as kindling in their gloved grip. The moon appears again and paints a winking passage of its own light through the black expanse, and both Keely and Finn stare along the length of it, as brittle looking as a stick of chalk, as if it will take them wherever it is they want to go.

*

ON THE 2ND, HAVING spent most of New Year's Day in bed together, Keely finds Finn a job. After going from shop to shop, she ends up asking Harry – the barrel-chested owner of the butcher's – if Finn can come for a chat and see if they might make something work. As it turns out, Harry does happen to have a position available, so she goes back to the flat and sends Finn down.

An hour later, Finn comes back through the door, grinning at her with his chipped smile.

You got it? she says.

I got it, he says.

But there's one condition: if Finn wants to start right away, then Harry has told him he'll have to cut his hair. They can't have customers coming back and complaining about finding great big dirty strands of it in their sausages and their giblets.

His hair means more to him than he's ever been willing to let on. He'd let it grow when at school out of pure laziness; but over time, after he'd found Evan and the band, it had come to represent a grander transition – from his solitude and the tyranny of his nickname to communing with crowds of people, the freedom in his mind to talk and feel and express himself. He felt as if his hair had started it all, and now that it was about to be cut, he was suffering from the irrational fear that he'd be returned to that perpetual state of anxiety and helplessness he'd known as a boy.

Keely can see the onset of panic in him. Already, she's familiar with his nervous tics, the little tremors in his left cheek, the distracted massaging of the parcel of flesh between his forefinger and thumb.

Why don't I do it for you? she says.

Since when have you cut hair?

With exaggerated sassiness, she puts her hands on her hips and scrunches up her nose.

I've cut plenty of hair in my time.

When she was a child, she'd used to cut Welty's hair when their da was too tired to do it, and she'd hack her way through the coarse tufts of her da's if he'd missed his appointment at the barber's in town. She wasn't great at it, but neither of them had complained. She doesn't see why she can't cut Finn's.

Come on, she says. It'll be fun.

Finn looks at her suspiciously, his large eyes narrowed, the corner of his upper lip twitching.

Fun?

She nods excessively, her eyes wide, her ponytail jostling up and down.

Fine, he says. But just don't—

Don't what?

Finn shakes his head.

I don't know, he says. Let's just get it over with.

Keely pulls out a chair from the kitchen table and stands it in the middle of the floor. Cold sunlight streams through the window above the sink. The sky outside has a blue, ceramic stillness to it, the tops of the bare trees yawing in the breeze.

Sit, she says.

Finn does as he's told. He places his hands flat on his thighs, breathes deeply in and out, as if he's about to have his photo taken.

Now take this off, Keely says, tugging at the shoulder of

his jumper before opening the kitchen drawer and rummaging around for the scissors. She returns with them to find that he's taken his T-shirt off as well, his skin looking almost translucent in the slant of winter light. She moves around to his front. His nipples are dark and hard, circled by a sparse growth of minutely glinting hairs.

Ready? she says.

Ready, he says.

She moves around him, delighting in his nervousness, taking small, playful snips here and there to tease him. His eyes are closed but she can see that he's stopping himself from smiling, his face passing under her shadow and then bathed once more as she dances her way around him.

Just get it over with, he says.

Don't get shirty with me, she says. I'm doing you a favour here.

But suddenly she begins to apply herself with a seriousness that surprises even her. Her movements become gentle, considered, deliberate. She begins to cut in earnest and hair feathers down on to Finn's neck and shoulders which she blows on to the floor with light gusts of breath. She's never seen the nape of his neck before, but here it is, long and pale and innocent as she bends down to kiss it.

What are you doing? he says.

I'm kissing you, she replies. Is that OK?

He nods and she does it again, breathing in the dry, sleepy scent of him. She starts cutting again, revealing his ears, which are surprisingly small, and then his fringe, which falls away in dark ribbons, landing in his lap and coating the floor in a surf of curls.

As she stoops and works to try and neatly frame his face, she's briefly blinded by memories of cutting Welty's hair, seeing it drop to the lino of the caravan by his bare, dangling feet. He would never be able to keep his head still, and she was constantly having to correct the position of it, gently at first and then more roughly, until they'd both start giggling, their da watching them from over the pages of the newspaper.

She blinks her tears back. All of this closeness with Finn – she knows it could drag her back to that time and those feelings of fear, of all the good she knows being taken away from her.

But she doesn't want that. She wants to make herself present and available to this boy before her now. She knows that he needs her and that he will keep on needing her. He's chosen to give himself to her, and she feels it important that she acknowledge the responsibility, not of making him happy, or of catering to his every need, but of trying to understand him as best she can, of learning the ways he receives the world and participates in it. It's not her duty to correct these things. She must simply look and listen. That, she thinks, is the best thing she can give him: her vigilance.

She stands back and stares at him. There is a saintly suffering to the sight: head bowed, eyes closed, fingers interleaved, the nimbus of finer hairs backlit by the window. She hasn't cut it too short, so it has a fluffy quality to it, the way it curls around his ears and lifts up in the fringe. He looks both radically different and exactly the same. His face has filled out a little, and his eyes look even larger, but it's still him. It's Finn.

He opens his eyes for the first time since she began and

squints against the hard slab of light. He looks at her, searching her face for the verdict.

Well? he says. How does it look?

Like I'm the best hairdresser in this whole town, she says.

ALL OF THEIR DAYS off together are like this: unfailingly bright and fresh, but tinctured with pockets of honeyed drowsiness in which hours pass without either of them moving, without the light seeming to change, without more than a handful of words being said. Keely reads with her feet tucked beneath her, the turning pages of her book the only sound other than Finn scribbling in his notebook, no longer writing lyrics but trying to chronicle the simple beauty of these days.

Days, weeks, months go by and the spell remains unbroken. They wake every morning in the grey-blue hour before work, and still half-asleep – with their bodies beginning to shift: fingers curling, feet arching, the quiet click and smack of dry mouths, the sweetly stale push of breath through the nostrils – they move toward one another, compelled.

When their skin touches there is an instant, electrical jolt detonated deep within, which then radiates out and charges the extremities – the lips, the fingers, Keely's nipples and the tip of Finn's penis pressing against the back of Keely's thigh – with an exhilarating, almost painful sensitivity.

Neither of them are experienced, and there's a clumsy, innocent greed to so many of their gestures, a breathless urgency that has as much to do with a fear of embarrassment as it does with the contagion of their lust. Their mouths lock or slide away from one another, just out of rhythm; the tip of a nose often presses and smears against a cheek or chin as if against glass; elbows and knees knock hard, so that Keely will sometimes find, when showering the next day, the slow spread of a bruise purpling the side of her thigh, or yellowing the ridgeline of one of her angular hips.

Afterward, they lie on their sides and stare at one another, their cheeks flushed, their hearts slowing. Sometimes they feign despair at the day of work that stretches out before them, and other times they say nothing, trading only facial expressions – smiles, frowns, raised eyebrows, toothy grins and gloomy sighs – that they've come to believe comprise their own secret language.

Over breakfast, in the growing light, they strive to perfect the kind of domestic ideal both have subconsciously absorbed over the years. They make one another cups of tea, pour milk over one another's cereal, whistle along with the radio that fuzzes softly in the background. Are either of them aware that they're playing these roles? It's a kind of acting that they revel in; playing parts that are both themselves and not themselves, heightened, more sophisticated versions that can only be realized in concert.

They leave for work and head out into bitterly cold winds sweeping in off the sea, the sky above them permanently bruised with low, ragged cloud. But their moods suffer no dip. They are living outside of the natural framework of existence, blessed, charmed, haloed by the strength and brightness of their love.

Spring arrives early in the last few days of March. The

sun is warm on the backs of their necks as they walk through the town on an evening after work. New leaves begin to whisper greenly in the shade of the trees they pass beneath, and they can hear the warble of the ice-cream van moving from street to street, children tearing after it, their pockets chiming with the scratched, broken tune of scrounged coins.

Keely wonders at the years in which she seemingly took no notice of the change in season. Not since she was a child, playing with Welty on the dunes, has she felt so connected to the rhythms of the world: the sounds and smells, the feel of the breeze lifting the hairs on her forearms, the songs of birds trilling sharply down from telephone wires.

And Finn is still adapting to the calm emptiness inside his head. His mind no longer wants to be in constant motion. After years of endlessly grinding against itself, there is stillness and space, no longer the sockets of gummy darkness he can get stuck in, but vast planes, horizons he will never be able to reach.

The summer is one of the warmest on record. In the town, there's a carnival atmosphere, with the sun blazing down, burning scalps and shoulders, turning the roads sticky underfoot.

The heat drives them both into a frenzy of fucking. Sweating on the sofa, even the faintest stir of breeze is enough to arouse in Keely a hunger to seek Finn out and march him into the bedroom, unpeeling layers of clammy clothes as she goes.

At the very beginning, the energy of their encounters had brought them both quickly toward a rushed, almost frenzied climax. But as the months have gone by, they've grown to move across one another's bodies with a precise, almost forensic intent, their sureness of pleasure so absolute that they will often smile at one another as they both undress, climbing into bed and grinning, though never without a slight, residual shyness that neither has yet felt fully ready to abandon.

These new forays can't be characterised by a slackening in desire. It's only that their desire is more evenly, carefully distributed, neither of them wanting to waste a single movement: touching and stroking and kneading flesh, listening to the other's breathing: feeling it dampen an ear, a hollow in the neck, stirring the swatch of hair leading down and down. It is the revelation that a body can be learned and played like an instrument, so that Keely knows when to roll Finn on to his back, when to hold his arms flat against the bed with her hands pinioning his thin wrists and then rest her full weight on him, her knees tucked close to his flanks, rocking slowly back and forth, her hair obscuring her vision so she can only see his face wrestling with itself; and she knows, by the impatient thrust of Finn's pelvis, when he wants her to ease herself off him, wants to have her bend over so he can lock himself behind her, his hands on her hips, until she can feel the spill of him dripping and cooling onto the bedsheets.

THE LATE DAYS OF autumn arrive, suffused with their characteristic mournfulness: the light is soft and indulgent, carrying with it a certain frisson, the quiet thrill that what they have between them is a fragile, vulnerable thing that might not be impervious to all they had at first believed it to be.

They have both felt it, these early stirrings of their fallibility. Silences stretch out for longer than before, and rather than arouse the pure and cloudless musings they once had, they invite unfounded, niggling suspicions of possible betrayal. Both begin to look back with increasing bitterness on the past selves that had so celebrated the sweetness of shared quiet; or they combust into rounds of aimless bickering that lead them both into their own vortex of self-pity, cruelly reimagining the lives they were living before they met one another as brighter, more fulfilling existences.

There are days that see-saw between the sublime and the despairing, but even these have their own particular charm, their own flavour that's worth relishing.

When Finn's with Keely in the evenings, he can feel it coming, this delicious sadness, creeping up on him when the sun drops behind the rooftops outside the flat, and the sky turns the colour of faded denim. He can hear her in the kitchen at the sink, her hands moving through the water, the chime of glasses as she leans them against one another to dry. And he's run through with tenderness, for himself, for her, for the way the world has worked to place him here, now, the wrecked, voiceless boy in the river that has somehow managed to survive, managed to find more of himself than he had ever thought possible.

He does not know Keely. He will never know her. And he's slowly coming to terms with this fact. But he is at her mercy, and if that can drive him to madness, if it can pollute his every waking minute with dread at the thought of losing her, then there's also peace in it. Because he knows that's the price to pay of loving someone: that you must place your faith and trust in the unknown. And what a privilege, he thinks. What a privilege that might be if only he will allow himself to do it.

He sees it in people all the time these days, when he's walking down the street, when he's waiting for a drink at the bar in the pub: what sad, lost, beautiful creatures human beings are. With nothing in them but the want to be seen and heard and touched and made to feel like every day isn't a terrifying, heart-wrenching, gut-punch of a mystery. Wanting to have it all handed to them on a plate: a reason for being here that doesn't vanish the moment they look it square in the eye; a reason for being here that doesn't soften and split like old fruit beneath the slightest touch.

But Finn knows there is no single, unifying reason out there. And what Keely makes him feel – made him feel – is that there doesn't need to be one. Is it not reason enough, he thinks, to wake every day and turn to face someone that was once a stranger – with a life all of her own, with a head full of memories, of laughter and bliss and sorrow – and find that she's prepared to wake and live her day by his side, moving together toward an end that neither of them can escape, that will be waiting for them at the end of all the days that will pass, all the suns that will rise and fall as their skins slacken and their muscles weary; through all the joyous fucks and bitter arguments and grinding silences that might yet stand between now and then? That, to him, is reason enough; and he is happy, so very happy that he has found her.

2

KEELY FINDS A LETTER ADDRESSED TO FINN TUCKED
away in the back of his bottom drawer. She isn't looking for
it. It's the first of her two days off and she's decided to give
the whole place a clean, which includes emptying all the
cupboards and all the drawers and hoovering up every last
speck of dust and dirt that's collected there over the past
three years of their living together.

She holds the letter and stares down at it. A map of heat
climbs her throat, so she opens the window of their bedroom, breathes in the warm spring air. She hears some
birdsong, and the more distant drone of cars on the high
street. Sunlight angles in, a neat little square that frames
her bare feet and seems to draw the motes up from the
floorboards.

She sits down on the edge of the bed. The date stamped
on the envelope is from over a week ago, nearly two. Normally, she sees everything he receives, but she doesn't
recognize this hand at all, has never seen it before.

She opens it and her eyes immediately sweep to the bottom to find the name written there. It's not what she fears. She'd thought, for the briefest moment, that it was from a girl he'd previously known, 'Amy', someone he'd been with before they'd met. He's talked about her before after she'd teased it out of him, and though she'd laughed and joked with him at the time, unease has always remained with her, more benign than jealousy, but a twinge all the same, a quiet shiver of panic that occasionally grips her when she thinks of the possibility that they might never have met.

The closer she and Finn have become over the years, the more difficult it's been to keep themselves from bleeding into one another: a being with the same thoughts and feelings, the same identity. There have been times when this has thrilled her. She's felt overwhelmed by the power of feeling that she has for him, and she's actively sought to absorb more of him into her, seeking to eliminate any doubts by wilfully ignoring the natural distance that separates any two individuals, all in the hope of arriving at a place of connection which she imagines to be unassailable.

And then there have been other times when this quest for intimacy has left her feeling more alone that she ever has before. His presence has offered no comfort, but has only aggravated her sense of isolation, and she's found herself wishing that they'd never met, cursing him for all the fresh, urgent worries and fears that his very existence has introduced into her life.

This is the first time she's ever discovered something that he's kept from her, that he's gone out of his way to hide. He's not a liar; she feels she knows this. The characteristics needed to create a person inclined toward slyness and deception are simply not in him. Not once before has she ever felt the need to question his honesty or his integrity.

Evan.

This is the name at the bottom of the letter. She's never met him, and she knows very little about him other than he was a part of the band that Finn had been in. She's seen only the one picture of him that Finn tacked to the fridge a year or so ago of them all on stage, though it's a blur of shadow and light, and she can only make out one side of Evan's face with any clarity, just the suggestion of sharpness to his nose and ear, and an intensity in his stare that she finds unnerving to meet.

She starts reading the letter. It isn't long, only a page with a small, final paragraph cramped right at the very bottom. His handwriting appears rushed and childish, and it takes her a little while to decipher. Still, she gets through it, and when she finishes, she places it to one side and stares down into her hands, her heart thudding dully in her chest.

Evan's leaving for a country all the way on the other side of the world. He wants a fresh start. He wants to get away from this place, which he describes as miserable and backward, and which he claims has had a stranglehold on his creative spirit for too long. But there's opportunity waiting on the other side of the world, and he wants Finn to go with him. He's willing to put their differences behind him. They're best friends. They belong in each other's lives. Think of the new life they could carve out for themselves, he writes.

At no point does Evan ever mention her, even though

she knows he's well aware of her. Finn hasn't seen him in over three years now, not since that very first day she and Finn had met, when Evan had left in the van without him and he'd stayed at hers, and that's where he's lived ever since.

She knows that it's caused Finn pain, and she suspects that it continues to do so. She's asked him about it, has pleaded with him to try and express himself, but he never wants to talk. He shakes his head and turns away, then makes some excuse about not being in the mood. Or heads out for another run, which has rapidly become an obsession for him.

This is the way it goes, she feels, with almost everything that she brings up these days. To begin with, he'd seemed so open and free with her; they'd talked for hours, through the night and into the morning, and he'd seemed to relish the feeling of having every last detail of his interior life exposed. She could see that there was relief in it for him, a weight that was being lifted away as he showed her his wounds. She can see him so clearly in those first few days and weeks, lying in bed, their eyes locked, each of them searching for more and more things to reveal, wallowing in the ecstasy of it all.

These days, Finn seems to have cauterized this part of himself. When they talk or argue, and he chooses to volunteer something, his voice is so flat and devoid of feeling that she can't help but be infuriated by it. He uses words like they're blunt instruments incapable of conveying anything of significance, or he sits in silence if he deems this to be an appropriate method of resolution.

A breeze blows in through the window, fragrant with the dust of the sun-warmed street outside. Keely stands and looks down at the impression her shape has left on the bed, at the slightly shifting creases of the duvet cover, then smooths them out with the flat of her palm. There had been a time when they would have sex almost every morning before work, their bodies snared in sleep and waking with the knowledge of one another's touch already at the surface, alive and waiting to be acted upon.

Now, it's not that they no longer have sex, or that it's in any way bad; but there's a distance that was never there before between them, that she's sure Finn has deliberately engineered. And after they've finished, without fail, he moves discreetly away from her toward his own side of the bed and he looks up at the ceiling or slantwise to the wall, seeming almost fearful that he might catch her eye.

She leaves the bedroom and takes the letter into the kitchen. She reads through it again and then one more time after that. There was a time when she knows she would have started drinking now. Any kind of pressure and it would be the first thing she would turn to. She can feel it, the same pull that she'd first felt after her da had just left, that ache at the back of the throat. There are bottles that she's sequestered away all over the flat – vodka and whiskey, rum and brandy – that she and Sarah had tapped into when running low. And there are tins, too, that she has stowed. She could find one now, and she could sip away at it until the sharp edge of the panic she's feeling starts to round itself out.

But since meeting Finn, she's felt the need for it much less intensely. It's not the same persistent drone that it once was at the back of her mind, but an occasional flare of long-ing that she can, more often than not, manage to quell. She'll still succumb – normally after an argument or if she's feeling particularly misunderstood or neglected – and when Finn's sleeping in bed or happens to be out, she'll find her-self drifting, as if on autopilot, toward places she can't even remember ever hiding anything, reaching up on to the top of the kitchen cabinet and groping about until her fingers find the dusted glass of a bottle.

Then she'll sit quietly at the table, never for long enough to sink into herself and the past so fully that she can't find her way back out, but just enough so that she can feel the tempo of her mind begin to change, and she once more becomes aware that there's a world beyond the one which is turning in her own head.

It was loneliness that had so readily steered her down that road. Loneliness and loss. She hadn't known how else to deal with such feelings, with the sheer weight and strength of them. And nothing else that she knew of could so swiftly obliterate them. These days, the losses of her mam, of Welty, her da have, to her occasional dismay, taken on a likeness, the margins between them blurring, so that she can push them away into the same dark corner, and only sometimes, when she allows it, do they rear up with their own distinct pain.

She sits down on the sofa beside the book that she's in the middle of, the spine cracked and the pages splayed. It's not as if there's anything terrible in the letter. There's no evidence of betrayal. But she wonders why he hasn't told her about it. Is it something that he and Evan have talked about before? Is Finn at work now considering taking Evan up on the offer?

She could go to the high street and ask him.

But she doesn't go to the butcher's.

Instead, she suddenly decides that she'll walk to the camp. She's been going there more and more recently. Now that it's been fully abandoned there's a stillness and a calmness that she feels to be restorative, and she often leaves with some clearer sense of the direction she needs to go next.

She walks out into the day. The buds are starting to open up in the trees and the sun punches some warmth through the breeze. She goes out of the town and twenty minutes later she finds the familiar long grey stretch of road that she'd used to ride down on her bike when she'd first got the job in the shop. She can recall how cold her hands would be in winter gripping the handlebars, her knuckles red and her fingers feeling fat with numbness.

The sea is in the distance, a blue-grey haze that winks minutely at her. It's the warmest day of the year by far, enough for her brow to prickle with sweat. She's wearing denim jeans that she's cut off and turned into shorts that do their best to hug her hips, but on her top she's wearing one of Finn's jumpers, so that she can smell him as she walks along. She's brought the letter with her in her pocket. She didn't want to leave it behind and then find herself thinking about it, trying to remember the exact wording of certain parts.

After another twenty minutes, the camp appears over the brow of the hill, though it has changed almost beyond recognition. Even a few years ago, she would've been able to see a small huddle of caravans and the corrugated shipping crates. Several horses would have been tethered up on the verge and cropping at the long grass there. She would have been able to hear the cries of children playing, the barking of dogs, the revving of engines being tinkered with.

Now, it's silent as she approaches the turn-off, crossed with old tyre tracks baked hard into the mud. She can see heaps of old belongings that have been abandoned to the wind and rain, looking shrunken and sad in the monstrous growth of weeds allowed to thrive on the borders. The ground's scorched black from all the fires that have been lit over the years, that might well have been lit when she was still here, that she and Welty might have gathered around on a night with their da and everyone else.

She'd spent a final day here a few weeks ago with Ruth, who'd been the very last to go. There'd been a time when she'd said that she'd never leave, that this was the only place to be. But she'd met someone in town, a new man, and suddenly living alone in the camp had been stripped of any appeal it had once had, and she'd left with next to no remorse, no tears welling out of nostalgia for what it had once been.

Keely walks into the dunes and visits all the places that she and Welty used to play, but she chooses not to dwell there. She looks out at the sea and she lets her mind empty, and she allows an hour to pass, and by the time she's strolled back to the old camp, she's decided that she'll bring up the letter with Finn. She thinks it's important that she knows how he feels about it, even if it's likely he'll be unhappy about her having found it and opened it.

When she returns to the flat, Finn's already home. She deliberately doesn't mention the letter right away. She wants to make sure she's given him every chance to broach the subject in his own time, just in case it should be this evening that he's planning on bringing it to her attention.

So she waits.

They have their tea together. They go for a brief walk before it gets dark, breathing in the sea which is always strong at this time of the year, and when they get back, they watch a few shows on the second-hand TV that they'd pooled their money together to buy.

But he says nothing, and when they climb into bed at the end of the night and switch the lights off, it's in the close darkness of their room that she turns to him and lays a hand on his chest. She opens her mouth to ask him about it, but the words don't come. Something stops her. Everything she'd decided at the camp goes out of her mind, and she closes her eyes to sleep.

WITH EACH CRACK OF bone as he brings the cleaver down, he sees a flash of some memory behind his eyes: a white, horned object nestled in the creases of his palm; the strings of his nan's apron turning idly in a draught; the shift of his grandad's tattoos as he rolls himself a cigarette; the slant of the roof above his head in his old bedroom.

The bell above the door rings and he looks up to see another customer joining the queue. It's busy and Harry's voice is booming out, dismissing some people and demanding others step up to make their order. There's the hum of chatter and the rustle of the white and blue striped plastic bags; the slap of mince and diced chicken on the scales; the earthy reek of the offal that hovers over everything.

In the morning, the smell is always at its most pungent: the red tiled floor, though swept and mopped before closing time, seems to gather up the iron-rich tang of blood overnight, and the scent of flesh from the cold, plucked chickens and pheasants that hang in the window, their thin necks cocked, their scaled feet neatly trussed. And when the door opens first thing, even if there's next to no breeze outside, little eddies of sawdust will blow and skirl about, coming to rest in corners until Finn gets down on his knees and sweeps them up with a dustpan and brush.

He likes working here. He likes Harry, likes the sheer size of him, the way his striped apron hugs his chest, the way he rests his thick forearms on the counter at quieter times, and places his chin on them, then talks away to whoever it is might be there. He's kind to Finn and has taken a paternal interest in him since he first started; he likes to ask about him, about how Keely is, about the plans they have for their future.

But something's changed in Finn recently. His days don't pass with the same ease and pleasure that he'd foolishly gotten used to. Instead, he's been plagued by the strange reopening of his past which he hasn't been able to control. He doesn't know what's happened to him that he should be so frequently visited by reel after reel of images he'd thought long buried. Most of them, on the surface, are of no consequence. They're not like the violent reimaginings that he knows Keely suffers of her brother some nights, when she wakes up with her face glistening with sweat and her whole body shaking.

The moment he'd met Keely, he'd felt the small, silent boy that he'd been – the one who'd trawled the river for hours on end, the one who'd been chased home by boys on their bikes, the one who'd sat and stared at the Bog People in the book from the library – start to drift away from him. There was something miraculous about the way her presence alone seemed to so vanquish the person he had been, the person he'd felt he was doomed to always be.

She freed him. He started talking. He could locate no desire in her to turn him into anything. She'd just allowed him to be, and that had seemed like the most precious gift he could ever have hoped to receive.

Now – and he doesn't know why – he can feel himself being sucked back into that boy, his fears, his anxieties. The same dread of words has crept back into him, and the alarm that he'll be led by them into places he isn't equipped to go alone; and he's started having these sudden, sniping attacks of fear and anxiety – even when he's around Keely. He has no way of anticipating them. He can be watching her just reading on the sofa or tying her hair up in the bathroom, and, in a heartbeat, he finds himself overwhelmed by the fact of her very existence: the rise and fall of her chest, the dart of her fingers as she reaches into a packet of crisps on the arm of the sofa, the arch of her back as she stretches herself out. He can't seem to escape her, this person with a head filled with thoughts, most of which she might never even utter to him. She's a mystery and always will be, and the uncertainty of it all, of her, is paralysing.

Is she happy? Does he make her happy?

He would blame all of it on the letter that he'd received from Evan a couple of months ago, but it's been going on for longer than that. The letter has maybe exacerbated it, if only because he could hear Evan so clearly in the words that he'd put down, in the subtle methods of manipulation that it seems so obvious now he'd been a victim of.

Finn believes now that his role in the band was more Evan's creation than any natural part of his own trajectory. He thinks he fell under the spell of someone who wanted something from him, who'd seen in him something that could be harnessed, something that could be used.

He has been worried that Keely wants something from him, too.

He doesn't know why he still hasn't told Keely about the letter. It's not that he ever took Evan's proposal seriously. He has no interest in leaving Keely and going to the other side of the world with someone he no longer considers a friend. Perhaps he just didn't want to worry himself or Keely. They are so close, and so rarely spend time with any other people, that sometimes even the most innocuous intrusion into their bubble feels like it has the capacity to derail them. Arguments flare up without either of them knowing what they're about, and each time it seems to take a little longer to get back to the place they'd been before.

It's not as if Keely has ever gone to any great lengths to hide her drinking from him, and it's not as if he's too ignorant to have remained completely unaware of it. In this way, he knows her drinking is something they collude in, part of a pact that they've made. It's just one of those things that he occasionally thinks about but has become used to pushing to the back of his mind.

They go out for a drink together at the weekend, and every three out of four he'll end up all but carrying her home. Then she has the odd night in between when she meets Sarah. These are always a little less extreme because she knows she has to turn up at the shop in the morning. But he'll still hear her key skipping over the lock in the door until she eventually fits it in, and she might only take her shoes and jeans off before getting into bed and falling asleep immediately, her breath smelling sharply of cider or wine.

But because Keely has spells – sometimes stringing a week or more together – in which she seems to be repelled by the idea of drinking, he allows himself to slip into believing that there isn't really anything to be concerned about. She'll grimace at the prospect of going to the pub, and they'll snuggle on the sofa and watch TV; or they might sit cross-legged on the rug and play cards or dominoes.

On these nights, she can be so quiet, so insular, so studious. She picks up a book from one of the stacks of beaten-up paperbacks that fill their flat. Settled on the sofa, she'll do little else until she's finished. Her powers of concentration are formidable, and any twinge of concern that he might have for her evaporates.

The day comes to an end. Harry claps him on the back. The old man looks around, pinches the nostrils of his large, rubbery nose shut and scratches at the greying stubble on his cheeks. He says the same thing that he says at the end of every day: Let's get this place shipshape and then the pair of us can be off into the sunset.

On his way back, after he's finished cleaning the surfaces and mopping the floor, Finn decides that he's going to try and tell Keely about how he's been feeling, about the flashes of his past, and maybe something about her drinking as well. After months of holding it in, now's the time. He knows that his reticence has been weighing heavily on her. She's told him before, has warned him that the silence he projects is still something that she's made to deal with, that she has to waste energy interpreting.

The late June sun is warm on his back. He runs a hand through his hair. It's still a shock sometimes to feel how short it is, for his fingers not to get tangled up in all the kinks and the knots. Whenever he goes back to visit his nan and grandad, his nan can't keep herself from remarking how much more handsome he looks, how she's been telling him for years to do it and now look at him. Why has he wasted so much time looking so scruffy?

He knows that Keely will be waiting for him at home. Not so long ago, these moments, just walking toward her, the quiet anticipation of seeing her, of smelling the nutty, slightly salty skin of her forehead, had been the best of his day. He'd open the door and she'd be on the sofa reading, or she'd be in the kitchen with her hair pushed back, her cheeks flushed from the steam lifting up from one or two or three simmering pans. He wants that feeling back. He wants to leave behind whatever this feeling is that's started to creep so insidiously back into his life.

He reaches the door and opens it, but there's no sign of her. The flat looks just as it did on the morning when he'd left. He calls out for her, pushes open their bedroom door and sticks his head in, only to find it as empty as the rest of the flat. It feels cold, unlived in, and he suddenly thinks back to the houses on his street that had been abandoned.

Perhaps she's ended up having to work a late shift in the shop. Or perhaps she's just out for a walk. Either way, since she's out, he thinks that maybe he'll try his hand at cooking something, something from the book that Keely has recently got in the charity shop. He has no natural talent for cooking, but he wants to make more effort with it, so he starts rummaging in the fridge, crouched down and peering into it with one hand on the door to keep the little light from going out.

He takes out nearly everything that's in there: some carrots, several sticks of celery, a jar of mustard, some chicken thighs Harry gave him the other night to bring home. Surely there must be something in the book that he can prepare out of this. He starts flicking through the pages, imagining Keely's surprise when she returns from wherever she's been to see him with her apron on, something bubbling away on the gas ring.

His finger stops on a page, slowly slithers down as he reads the words. He thinks he might have found something. It's a French-sounding dish that might surrender to his amateur impulses. He's just about to flick the radio on for some music when he hears a knock at the door.

They so rarely have visitors that the sound makes him jump. He stays very still, listening to the thrum of his heartbeat in his ears. He thinks he might be mistaken, that maybe it's just someone out in the hall; but he hears it again, louder this time, and he moves over to open it.

He finds Mr Lister standing there. He knows Mr Lister

from when he occasionally pops into the shop to see Keely, and either Mr Lister or his wife are normally hovering around somewhere, walking along the aisles with a clip-board in hand, or simply sipping at a cup of tea and chatting away to customers while Keely serves people at the till.

He's a small man with a thin head of hair, wire-frame spectacles, and a moustache that he keeps impeccably trimmed. He wears a startled expression permanently on his face, the very same one that he has now when he looks up at Finn, his eyes wide and his small hand lifting to worry the top button of his green cardigan.

There's been a problem, he says.

Finn says nothing in response. He just stares down at Mr Lister, at the freckles and liver spots that he can see mapping his pate.

Mr Lister shuffles anxiously. He redistributes his weight from one small foot to the other. He doesn't know what to make of Finn's silence, so he simply starts talking: he tells Finn all that he knows, which isn't much, but that Keely was feeling unwell in the shop and she's been taken away in an ambulance. He tells Finn that he'll drive them both to the hospital now in his car.

They drive in silence for the first five miles until Mr Lister eventually reaches over and turns on the radio. Classical music starts up: a moan of violins followed by a darting ripple of piano. Finn keeps his eyes on the road, on the approaching beams of light that paint his and Mr Lister's face with stripes of lurid yellow light.

It's only after another five miles that Finn feels his brain start to thaw from the shock.

You don't know what's wrong with her? he asks.

Mr Lister shakes his head.

I've told you everything I know, he says.

Finn feels his eyes well with tears.

Is she going to be all right? he asks.

But Mr Lister can only shrug his small shoulders and repeat himself.

I've told you everything I know, he says.

It takes nearly an hour to get to the hospital. There's traffic along the way. Twice Finn sees the blue flash and flare of sirens up ahead. He can't keep himself from thinking that they have something to do with Keely. He sees her face and her blue eyes so clearly in his mind that he can't keep thick, soupy tears from running down his cheeks.

He can feel Mr Lister looking at him.

A moment later, he feels a tentative hand on his shoulder.

It'll be all right, Mr Lister says. It'll all be fine.

They arrive in the hospital car park. Mr Lister says that he'll find a space for the car as he lets Finn out at the hospital entrance. Finn's never been to a hospital before in his life, he realizes. The long corridors, mint-green walls and floors, the sharp smell of antiseptic, the crowded waiting rooms full of slumped, pale-faced people, the strip lights that glare blindingly down on the endless convoy of nurses and doctors and gowned patients – all of it shocks him.

His mind is feverish with worry. All he wants is to find Keely, to see her and know that nothing terrible has happened to her, that she's not going to leave him on his own. He's not sure if he's ever prayed with any kind of sincerity before, but he finds himself repeating the words, Please God, over and over and over and over again.

He locates a reception, though there's a queue that he has to wait in. He wishes he were the sort of person who knew how to push to the front of a queue – to walk past the stooped old woman who's so small that she can barely see over the counter, her white hair the same texture as candyfloss.

But all he can do is wait.

When he finally gets to the front, he stares through the glass at the tired, frayed-looking woman at the desk. He doesn't know what to say other than Keely's name. The woman asks him what he's here for, but all he can say is Keely's name again.

Has she been admitted here? asks the woman.

He nods.

He doesn't think that he's talking loudly or that he's behaving in any way erratically, but the woman tells him to calm down.

I'll only be able to help you if you calm down, she says.

She points to a chair and tells him to have a seat.

Someone will be with you shortly.

He walks over to the chair. He feels as if he's floating, as if his limbs aren't his own but have been sewn on like a doll's. He can hear the lights above him humming. Someone coughs and groans behind him. He's not sure how he's come to be here, what events have occurred to land him in this seat, his mind a bleached and empty shell.

Another woman, perhaps only a few years older than himself, with ginger hair and freckles clustered on her cheeks and forearms, offers him a paper cone of water, which he drinks in one and then holds, looking down at the floor like a small boy who's spilled his ice cream.

Is it Keely you're looking for? says the ginger-haired nurse.

He looks up at her and nods.

There's no need for you to panic. She's just getting herself ready and then she'll be with you soon.

His eyes widen in disbelief.

She's OK? he asks.

The woman with ginger hair nods. She's going to be fine. She'll be with you as soon as she's got herself ready.

He watches the woman leave, her strange blue outfit rustling as she goes. He doesn't want to be sitting down anymore, so he stands up, his eyes scanning every direction.

When he finally sees Keely, she's smiling slightly, almost sheepishly. Her skin looks pale and the soft pouches beneath her eyes are a deep, livid purple. She's brought the sleeves of her jumper over her hands and she moves toward him with the short, tender steps of somebody just learning to walk.

Mrs Lister is beside her, her hand lightly grasping Keely's forearm, gently steering her toward him. He wants to take Keely in his arms. He wants to ask her what happened and if she's OK, but he feels suddenly embarrassed in front of Mrs Lister, who's looking at him strangely now, the fine lines at the corners of her mouth deepening as she gently pushes Keely toward him, who presses herself against him, the top of her head tucked beneath his chin, the nutty, slightly salty smell of her brow rushing his nose.

*

FOR THE FIRST FEW weeks after finding out that something's growing inside her, Keely feels nothing. Her body is hard and cold and unchanged, and she takes this to mean that she's unfit to be a mother, that there's something fundamentally missing in her genetic makeup, a flaw that would, should she choose to have it, deny her access to the love that all other mothers have for their children.

She'd had the conversation with the nurse in the little cubicle about what her options were regarding the baby. She doesn't really remember much of it. The bleeding that she'd experienced had been enough to make her feel faint, and she'd struggled to concentrate, only half listening as the nurse tried to talk her through the possibility of arranging an abortion, handing her a small stack of leaflets that she'd been encouraged to look through at home.

Abortion: it's ugly sounding and ugly looking, and she spends fruitless hours trying to will it away; but it has stuck fast in her mind, a darkly gleaming presence on the periphery of every thought. Finn has made sure that she knows she has his support, whatever it is she chooses to do. But still, when she lies awake in bed thinking about it, she never arrives at a point where the prospect of actually terminating her pregnancy seems like a realistic one. She feels the suck of guilt dragging her deeper and deeper into herself.

She rarely sleeps and when she does, she dreams frequently of Welty's red windbreaker. It's tied to a length of twine or string, and she holds it like a kite. She's out on the dunes and she has it in her hand. The wind is up, and the red windbreaker is above her, the sleeves darting and shifting. She can hear the noise it makes, flapping and rustling just as it had when he'd worn it. And then there are times when the hood fills with air, so that it looks as if there's a headless body staring down at her, and she desperately wills Welty's face to appear, wills his dark eyes to find her own.

And when she wakes, she does so with a keen, painful sense of shame. She doesn't know why, but it lingers for the entire day while she's at the shop, following her around like a leak of noxious gas.

She knows she doesn't have much longer to decide. There's a time limit that she's working within. If the baby grows past a certain point, then it becomes dangerous. More than once, this clock inside of her has stoked a fierce anger in her. It's the horrible realization that she has such little control over her body. She and Finn had almost stopped having sex altogether, and even then they had been so careful not to conceive – but it had happened anyway; and now her body has taken over, has acted without her consent, a force that can't be contained no matter how much she wants it to be.

Before all of this, they had only ever talked about having children the once, and neither of them had really been in favour of the idea, at least not any time soon. The practicalities – the space in the flat, the lack of money, the general immaturity of their own lives – were enough to put them off considering it with any seriousness. Maybe someday, they'd agreed, but even then she'd not felt as if it was something they'd really ever do.

Now, whenever she asks him about it, all Finn repeats to her is that he'll support whatever it is she wants to do. She's thankful for this, but she also can't keep from trying to gauge if he's keeping something from her. Whether there's some germ of longing in him to be a father or whether he's utterly repelled by the idea, she can't tell. She presses him on the matter, but he won't budge. He explains that he feels as if the decision has to come from her, and that whatever it is she chooses he knows will be right for both of them. She nods and smiles, but she does her best to keep a close eye on him, watches him moving around the flat when he returns from the butcher's, trying to understand this man, part of whom she's now carrying inside her.

It's the first time that the future, their future, has lost its shapelessness, the wonderful porousness that had once stretched out before them. Now, it's started to harden at the edges, narrowing like a tunnel down which there's no obvious exit, no hoop of light they might easily jump back through into the scroll of days that had once seemed endless, as if they were made for them and them alone.

She trudges through the final days of August, each one indistinguishable from the last. It remains warm, and everything – the grass, the sky, the pavements, the trees – has a bleached quality to it, a tiredness that seems to bleed into her. Even the moss that so often thrives on the ledge of the window above the sink has hardened and yellowed, and it comes away with ease when she nudges it with the tip of her finger.

When she wakes in the morning next to Finn, she barely notices him. Before she'd been rushed to the hospital with Mrs Lister after the bleeding, she'd been planning on bringing up the letter with him. She'd spent weeks feeling angry about it, feeling weak for allowing him not to engage with her about it, suffering terrible spells of fear that he was going to leave, that he'd do the very same as her da and just start packing one day.

She finds that her mind often returns to her own child-hood. She tries to recall if she'd ever thought about mother-hood when she was a young girl, but she has no memory of it. Perhaps, she thinks, this is because in some ways she already was one. In the absence of their mam, this was the role that had been thrust upon her, and though she'd loved taking care of Welty, she's never been able to fully escape the fact that she'd failed at it. It had been her duty to protect him, but she'd allowed the very worst to happen to him. She can't face going through such a thing ever again.

This is the conclusion she reaches at last: she can't risk bringing a life into the world, only to have it be taken away from her because of her own incompetence. She explains this early one morning to Finn when they're still in bed. The light from outside creeps under the curtains and washes the lower quarter of their sheets blue. She knows that he's awake because she can see his toes clenching and unclench-ing beneath the cover, something he does every day before he places his feet down on the chill floor.

She's lying on her back, staring straight up at the ceil-ing, when she comes straight out with it. She doesn't shake or sob, but she feels tears slip from the corners of her eyes and run into her hairline.

I can't have it, she whispers.

He turns on to his side to face her, but he says nothing. He brings her close to him so that she can smell him, his sweat, the slight staleness of his breath. His arms wrap around her.

It's OK, he says, and he holds her while she quietly cries. With her hand at the small of his back and one finger slipped beneath the waistband of his boxer shorts, she feels a small shiver of desire for him, something she would once have acted on immediately, but then it's gone, and they simply hold one another until it's time for them both to get up for work.

She spends the day in the shop wondering if she'll change her mind, but she feels no special stirring. The guilt is still with her, but it's something that she knows she has to ignore, because the truth is that she still feels no attachment toward what's growing inside her. It seems impossible for her to care for something so small, something that, to her mind, can have no understanding about the fate that's been decided for it. She takes all this to mean that she's made the right decision.

That evening, she rings the number on the leaflet that she was given by the nurse. She speaks to a woman who asks her a series of questions. She answers them, hearing the flatness in her own voice, and an appointment is arranged for three days' time. She's advised that she should be accompanied, but she already knows that she'll go alone. She puts down the phone and decides to go on another walk.

Do you want me to come? Finn asks her, half standing.

She shakes her head.

I'll be back in a while, she says.

As she weaves between the people on the high street, for the first time in a long time, she finds herself thinking about her da. What if she were to bump into him now and she revealed everything that had happened to her, everything that was happening? What would her da say? Would he have an opinion on the matter? Would he try and persuade her to keep it?

She could go and visit him. She still has the address. She could just turn up and it could be the first thing that she blurts out. She could ignore the fact that they've not seen each other in years; she could ignore that he's standing in a different house, that he's standing next to a woman she doesn't know, and she could tell him that she's carrying his grandchild inside of her.

But what would be the use of any of it? He doesn't care enough to be with her, so why would he care enough to be with his grandchild?

She and Finn try to carry on with their lives as if nothing has happened, as if nothing is about to happen. Her appointment draws closer. It's marked down in the diary in the kitchen with a little cross. She's become positive that nothing will change her mind. All she has to do is get through these next few days, and then they can both put it behind them. In a year's time, she convinces herself, they'll barely be able to remember how they felt.

But something happens the day before she has her appointment. She's at the shop on her lunchbreak. She goes into the back room with her sandwich and her book. She takes her seat just as she normally does on the chair that she likes to read on, the one that she likes to rock back on and lean against the wall. She's about to push back and lift the front two legs of the chair off the ground, when she suddenly stops herself.

At first, she doesn't know why.

It's almost as if she hasn't made the choice, as if some other force has commandeered her body. But then she realizes. It's because she's afraid of falling off. Not for herself – she's never worried about that once before – she's afraid for the baby, afraid that the chair might come out from under her and the baby would be harmed. Without her knowing when or how, it's become real to her that she has the potential to care for the life that's growing inside, and she knows she's willing to protect it for the rest of her days.

She goes home that evening and tells Finn. She has to explain to him that it's not that she suddenly thinks what they were going to do is bad.

He stands at the sink, his arms folded, listening quietly.

What does this mean? he asks when she's finished.

What it means, she says, is that I want to have it.

She hasn't uttered the words out loud yet, and to do it shocks her, takes the air from her lungs so that she has to take a deep breath and keep very still.

Is this what you want? she asks Finn.

It is if you want it, he says.

SHE CLEARS OUT THE flat of all the bottles and tins that she knows are still hidden away, rooting through cupboards, standing on chairs, sweeping her hand through the darkness beneath the bed. She finds more than she thought she would, and she carries them, clinking away, in two bin bags. She leaves them on the street and stands a while to look at them, wiping the stickiness of her hands on her jeans, and breathing in the air through her nose, not wanting to catch another whiff of the liquid now leaking darkly across the pavement from a tear in the bag. She hasn't touched a drink since she found out, not even when she was planning to have the abortion. She hasn't felt the slightest craving for one. It's like a switch has been flicked off inside her head.

Her bump grows and people start to notice it. They congratulate her and ask when it's due. They have been to the first few scans: Finn takes time off work to go with her, and Harry pays him all the same. The baby is healthy and well, but they've declined to learn the sex. It's Keely's opinion that there are too few good surprises in the world, and that they should wait for this one, whatever it may be.

Her skin is stretched taut and hard, and her shirt lifts a fraction every time a fist or heel or toe prods from inside her. She delights in every nudge that she feels. She tries to imagine the baby inside her, but the strangeness of it makes it almost impossible, and she has moments where none of it seems real, as if the whole process is some elaborate joke, and that there must be some other, more natural way of producing a child.

Mr and Mrs Lister allow her a chair to sit on when she isn't serving people, just so her feet don't get too sore. In the early afternoons, before people finish work, she's often able to read a few chapters. She rests the spine of the book on her bump and allows herself to be absorbed into the story. So much so that on occasions she doesn't notice the tinkle of the little bell above the door when it opens, and her head snaps up to hear a customer clearing their throat and waiting with a pint of milk or a cut loaf.

She's six months along when one day she looks up to find that her old teacher, Miss Collins, is staring down at her. She looks no different, with her brown hair tied up, her soft brown eyes and the kind smile that stretches wide enough for two little pockets of darkness to show at the corners of her lips. She's wearing the same beige coat that she'd worn the day she dropped off the bag of books at the caravan door all those years before.

You're still reading, she says.

Keely looks down at the book in her hands. She doesn't know why she feels so shy, why her cheeks flush with colour, why she wants to creep away and find Mr or Mrs Lister so that they can serve at the till. For a moment, neither she nor Miss Collins say a word. Just their eyes meeting, scanning, smiling.

And then Keely sees Miss Collins's gaze drift down to her bump. She expects a flicker of disappointment to cross her old teacher's face, to see that she's already limited her horizons in such a way, that she's thrown away the 'potential' that Miss Collins had once expressly said Keely was in possession of.

But Miss Collins's eyes only widen, and she launches into all the usual questions, and through them Keely learns that Miss Collins has a child of her own, a seven-year-old girl called Alice that she'll soon be going to pick up from primary school.

I'm glad that you've stuck with it, says Miss Collins, her

eyes turning down to the book that Keely still has in her hand. You were always good.

Keely feels her cheeks flush for a second time. What is this embarrassment that she's feeling? She can barely bring herself to speak.

But then she does speak.

She opens her mouth, and she starts telling Miss Collins about all of the books she's read, about the ones she's bought from the charity shop, about the stacks and stacks of them in her flat, about how she reads one after another, and sometimes she struggles to get them out of her head, the stories that live there and continue to play out, a dialogue without end.

When Keely finishes talking, her head feels light and her fingers are tingling. The baby kicks inside her, a sharp jab with a fist or foot. She might have talked for a minute or ten, she doesn't know, but it feels to her as if she's been waiting to say all those things for a long time.

She looks at Miss Collins, who's staring at her strangely, her head slightly cocked, the beginnings of a smile on her lips.

Have you ever thought about teaching? she says.

FINN'S NAN DIES SUDDENLY on a Wednesday evening. By the following Friday, she's being lowered into the ground, and he and Keely and his grandad are standing on the lip of the grave. They watch as this woman, who'd only a few days earlier been on the phone to Finn telling him about what Keely should be eating to keep the baby healthy, is about to have heaps of earth tipped on top of her, never to be seen again.

Some of his nan's bingo friends are there. They introduce themselves and he allows their papery, darkly veined hands to linger on his wrist, his shoulder. They tell him what a wonderful person his nan was, how much she'll be missed. He notices that almost all of them are crying, their creased, sunken cheeks tracked by slicks of watery light. His and his grandad's eyes are dry. Keely's the only one out of the three of them that sheds a tear, her hands folded over the new life that's so nearly ready to begin.

Finn looks around for his mam. Now that he's about to become a parent, he's been thinking about his own more and more of late. He still knows nothing about either of them. Once or twice over the past few years, he's considered asking his nan or grandad about them, just a little so that he could start to create a picture to work with.

But every time he's come close, something has stopped him. He wants to keep getting on with his life. He's tired of having to look back. He only wants to look forward, to keep moving in a direction that takes him away from more things that will weigh him down. So he's said nothing, and now his nan is dead, and he can only guess at the knowledge and the memories that she's taken with her.

They have drinks and food in the same pub his grandad drinks at. It doesn't look any different from the last time Finn was there, aside from the fact that everyone's dressed in black, pecking like crows at the wilted buffet. Keely hovers near him. She'd grown fond of his nan over the years that they'd visited, and he can feel her looking at him. He knows she wants him to cry, but he can't do it.

They return to the house with his grandad after the wake. Keely, even though her bump has started to make moving awkward for her, boils the kettle for tea. Finn sees his nan's apron hanging on the kitchen door. He asks his grandad if he wants help clearing some things out at some point, but he shakes his head. After years of looking so robust, he looks suddenly frail, tired. He sits in his chair and lights a cigarette, hunches over it, blows the smoke weakly away from himself. The light is dimming outside. His grandad stares at the grey TV screen, at his dark reflection there. He's alone and he knows he is.

At the door, before they're about to go, Finn turns and asks if his grandad would like him to stay in his old room, just for the night, but again the old man shakes his head. He's rolled up the sleeves of his shirt so that his old tattoos are on show. Everything about him looks thinner, slacker. His teeth, stained brown from the tobacco, look as if they might be about to fall out. He thanks them and closes the door behind him.

Finn drives back in their car. Since Keely fell pregnant, he wanted to be able to drive her to the hospital, and now that he's passed his test, he enjoys being out on the road, thinking and listening to music. Occasionally, Keely reaches over and places her hand on his lap. Neither of them says anything. The light continues to fade until darkness falls and the roads are lit by the searching beams of cars, the red glow of taillights pulsing on and off like creatures in the very depths of the sea.

Finn doesn't cry until four days later when he's on a run. He reaches the top of the hill that's around a mile out of town. His lungs are heaving, burning. The night he'd been chased by the group of boys comes back to him in a volley of bright, hard-edged images: his grandad's wedding band tapping against the dark wood of the pub table; the flashing neon red sign outside the chippy; a sheet of greasy newspaper drifting to the ground; and then him running and running and running, his feet slapping the pavement and then tearing through the long grass of the playing fields, the darkness all around him, hearing the panting and cursing of his pursuers.

He can see the sea, the flat grey line of it just below the horizon. Normally he only pauses for a moment here to savour the feeling of being so high up, but now he crouches down and he thinks about his nan, this woman that did so much for him, fed him and clothed him and loved him, reluctantly sent him out into the world and never let him forget that she always wanted him back. He thinks how lucky he is to have had her. He knows there are so many people out there, on this island and across the water on scores of other lumps of rock, who have had nothing close to the amount of care and affection he's had over the years, who would never have someone like his nan in their life.

What had she wanted to say to him that night after she'd caught up with them both on his old street? Why had he not just let her take him to one side? Now that she's gone, he feels as if he didn't know who she was. He wishes he'd asked her things. Not just about his mam, but about herself and her own life: what she'd wanted from it, what she'd ended up with. He went through those days of his child-hood as quietly as he could, not wanting to disturb anyone, not wanting to be disturbed himself. He remembers the times that his nan had tried to hug him and he'd shrunk away, so afraid of being touched, and he feels the tears start to stream down his face. Then he's crying, properly crying, in a way he hasn't done since he was in the car with Mr Lister, his nose thick with snot and his chin bunched and dimpled and red. He stands up, wipes his nose, his eyes. He breathes in the gust of wind that blows in from the sea.

Only two weeks after the funeral, he goes back to visit his grandad to see how he's getting on. He doesn't tell him that he's coming, because whenever he's spoken to him recently, his grandad comes up with some excuse as to why he won't be there.

He knocks at the door like he's done ever since he left, but when it opens it isn't his grandad standing there. It's a woman around his age, small with pale skin, dark hair and dark eyes. She's wearing a white nurse's uniform, soft-soled black shoes, a black cardigan that somehow doesn't look dated but hugs the contours of her body.

Hello, Finn, she says.

He blinks rapidly in surprise, and it takes him another moment to realize that he knows who this woman is. It is Amy, the girl that he'd once dated, who he'd never had the courage to write to once he'd met Keely and turned his back on the band.

Finn offers his hand, but they end up embracing a little awkwardly on the step of his old home, Amy still inside and him still out.

What are you doing here? he asks.

I'm here for your grandad, she says.

Finn's nonplussed. He shakes his head and raises his eyebrows.

You don't know? Amy asks. He said he'd told you.

Know what? Finn replies.

Inside, all of his nan's stuff is still in the house, nothing changed, as if she might suddenly reappear and pick up her life where she left it. He wonders if maybe this is what his grandad is half expecting.

He won't let me touch any of it, Amy whispers to him as he steps inside.

His grandad is sitting watching the TV and Finn can't believe that it's him. He's sunken down into himself and he's wearing a bib. He looks so much thinner and older than he did only two weeks before, and Finn wonders what he's been feeding himself, or if he's been eating at all. His clothes seem to hang off him now, and everything that he's wearing looks faded, dishevelled. This is the man who used to have his clothes ironed and his shoes polished, who was forever talking about how important it was to look smart and make a favourable impression.

He turns to study Finn, his purple lips trembling slightly.

What are you doing here?

These are his grandad's first words to him. Finn can see that he's embarrassed, ashamed. His grandad struggles to push himself up from out of his slump, tries to stand but then falls back, so that Amy has to hurry over to him and help him rearrange himself as Finn stands back, too stunned to move.

There's no need for you to be getting up, Amy tells his grandad, who's still looking at Finn, his eyes wide and beseeching. Don't look at me, they say. Look away now.

They leave his grandad in front of the TV, and he follows Amy through to the kitchen. The carpet tiles are soft beneath his feet. Outside, the wind blows the washing line and the coloured pegs dangling from it bob gently up and down. He sees a sparrow peck at something on the patio, then fly away. Since his nan died, weeds have shot up through the grouting, some that would reach up to his knees.

He watches as Amy moves about the kitchen as if it were her own. She fills the kettle, takes down two mugs. The sound of the TV reaches them: laughter on a gameshow. As she busies herself with the tea, she tells Finn that his grandad has been very ill for a while now, at least a year, maybe a few months more. She's a community nurse these days, and she's been coming here to help out with him. Even when his nan was alive, she would come here to check up on his grandad's general wellbeing, take his blood pressure, listen to his chest, try and make him feel as comfortable as he could.

The kettle boils and she turns to Finn.

He isn't going to get any better, she says.

Finn goes back into the lounge and sits on the sofa, in the very place his nan used to sit. There's still an ashtray on the arm, though it's empty. He presumes that his grandad refuses to allow this to be moved either. He wonders at the love his grandad's had for her all these years, must still have for her now. He remembers when he'd first met Keely and he'd thought that his grandad couldn't possibly have felt about his nan the way he did about Keely. He thinks how wrong he was.

Why didn't you tell me? he asks.

His grandad doesn't turn from the TV and Finn thinks that he must not have heard him. He asks the question again and this time he sees the slack muscle of his grandad's stubbled cheek flicker slightly, and his left eye swivel a fraction to look at him before returning to the TV. Finn knows that he can hear him, it's just that he doesn't want to answer the question. He doesn't want to do anything that he doesn't have to.

After talking with Amy a little more in the kitchen, he says goodbye to his grandad, but his grandad still refuses to look at him, says not a word in response. Amy follows him to the door and stands with her arms folded across her chest. Finn puts his hands in his pockets. He's surprised to find that he's on the brink of tears, his throat thick and his eyes misting a little.

He doesn't want Amy to see him, turns away slightly, but she's already stepped out on to the street, and before he knows it, she's next to him and he's leaning down to embrace her, smelling her dark hair, the perfumed collar of her nurse's uniform against his nose.

Finn starts visiting his grandad every Tuesday after work. He leaves Keely at the kitchen table, her head bent to study for the course she's started to be a teacher. He's amazed at how she's managed to take on this work, all while still being at the shop and carrying the weight of their unborn child around with her. In many ways, this is the closest he's felt to her for a while. What they've made between them, this life that's soon to announce itself, he truly believes will knit them together in ways that are beyond his imagination.

And yet there's still some lingering distance between them. When they touch, it feels formal, and when they sleep together at night, she no longer twines herself around him but keeps to her side, cradling her bump, and they wake seeming further apart than when they went to sleep. He knows there was a time when they'd wake and be touching, and that their touching was a charged moment, as if they'd spent all night held in a state of arrested desire, only allowed to act upon it in those first few moments.

He still longs for her, still finds himself at work or shopping for groceries and fantasizing about her, feeling himself harden at the thought of them in bed, of her hands on him, his mouth on her mouth, on her neck, pulling at her nipples, kissing the taut, pale flesh of her stomach until he can begin to taste the sweet, briny scent of her.

But they move these days so differently, always around each other, never touching, as if they've not known intimacy. And the same goes for how they communicate. He never got to tell her about the strange flashes back to his past that he'd started experiencing, and now that they seem to have calmed down a little, he doesn't think it's worth the hassle. And now that she no longer drinks, he doesn't have to worry about that anymore. He can push everything down, where he hopes that it'll stay, where he can't see it anymore.

He never fails to ring his grandad's house before he sets off. His grandad never picks up, but Amy does and he speaks quietly into the phone. He doesn't know why, but he hasn't told Keely about Amy being there. She knows that there's a community nurse, but he's told her that it's a woman named Philippa, someone different entirely, someone he's described as old and frumpy, not the same age as them.

He reasons with himself that he's doing it to protect her. She's in a fragile position. He doesn't want to worry Keely with nonsense from his past, things that have no bearing whatsoever on their present or their future. But no sooner has he told himself this, than he's forced to reckon with the flutter of excitement that he feels in his stomach whenever he's approaching his grandad's house. He finds that he's looking forward to talking with Amy. He looks in the windows of cars he passes to make sure he doesn't have anything around his mouth from the sandwich that he's eaten on the way, or to make sure his hair isn't looking peculiar.

Then, whenever the door opens and he sees her, they always hug. He likes the smell of her perfume, which is the same one she'd used at the time they'd first met. Her hair looks even darker to him, and he finds himself admiring how it contrasts with the paleness of her throat, the way it brushes against her cheeks as she leans over to plump the cushions in his grandad's chair.

His grandad's decline is a curious thing. Sometimes, Finn starts to believe that he surely must be nearing his end. At these times, his grandad sleeps for hours on end, and sometimes doesn't even wake up to see Finn before he has to go again.

But then there are other times when he walks in to find his grandad on his feet, dressed almost as smartly as he used to be, shoes polished and trousers pressed. He's more talkative than he was the first time he'd visited, but they still don't talk about the illness he's suffering from. What his grandad wants to do is carry on as if nothing has changed, and even if Finn would like this to be different, would like to sit and discuss what his grandad is feeling, he also must respect what this man wants: to go through to the end of his days without having his suffering become an attraction, without having his grandson look at him and see any weakness.

The times when his grandad is asleep are the visits Finn enjoys the most. He sits with Amy in the kitchen, taking it in turns to make cups of tea. They talk about anything and everything. Amy knows about Keely, knows that she's now in the final stage of her pregnancy. Finn had said as much on their first meeting a while ago. But since then neither of them have ever brought her up again. Still, Keely's presence in their conversations is a solid shadow at the corners of their vision which they both must do their best to avoid.

Just as when they were younger, Finn finds Amy easy to be around. She asks him about the band and why it came to an end, and he finds himself explaining his relationship with Evan in a way that he never has with Keely. What he discovers is the horrible fact that, in some indefinable way, Amy's presence is far more soothing to him than Keely's at this present time. He thinks: even in those first days when he and Keely had shared their whole lives, there'd been a simmering, bristling energy to their confessions, an undirected splurging of them rather than a considered, measured decanting. But with Amy, he finds that he can talk about himself without feeling charged with jittery energy. He feels he can look at himself from a more comfortable distance, and he can see a little more clearly the man he is.

On his drives back, he tries not to think about Amy. He tries to convince himself that he doesn't have any longing for her physically, that their hugs are innocent of any meaning; but he can't keep himself from summoning up old memories of them together, their clothes strewn about and the full roundness of Amy's hips and thighs, the creaminess of her skin.

He drives and tries to blink the images away, turns up the music so loud that his chest rattles and hums. But nothing works. He imagines Keely discovering these thoughts, having them laid out before her like photographs, and his face flushes so violently with shame that more than once he has to pull over on to the hard shoulder, where he rests his head against the steering wheel and hammers his fists against the dashboard, spitting out curse after furious curse against himself.

KEELY IS THREE DAYS past her due date. She's tired and restless and she wants the baby out of her. She snaps at Finn whenever he asks if he can do anything to make her more comfortable, asks him to leave her alone for a few hours, just until she starts feeling a little more sociable.

He tells her that he doesn't want to leave her alone, doesn't want to be away when something happens and it's time to go to the hospital. But she shoos him away, and she reminds him of what the midwife had told them just two days before, that it's very common for first time pregnancies to go over by at least a week, sometimes more, and she thought Keely might not start her labour for a few days yet.

So he acquiesces. He tells her that he'll drive down to see his grandad, since he hasn't been for a week. He looks at her lying on the sofa, a pale sliver of the great drum of her belly showing between her T-shirt and pants. Her eyes are closed and she has the back of one hand resting on her brow. She's been like this more and more of late, asking for space, and though the nurse has told him many times about the hormones, it still smarts to suffer her rejection, to feel as though she wants no part of him in these final moments. He risks stooping down and kissing her lightly on the top of her head, and then he's away, the car rattling down the motorway and the radio on.

Amy opens the door and immediately brings her finger up to her lips. She mouths the words, He's sleeping, then turns around and tiptoes through to the kitchen. The TV is on as Finn passes the lounge, but the volume is off. He steps in and looks at his grandad. His face is sunken and his hair, once combed thickly back, is thin and wispy, gathering about his ears like the down of a baby bird. His mouth is open and there's a thin slick of drool on his chin that catches the flashing lights of the TV. Finn picks up a tissue from the box on the arm of his chair and very lightly dabs it away, then heads through to the kitchen.

The kettle has boiled and Amy is just reaching up into the cupboard. He notices that she's not wearing her nurse's uniform for some reason, but her own clothes. He can see a half-moon of soft, pale skin over the band of her jeans. He tries to move around her to take a seat at the table where they usually talk, but as he does so Amy turns with the mugs and they collide awkwardly, his arms pressed against her chest, and hers down by his crotch.

They smile and laugh, but before either of them know it, it's happening. Their lips are together and he can taste her mouth, can feel her tongue probing against his chipped tooth. A shard of a memory digs at him behind his eyes, and he sees Keely's hands on his cheeks and he hears her voice – So you'll leave it as it is? – but then he's back with Amy, and it's familiar, and the familiarity makes it natural, almost as if no time has passed since they were last kissing, when Finn was still in the band with his long hair and his trench coat, and she was in the first row of the audience, waiting to take him back to her flat.

They move as if underwater, wrestling with one another, breathing fierce jets of air only through their noses. Finn's heart is pounding and he can feel Amy's doing the same, and when he opens his eyes, he's surprised to find himself in the hallway, the same patterned wallpaper, the clock ticking away. An image of himself standing in his nan's purple and green cagoule briefly flashes across his mind, and still with his lips pressed and greedily twisting, he looks over Amy's shoulder to see his grandad asleep in his chair, his head cocked to one side, oblivious to what's happening just a few steps away from him.

He is following Amy upstairs into his old room. He flicks the light on. He hasn't been in here since he, with Keely, packed everything up and moved out. It's just as he left it: his single bed, his chest of drawers, the same blue and yellow on the walls, the slant of the roof and the small window. Now here he is, a grown man, with his girlfriend at home and their child inside of her, and him here with Amy, a woman he'd once known who's now caring for his terminally ill grandad.

A moment arrives, a shiver of clarity in the fug of his brain. He knows this is his chance to stop it. He can walk away from Amy, he can go back downstairs. He can drive home and nothing much will have changed. Nothing irreparable will have happened, and his life will continue as it has been, his life with a woman that he knows he loves and knows and wants.

But then Amy's mouth is on his again, and the moment passes, and he is being lifted out of himself, out of his body, and it's only when they're lying in the darkness, with their limbs still snared together and the cooling run of his seed tracking down his inner thigh, that he hears the phone ringing downstairs, and he's returned to a world that's now entirely different to the one it had been.

3

KEELY'S IN FRONT OF A CLASS OF NEARLY THIRTY children. It's the final day of term, then she'll have three weeks off with Anna, who'll soon be turning three. She has a book in her hand, one that she'd first picked out from one of the bags that Miss Collins had dropped off outside her caravan door. She's listening to a small girl at one of the front desks read from the final chapter. The girl's voice is quiet and a little shaky, but she has a good command of the language, rarely tripping up on the longer words.

She's now officially a teacher of English. It's Miss Collins's position that she's taken at the local school. Keely had come to know her as Claire over the years that she'd studied and was helped along the way to get to where she is now. They are friends these days.

Keely loves working with stories and language every day, and even though she only took over her own class a couple of months ago, she's yet to arrive in the morning without a tremendous sense of excitement about the day ahead, and without immense pride about how she's managed to transform her life.

There are two windows that look out on to the playing fields. The sky is low and grey, and the grass of the field looks soupy after a few days of steady rainfall. It's getting toward dark, but inside the classroom is warm and bright. It smells faintly of orange peel. There are Christmas decorations up, some of which the children have made in their art class, snowmen and reindeer cut out from coloured card and rendered 3D with scrunched-up balls of tissue paper.

This is the same classroom that she'd once studied in, and she can remember looking out of these same windows, urging time to move faster, desperate to be set free. In summer, she'd long to get back to the camp so that she could head on to the dunes with Welty, and in winter she'd hope to get back to cosy up next to her da in the caravan, with a plate of hot chips in her lap and the TV on.

Now she's standing, dressed in one of the few new outfits that she's been able to afford, and she's looking out over the rows and rows of small faces that occasionally lift to stare at her or at a friend or at the clock. For the first few weeks, she'd felt nervous, as if she had no right to be here. What could she possibly impart to these young people? What did she know that they didn't?

But as time has passed, she's started to feel more and more in control. She knows the books that she's teaching inside out. She's read them so many times that she can recite some passages without fault and has done so to amuse and engage her classes, who follow the words on the page with their fingers as she narrates, checking to see if she makes a mistake.

Just as the girl finishes reading, the bell sounds out and the children start talking excitedly, pushing their chairs back and packing their books and pencil cases away in their bags. Normally she'd raise her voice and tell them not to rush, then remind them of any homework that she's set; but since it's the last day, she says nothing, just stands by the door as they file out, smiling, wishing each one of them a happy Christmas.

When they've gone, she sits at her desk and just holds herself there. The corridors are busy and loud with footsteps and chatter. She remembers walking down these corridors after Welty had died and feeling every pair of eyes on her. She remembers not wanting to be there with such a passion that she'd simply stopped going. That was when Miss Collins, or Claire, had turned up. Maybe, she thinks, if she hadn't dropped out, then she wouldn't be here now.

She wishes the other teachers a happy Christmas in the staff room. Smoke wafts near the ceiling and there's a plate of custard creams on one of the tables. She gets along with most of her colleagues, and there's one, the art teacher named Dan, who – she was told at the Christmas party – fancies her. She waves goodbye to him last, and then heads out.

She gets in the car to drive home. As soon as she starts the engine, the first flakes of snow start to fall, feathering the windscreen and melting a second later. As she turns out of the parking lot, some of the children are still hanging around the front gates. She can see one or two of them with their tongues out, trying to catch the drifting snowflakes. A clutch of girls wave to her. She waves back and then hoots her horn. Even over the rattle and groan of the engine, she can hear a cheer go up.

The car is old now, is clinging on, surely on the brink of heading for the scrapheap soon. Sometimes it doesn't start, and once it had simply puttered out when she was driving, so that she'd had to put on her hazard lights to pull over and start it up again. She slows and prepares to turn on to the road that Anna's nursery is on. A Christmas song is playing on the radio, but she can still hear the tick tock tick tock tick tock of the indicator, like a syncopated backing to the song.

The snow starts to fall, heavier and faster, so she increases the speed of her windscreen wipers. She hasn't seen snow for years, not since those first months when she'd met Finn. She thinks about him now, sees his face in her mind, his wide-set eyes. It sometimes happens at work, his face appearing like this; it takes her by surprise, and she has to place her palms flat on the desk to keep her hands from shaking.

Anna is over on the other side of the room next to the little sandpit they use for burying treats that the kids have to reach in and dig out. Her hands are just being cleaned with a wet wipe by Andrea, the woman who runs the nursery. Anna already has her duffel coat on and her yellow wellies. Her hair is light like Keely's, but her eyes are the same as Finn's, a sharp, piercing green that she sometimes struggles to look at without Finn's face darting in and out of her mind.

When Anna turns and sees Keely, she smiles and waves with the hand that isn't being cleaned. Keely can see her mouth move to form the word Mummy, but she can't hear it over the noise of the other children playing. Her body is small and compact, and sometimes reminds her of Welty, the way she can contort it to wriggle and slip her way around the house, under the bed and behind doors, where she hides to spring out and surprise Keely.

Andrea looks up to see Keely and smiles. She leads Anna, who's half walking, half skipping, by her hand.

Keely drives them back to the house with Anna in the backseat chattering away about her day and pointing at the snow that's already starting to gather on the ground here and there. Two months after Anna's birth, Finn's grandad died and he and Keely had used the money left to him and from the sale of the house to buy their own, though Finn no longer lives with them – she asked him to leave, and she has no plans to ever ask him back.

The thought of him with that girl shocks her even now, can bring a wave of nausea over her that can last the whole day. Her imagination turns on her in an instant, and before she knows it she's watching Finn's hands work their way around a body that looks fuller, tauter, sexier than her own. The body always remains faceless, but Keely can see her tongue, and she can see how it climbs like a vine into his mouth, its tip running along the scarp of his broken tooth, the tooth that he'd kept for her.

But what she hates him for most is how utterly stupid he's made her feel. For years, she'd believed him to be the kind of person who would never consider doing such a thing, who would have rather died than cause her any harm. But she'd been wrong, and she knows now, if she hadn't already known it deep down, that there's not one person on this earth that can ever be truly trusted.

The house is cold and dark when she leads Anna in by the hand. Since Finn moved out, she's worked hard to make sure it feels as homely as possible. Money's always tight and what little she does have she spends on trying to make Anna as happy and comfortable as possible. She wants her to have nice clothes, a nice bedroom where she can play with her friends, a tidy little garden that they can both be out in in the summer.

Even though Anna was still a baby – only six months old when she and Finn parted – she still seems to be almost preternaturally aware of the rift between them. Finn's absence is something that Anna remarks on almost daily, and there are nights when she walks sleepily into Keely's room, crying quietly, saying that she misses her daddy. There's nothing Keely can say at such times other than to draw back the covers for Anna and haul her small body into the warmth, just as her own mam had once done with her, and to promise her that she'll see her daddy at the weekend.

Keely flicks on the lights and the heating, then sits Anna down on the toilet to have a wee. The bathroom smells of the airing cupboard which has been left open all day, a clean, woody scent that she likes. There are towels neatly folded across the wooden slats, and also a small plastic duck with a red beak that Anna likes to play with in the bath.

She makes Anna her tea: mashed potato, fish fingers

and a few scoops of baked beans. She sits opposite her at the table and asks her questions about her day. It still seems remarkable to her that this little person understands her, that she has thoughts of her own, that she can articulate her pleasures and displeasures so clearly, and often so amusingly. It seems utterly unfathomable now that Keely had come so close to vanquishing this life that she's created, that's been added to the world and makes her own so much brighter and happier.

Anna tells her about a painting that she did. She has a friend, a little boy named Sebastian, that she spends most of her time with. Keely has taken Anna over to their home in a little village a few miles away. It's a large white house with its own drive and garage, and it has a garden so big that the lawns have to be mowed by a sit-on machine.

Keely will often have a cup of tea in the kitchen while Anna plays for a bit longer, and she'll sit at a large wooden table and stare at the dark gloss of the granite surfaces, at the pleasingly distressed tiles of the floor. This is the first house she's been in that belongs to people who have money.

Sebastian's parents are called Louise and Jonathan. Louise grew up in the town but she met Jonathan when she went to university. Keely assumes that's how she lost her accent, though sometimes the occasional word slips out of her mouth that has the same musical lilt to it as her own. Jonathan, a tall, fair-haired man with bright teeth and spectacles, is from somewhere down South and does a job that Keely doesn't understand but must earn him a hefty salary. He doesn't say much, and often seems a little wary around her, as if she might be considering attacking him.

Anna sometimes asks if Sebastian can come over to their house to play, but she always comes up with an excuse why this isn't possible. She would love to have Sebastian round, to hear him and Anna playing upstairs in her room, but she's simply too ashamed to have Louise or Jonathan see how small and grubby her house is compared to their own. She'd love to have a great big kitchen with a tiled floor and cupboards that go up to the ceiling, but she has only enough room to fit in a small plastic table that she knows is actually patio furniture. It was all she could afford at the time, but she's promised Anna that they'll have a big wooden one like Sebastian's one day.

Anna leaves some of her tea – half a fish finger and a dollop of beans – which Keely finishes off while stood over the sink. The windows are all dark now, though when she's rinsing the plate under the sink, she can still see the snow landing on the glass and then disappearing.

Finn recently bought Anna a video player and some videos. She has no idea how he scraped the money together, but Anna loves them. She wants to watch one now, one they must both have watched a hundred times. Like some of the books she's read, Keely can remember nearly all of the dialogue, and she can time some of the lines perfectly with the characters on the screen to make Anna laugh.

She switches on the old, ugly electric fire that she'd like to remove at some point, but which now warms them, the bars glowing red after a few minutes. The sofa is lumpy but comfortable enough. Anna fetches her blanket from upstairs and then comes back down with it trailing after her, still in her nursery uniform but with her pink dressing gown over the top.

They nestle up together in the corner of the sofa. Keely loves to feel her daughter's body pressed against her own, the solid weight of her. When Anna sleeps at night, Keely never goes to bed without tiptoeing into her room. She'll watch her daughter's chest rise and fall, but still she'll lower her hand to hover over her mouth just so she can feel the soft warmth of her breath against the tips of her fingers.

Sometimes, if she's not too fearful of waking her up, she'll rest her hand on her chest and feel the steady drum of her heart. It can send a shiver of worry through her, all of this precious life supported by something she can't see, can't touch, can't protect. She'd like to keep that heart locked away from harm, for it to be always with her, never not within her reach, and it's only recently that she's felt a little more comfortable handing Anna over to be looked after by someone else.

They watch the video. The bright colours splash across Anna's face. She laughs at all the same parts, sings along with the songs, sometimes getting the words mixed up in ways that make Keely smile. There's the occasional suggestion – the way she brings her small fists up to rub at her eyes, or starts sucking on the tip of her thumb – that lets Keely know Anna's tired, and she hopes that she'll at least sleep through the first part of the night before climbing into her bed, where Keely herself is often still awake, swarmed by thoughts of Finn, reliving the terrible conversation that led to him leaving.

The video ends and then they go upstairs, Anna placing her hands on each tread and counting them, her bum raised up in the air. Keely runs a bath and watches the mirror steam up, then she lifts Anna up so that she can draw on it with her finger. She draws squiggles and claims them to be clouds. Then she draws both the sun and the moon, two uneven circles on opposite sides of the glass.

You can't have the sun and the moon out at the same time, Keely tells her. Or you can, she corrects herself, but only one of them can really shine its light.

But Anna shakes her head. She's stripped down to just her white vest and her knickers with the frilly trim. Her legs are thin and lean like Keely's were at that age, but there's also a suggestion of Finn, in the knobbly awkwardness of knees and ankles.

Some people are in the light, Anna says, and some people are in the dark.

It's not uncommon for Anna to say such things. She has an uncanny knack for aphorism, like a miniature sage. These moments can be funny, or they can unnerve Keely, and she can convince herself that Anna has been gifted with some prophetic foresight, as if she might one day reveal her destiny as she's pawing yoghurt into her mouth with her fingers.

Sometimes Keely will get in the bath with her, but now she just kneels down next to it, still wearing her work skirt, so that it's stretched tight across her thighs. Her left sleeve is rolled up, so she can dangle her fingers in the water and help fish out some of the toys that sink to the bottom. The duck with the red beak is in there, bobbing on the surface, but what Anna seems to enjoy the most is an ordinary plastic measuring jug, which she fills up and pours out over her own head, and sometimes drinks from when she believes Keely isn't looking. Whenever Keely catches her, Anna claims to like the taste of it more than normal water.

She tells Anna that she didn't have a bath when she was her age.

Then what did you get clean in? Anna asks her.

We had a little shower in the caravan.

Keely does her best to explain what a caravan is. She wants to take Anna to the camp someday soon. She went recently, the last time Finn was looking after Anna, and she walked up into the dunes and down on to the beach. No one was there, and it seemed like no one ever had been, and she'd left not knowing whether this was a good thing or a bad thing.

Keely looks at her daughter, with her hair dark and flat, her skin glistening. Her green eyes always seem to look bigger in the bath, at a glance taking up half of her face. When Keely drops her off at Finn's and Finn lifts her into his arms so that their faces are level, it can still shock her to see how similar they look; and she can't help but feel a small part of herself resent this. She doesn't want to be reminded of him or what he did for the rest of her life, and this is going to be the case.

Anna is asking to get out of the bath because she's feeling cold. Keely lifts her out, wraps her in a towel so that only her face is showing, her eyes peering up at her. She picks her up and carries her into her small bedroom. The walls are painted a shade of light blue, because Anna had said that she wanted it to feel like she was surrounded by the sky. Keely hadn't been able to afford to get a decorator in, so she'd painted it herself. But even with a stepladder, she hadn't been able to reach certain corners, and so one afternoon when Finn was dropping Anna back off, she'd asked him if he could do the last touches.

This was the first time they'd been in the same room together for longer than thirty seconds since they'd split, except for when she had gone round to his flat to check it was suitable for Anna. He looked paler and thinner, and when he'd climbed the ladder and reached up, she saw the hard bones of his hips poke out over his jeans.

They'd talked, but not about anything other than what he'd done with Anna that day. Still, the exchange had been calm and without incident. It's only ever her that gets angry. It always has been.

Finn hadn't been able to finish it all that night, so he'd come back the following week, and it was only a few nights after that that Keely had seen that he'd painted a little yellow sun in one corner of the room, with a face – two eyes and a nose and a gentle, beatific smile – that was looking down on Anna's bed. He must have snuck a small tin of paint in with him, just a sample maybe, in his coat pocket. She'd pointed it out to Anna, and now Anna looks up every night and says goodnight to it. Keely likes to look at it at night too, though she's never mentioned it to him, and he's not mentioned it to her.

She tucks Anna in bed. She's wearing her pyjamas, the ones with the little red truck motif, because she likes anything red and things that go fast. Her hair is still damp to the touch behind her ears, so Keely lays a small hand towel on the pillow that she keeps warming on the radiator.

She asks for a story, and picks up the one about a boy who helps a bear build a den in return for being taught to ride a unicycle. The story always prompts Anna to say that she'd like to have a garden big enough for a bear to build a den in, and Keely tells her that one day they will, but she can't promise the bear.

Anna falls asleep before Keely's even halfway through the story. She must have been tired. She lifts up the duvet so that it's snug beneath her chin, and then she just sits for a few minutes and looks at her. She hovers her fingers over her mouth to feel her breath. The fact that she's a part of her is yet to lose its potency, and she hopes it never will.

Downstairs it's cold and empty now that Anna's in bed. These are the hours, the empty hours of her day in which she's alone with her thoughts. This is when they can pick at her, when they know she's vulnerable, swarming her like ants on a dropped cone of ice cream.

The only thing that soothes them is the few mugs of whiskey – never more than three – that she pours now, sitting herself at the table and watching the clock on the wall until it's time for her to go to bed.

HE'S STILL AT THE butcher's in the day, though at night he's studying. It's not a course that he's a part of or paying to do, but something that he's taken on himself, that he's entirely responsible for. He has stacks and stacks of books, most of them borrowed, some of them bought, but they've come to feel like the only things that are keeping him going, that are saving him from despair.

He can see snow starting to fall from the darkling sky outside. He serves the last customer of the day and then begins clearing away, wiping down the surfaces and mopping the floor, spreading out the little fistfuls of sawdust where necessary.

For the first few weeks after he'd split from Keely, Harry had offered him the spare room in his and his wife's house. Every night, they'd walked back together and sat down at the table as Linda, Harry's wife, would serve them up a meal, and then Harry would do his best to ask Finn about everything that had happened between him and Keely, which he described almost every night in the same way, as being like pulling teeth.

Finn knows that Harry worries about him. When he'd found a place to live and move his stuff to, Harry had tried to convince him to stay a little longer. It was Linda who'd had to convince Harry that Finn was ready to be on his own again, and only then had he let Finn out the door.

Around a year ago, Finn went into the charity shop that Keely used to go into all the time on the high street. Since he saw so little of her now, it was somewhere that he could go to sense her presence, to feel near her and all the small moments they'd shared together there.

He'd been looking at nothing in particular when he'd seen a spine on the shelf that his eye had been immediately drawn to. When he'd pulled it out and turned it in his hands, he found that it was the same book he'd been obsessed with as a boy, the one he'd found in the library at school about the Bog People.

He hadn't seen the pictures in so long that when he opened the pages, he'd had to fight to hold back the tears. They brought with them a such a vivid rush of memories, and almost every thought that had ever skimmed through his mind at that age seemed to flow through him again, as if his entire life was somehow contained within this book, as if it was a portal into a past version of himself.

Just as when he was a boy, he started to spend whole days thinking about the book. It became his primary means of distraction. Whenever he was thinking about how he'd betrayed Keely, or about how Anna was now living most of her life without him there to be with her, he'd force himself to think about the book, using it as a beacon, like a lighthouse to guide him safely around the spearing rocks and safely on to shore.

For weeks, maybe over a month, the distraction worked; but then times started to creep in when it didn't work, when no matter how hard he tried, he couldn't control what his mind wished to summon forth. He'd wake and the first thing that he'd see would be the faces of Keely and Anna. It always felt to him as if they'd been waiting there for him; he never had any memory of dreaming of them, but there they'd be, staring at him, their faces always expressionless, seeming to expect both something from him and nothing at all.

On these days, he could barely bring himself to get out of bed. The knot in his stomach would be as tight as it was when he was a boy. He'd try to calm himself by imagining the river that he'd used to wade through, but it never worked. He remembered back then that he used to feel a kind of emptiness, but the feeling that took over him now would more often than not strike him as the opposite, as a fullness, a fullness that was stretching his muscles and his skin, as if something was growing inside him, a malignant life force seeking its freedom.

It altered the way he moved around. His gait became slower, clumsier. His head was permanently foggy. He felt as if his body was shutting down, as if it was no longer truly his own. To try and counter it, he started to run more than ever, sometimes doing five miles on a morning before work, and then heading back out for another five after. It's not as if he'd had much fat to lose, but he became dangerously thin. His eyes bulged. His teeth pressed against his lips. The strings of his apron could be fastened twice over around his waist.

There were many nights when he'd go without eating. He barely recognized the sensations of hunger. Everything he ate came out of a tin: baked beans, carrots, potatoes. Sometimes, if he couldn't face the very simple task of standing and stirring the beans, he'd warm the tin on the radiator and then dig in with a spoon. By the end of the week, he'd have a stack of tins and lids that he'd then have to clear away before Anna arrived on the Sunday.

It was always at night that he was at his worst. The darkness invited every spectre his mind could conjure up. He desperately struggled to make sense of what he'd done, how he'd so thoroughly ruined his life. The fault was all his own, and it made him feel so wretched that he wanted to tear at himself, and often he would, dragging his nails down his forearms until the skin broke open, so that the next day he'd have to make sure to wear a long-sleeved top to keep Harry from seeing.

How? Why? These were the questions that haunted him. He'd had no desire to do it, no secret motive propelling him forward. It wasn't that he hadn't loved Keely; it wasn't that he'd thought of Anna in any way other than that she was the most beautiful, astonishing creature that he'd ever set eyes on. These were the things that life had presented to him without his having to make a decision, without his having to really work for them. They'd appeared purely out of luck and chance and good fortune. And yet he'd spat them back and now here he was, alone, in a room with walls black with mould, and a toilet down the hall that he had to share with other tenants, some of whom didn't seem to sleep for days on end.

I NEED TO TAKE three days off work next week, he'd said to Harry, who'd looked up at him surprised before nodding lightly and saying that he'd cover the time himself if he had to.

It was the beginning of November, and Finn had read about a local dig that was happening a few miles away. A team of archaeologists were expecting to discover something of great importance. From the air, they'd managed to discern patterns on the ground below that suggested an ancient town, shapes of walls and pathways pressing up beneath the grass. He cut out the pictures and studied them by lamplight.

The article – which he had stumbled across in the local paper – gripped him in a way that was physical. His body was tense, and when he'd got to the end, he realized that his heart was hammering and that his fists were bunched together so hard that his knuckles shone white, like hard, pale fruit.

Finn didn't quite know what he was going to do when he got to the site. He just knew that he needed to be there. It was a feeling like the one he used to get as a boy when he'd run his hands through the treasure in the box under his bed, a feeling which remained inside him long after he'd put the paper to one side, humming like the final note struck on a piano.

Keely now had the car that they'd shared, so he decided that he'd run there, packing a backpack with a map, some water and a small amount of food – a banana sandwich and an apple – then setting off early in the morning when it was still dark and the air cold enough for his breath to mist from his nose and mouth.

As he ran and the sky got brighter, his lungs seemed to expand. He'd not felt so light on his feet for a long time. The sun rose up and washed him in light. The wind tore at him, reddening his thighs. His fingers ached with the cold, but he was alive, and for the first time in many months, years, he felt glad of it.

For the first two days, he just stood there at the edge of the field by an old fencepost that was driven lopsidedly into the soft earth. Even though it was cold in the crosswind that was whipping from the sea over the land, and he couldn't see anything that was happening with any real clarity, he'd felt elated to simply be near the activity, to see the tape flapping in the wind, the small bodies crouched low with tools in hand, the occasional shout that went up and brought more bodies over to huddle around.

On the nights after he'd run home, it seemed strange to him that he'd never considered his passion as a child – all the digging around in the river and in the playground, the retrieving bits and pieces of lives that had gone before him – had the potential to be manipulated into something bigger. He'd always thought this habit an aberration, something worthy only of ridicule, not that there were other people out there who shared his interest and could turn it into a career.

He started – gradually – to feel again: he had thoughts and ideas that knitted together in a way they hadn't for a long time. He realized this was his imagination firing up again after a long period of dormancy. It had vanished, but now it was back, and he was given his first glimpse of a possible future, his first taste of hope.

On the third day, he arrived just as he'd done on the previous two, though this time he'd been surprised after an hour to hear the sound of footsteps behind him. He'd turned to see a man, older than him by at least twenty years, approaching with a brisk, official stride. Finn had wanted to run; he'd thought that maybe he was about to be castigated, was perhaps in trouble with the law.

But the man had raised an arm and he'd smiled. Grey hair poked out from beneath a cap; his skin was ruddy, as if he'd just removed himself from a warm hearth. He asked Finn if he was interested in what was going on, and the moment Finn confirmed that he was, the man asked him to join him in having a look around the site.

His name was Graham and he was one of the people in charge of the whole operation. Finn, still in his running shorts, stalked after him, listening to Graham talk about what they were looking for, what they'd already discovered, and what the impact of some of the discoveries could turn out to be.

They approached the trenches that had been dug. He was shown the marvel of a perfectly intact wall built thousands of years ago. He was shown pieces of old pottery, some jewellery and, most remarkably, an old leather shoe. People looked up at him and nodded or smiled, then went back to their digging with little trowels or delicate brushes. None of them seemed to be talking, completely absorbed as they were in their own worlds.

He'd stayed there all day. He'd witnessed the discovery of two more things: a small pendant, and a great chunk of wood that was thought to be a part of a door. The thrill that had attended these moments was like an old, forgotten flame burning through him, and he'd known that this was what he must do with the rest of his life.

Now, a month later, as he returns from the butcher's through the falling snow, it's with a renewed sense of purpose. It's a Friday and he's off tomorrow. He knows that Keely breaks up for the Christmas holidays today. He's spoken to her on the phone recently. She wants him to have Anna on the Saturday rather than the Sunday. It's the third week in a row that she's asked this; he doesn't know why for sure, but the previous week Anna had said something to him that he'd not understood, and he'd felt an ache of jealousy before she'd said something more about a church and Mummy's brother, only for him to realize, pricked by his own selfishness, that Keely must have taken her to visit Welty's grave at some point.

On his bed beneath the lamp, he opens the books that Graham gave him and he sets to work, making notes and small drawings, jotting down dates and words that are long and complex and require him to make a few stumbling attempts before he can pronounce them properly. He eats while he works, not looking at the spoon that he fills up with scrambled egg and beans and lifts to his mouth. He must learn, learn, learn. This is all he wants to do.

He's not sure how, but the whole enterprise has become more and more closely linked with Keely and Anna. The more he reads and learns, the more he feels he's clawing his way back to them. Every note he makes strikes him as an attempt at communicating, like he's tapping out a message, knowing that one day they'll hear it and respond. He has the rare, addictive feeling that he's improving himself. Even if he wanted to stop, he wouldn't be able to.

He switches off the lamp and closes his eyes. With Anna arriving tomorrow, this is the only night he ever truly sleeps well, when he knows he'll wake up and be able to lift his daughter into his arms.

SHE'S GOING TO VISIT Welty's grave for the third time in as many weeks. It's hit her very suddenly, this need to feel him near her again. After years of not visiting, of trying to keep him at the edge of her thoughts, the sense of his presence struck her so powerfully one morning as she was pouring out Anna's cereal that she'd had to stop and brace her arm against the work surface for fear she was about to drop to her knees.

She's tried to make sense of it, this peculiar resurgence of Welty's energy, and the conclusion that she's reached is that it's to do with Finn. She can't endure the loss of him without fighting to gain something back. She refuses to let her life be defined by absences, by the disintegration of relationships rather than the strengthening of them. And if she can't rely and lean on the living, then she'll do it with the dead.

The snow must have stopped just after she'd gone to bed because it's not that deep. She'd thought that the engine wasn't going to start this morning, but it had fired up right away. The roads have been gritted and, though she didn't manage to catch the forecast, the temperature feels slightly warmer, so that what snow is still on the ground might soon melt away.

She pulls up outside Finn's flat on the edge of town. The area is horribly run-down. It's at the very top of an old, shoddy house with weeds that slink out from the gutters and several slates missing from the roof. The windows are so thin they rattle whenever a car drives by. She knows this because she's been in there. She'd wanted to see where Anna would be spending her time, if it was clean and safe for her, and she'd asked Finn if she could follow them up the dark, cavernous stairs.

He'd let her walk around, neither of them saying anything. It was dark and the wallpaper was peeling away at the corners, with only a single bed pressed against the wall in the corner. But he kept it clean, and he'd bought an oil heater that he plugged in and used to keep it warm.

Still, she never feels comfortable leaving Anna here. She unbuckles her small body from the car seat and lifts her out, feeling the fleece of her coat against her cheek. Anna is happily jibbering away about what she and her daddy are going to be doing today. She's brought her drawing pad and pencils with her. She often comes home having made drawings of things that Keely doesn't recognize and that Anna doesn't seem to know herself. The only answer she ever offers is that they're from Daddy's books.

Keely rings the buzzer, holding Anna's mittened hand. The sky is still grey and the clouds low, the sun sulking behind them. Even though it's a little warmer, Keely has dressed Anna in all of her thickest clothes.

Finn answers the door and immediately Keely's eyes meet his, though only for a second before they dart away. She's yet to be able to look at him without her heart thumping and the feeling of nausea rushing up her gullet. He's dressed in his running shorts and trainers and a large knitted sweatshirt, one that she used to wear. He's let his hair grow out a bit more. She thinks he looks a little better than he has done recently, not quite so pale, not so painfully thin. His knees are red and the hairs on his shins dark. He presses himself close to the door like a shy child might press themselves close to the leg of a parent.

Anna rushes toward him and he lifts her up, kisses her

cheeks, knocking her hat askew as he does so, so that Keely reaches over and pulls it straight, then retreats back outside again.

I'll be back at four, she says.

They never exchange any words beyond the practicalities of their day or how Anna has been. Not once has she enquired after any details of his life. She's still too angry with him; and, if she admits it to herself, she's also afraid to hear that he might be happy, happier in a life without her, with a life that he's realized she was holding him back from.

He nods his head.

I'll have her ready for four, he says.

She leans over and kisses Anna, but also catches the slightest smell of Finn, of his breath, and she's briefly transported back to the bed they'd shared in their old flat, when they'd wake in those cold blue hours before work. What would he say if she articulated this? Does anything like that ever go through his mind when he sees her?

She turns to wave before she gets into the car, but the door has already been shut. She climbs in, turns the key, feels the engine thrum surprisingly to life again. The drive to the cemetery isn't far, twenty minutes at the most. She can remember the few times her da took her and Welty to lay what they'd picked from the dunes on their mam's grave. And she remembers Welty's funeral, when nearly everyone from the camp had turned up in their black and musty clothes, and they'd all stood and watched as the small casket was lowered into the ground. She can see in her mind's eye the light being blown about the surface of the sea, the smoke from the power station drifting darkly away.

The roads are wet and dark. Spray kicks up from the tyres of the cars in front of her and her windscreen wipers drag across the pane. The radio plays Christmas songs. She's already done all her shopping for Anna. She asked for a small amount of money from Finn as a contribution. She's aware that he's in a poor financial position, but he's not once failed to cough up the amount they'd agreed on for Anna's keep.

The engine rattles and churns as she speeds out of the town and through the fields quilted in snow. She peers up at the sky, feels the weight of the clouds that are heaped one on top of the other. She wonders again about the forecast and hopes she might catch it at some point on the radio.

Before she knows it, she's arrived. There's only one other car here, parked on the other side of the lot. She pulls up and looks out at the cemetery. It feels different covered in snow, older, more innocent. She doesn't believe in ghosts, and yet the past few times she's been here, she's felt restless when walking between the rows of canted headstones. The air becomes charged with a different quality, almost a hum rising up from the ground, as if the buried are muttering to one another below.

She doesn't find the feeling unpleasant or disquieting; rather, it's almost comforting. She imagines what Welty would be saying. She tries to recall his voice, the tone of it, the various inflections. Sometimes she can hear him, a kind of echo in her head, and she holds it there, listening as closely as she can until it fades.

The church looks dark and empty through the stained

glass of its windows. The roof is covered in an even layer of snow, the spire poking out above. She can see the steady silver drip of meltwater staining the old stone wall. Moss has mapped itself across entire swathes of it. The door, made of thick, roughly hewn wood, boasts a large wrought-iron knocker. The last time she came here, she'd taken it in her hands and was surprised to find it open.

Inside, she'd sat down on the back pew. No one else appeared to be there. Candles that she'd failed to notice from outside were burning on the high window ledges. The sound of her own small movements rang out in the air, which was scented with stone and busy with motes that were held and kneaded by the light that sluiced in through the glass. She'd closed her eyes and done nothing but think of Welty, and she'd been rewarded with a volley of bright, vivid memories of him in the dunes, in the coal cart on the beach, looking up at her from the little pallet that was his bed.

She's about to get out of the car, when she sees someone weaving between the graves, a tall man with his hands buried deep in his pockets and a head of grey, springy-looking hair, his eyes lowered to the ground. There's some small, vital part of her that knows it's her da before her mind allows her to fully comprehend it. Her hands, seemingly of their own accord, lift themselves from her lap and grip the steering wheel.

She holds her breath as she watches him step past the last of the graves, her blood thundering in her ears. He doesn't look up until he gets to the lone green car on the other side of the lot. It must be his, a new one; or it belongs to Angela, the woman with the auburn hair she'd stared at through the window years back, the stone clenched in her hand.

His eyes don't seek her but the sky, pausing for ten seconds or more, his hand on the door, to study the grey trudge of the clouds above. She's far away, but she can still make out the dark grooves that now cut across his face, that tug at the corners of his mouth, and she can see the skin under his chin is looser.

He looks like he could be older than his fifty-odd years, but it's definitely him, the man from whom her own life has sprung. The man that she loved and was loved by for so many years, that she hasn't seen or spoken to since she left him lying on the floor of the first flat that they'd moved into in town. The man who's come to visit the grave of his dead son, his long-dead wife.

She watches as he gets into his car and she can hear him then in her head, hears the groan that she knows he'll be making as his knees bend and click as he settles himself into his seat. How many times has she heard it before, in the truck with him and Gordon and the coal rattling behind them. When he'd sit down at the table in the caravan with his cup of tea. Through the wall when he'd get out of the bed to face the cold dark winter mornings.

He starts the engine and reverses, and then he's driving toward her. She could wave. She could get out and stand in the middle of the road. She could throw herself down in front of the car. But she stays as she is. Surely his eyes will be drawn to hers. Surely he'll sense her there and turn his head. He'll see her. He'll see her and then he'll stop and get out. He'll walk over to her door and open it. And everything, everything between them will be resolved.

But as he draws level with her, she sees that he's distracted by something, flicking some dial on the dashboard or adjusting the heating, and she watches, turning her head one way and then the other, as he simply drives past her. His brake lights pulse red as he reaches the exit of the cemetery, and she catches one last glimpse of his face – a sliver of the long, pale cheek and the dark, curving line of his mouth – and then he's gone, his life continuing as if she'd not been there at all, so in that moment she feels like a glitch in the universe, a window that's been opened up and through which she's watching, but from somewhere else entirely.

He was here and now he's not.

This is a fact. Her life has been made up of facts and here is another one to add to the pile. She sits, still gripping the wheel, minutes passing before her heart finally starts to slow. She lets her hands fall back into her lap. She looks down at them. They're pale and wrung out, suddenly empty of whatever crackle of tension and strength had fastened them so firmly to the scuffed plastic of the wheel.

She looks out the window at the empty parking lot, at the church, the rows of snow-capped headstones. Her da was just here with her. So clearly, vividly here; and yet now it seems as if it might have never happened, as if what she's just experienced was a projection beamed down from some orbiting portion of her own mind.

She hears a bird call out from somewhere, then silence. There's a stand of black-limbed trees reflected in her wing mirror, the twist and mesh of their branches reaching darkly against the pale expanse of sky. Might these be considered witnesses? She's never thought of a tree in such a way, and yet now she finds herself willing a sentience upon them, because she can't stand to have been the only being present for what's just happened, for the weight of it all to come down on her shoulders.

The thought overwhelms her, and she reaches for the handle to roll down the window, takes greedy gulps of the slightly metallic-tasting air that rushes in. She closes her eyes and tries to calm herself. It's not that she thinks it so unlikely that she should see her da here. She's often wondered if this might be the place where they finally meet. The strangeness is that it should happen without consequence; it's that these two people, with everything they've had and lost between them, can share the same space and there be no stirring of the atmosphere, no breaking of the silence, no meaning beyond a series of fleeting impressions, of movement and colour, light and sound.

It's like dropping a kerosene-soaked rag on to a heap of dry brush, lighting it, and seeing no swell of fire but only a thin twist of smoke. She suspects, in reality, that every second of her life has been like this, holds within it the potential for the profound, the shattering, and that there's no moment in time that doesn't have the possibility for some kind of beginning or some kind of end. It's just that most of them go by without making themselves known.

But this moment should have made itself known; and the space holding all the possibilities of what could have happened feels tangible to her now. The space around her, in the car and in the parking lot, feels boundless, as if it's not a part of the world but the world itself, and she's at the very centre of it.

She opens her eyes and finds that it's started to snow again. She pulls the handle and climbs out, stands and looks up at the drifting flakes coming down. They land on her, on her lashes and nose, her cheeks, her hair. She watches them melt on the sleeve of her coat, in the almost green, thinly lined basin of her open palm.

She knows where Welty's grave is without having to stoop and brush away the snow to read the identities of any others. She finds the path that her da had walked along moments before and looks down to see his footprints in the snow. She knows by the tread that he was wearing the same boots that he's had for years, the same ones that he would pull off at the door of the caravan and leave there, the laces snaking out and sometimes tripping her or Welty up.

She follows them, follows his loping stride that her own can't match. The snow continues to fall, the flakes fatter now, busier. She thrusts her hands into her pockets. Her head is lowered to look at her da's prints, her chin tucked into the collar of her coat, her head strangely empty of thought. All she wants is to be by Welty's grave, to kneel down by it, to touch the cold stone with her fingers.

When she reaches Welty's grave, she can see her mam's too. There's a small clutch of flowers that her da must have laid there, the red of the petals and the green of the stems already gathering snow. She imagines her mam beneath the earth, deep in the cold chill dark. She moves over to it, lifts up the flowers and shakes them free of the snow, then places them back down and returns to Welty's grave.

Keely looks down and finds her da's footprints pointing directly at it. She steps into them, looks down at where her da would have just been looking, his eyes taking in the very same scene. The same bunch of flowers, which she nudges ever so slightly with her boot to shake free the snow.

And then she begins to talk. She's never done this before, has always been silent. But now she's telling Welty everything, every detail about her life that he's missed. She wants him to know her, wants to feel that he's not trapped in time but in the here and now, with her, alongside her.

She doesn't even think about whether he can hear her or not. There's no pang of self-consciousness. She's just talking, telling him about having just seen their da. She wants him to take some of the weight from her, and as the words leave her mouth, she feels lighter. He's obliging her. He's doing what brothers should do. She tells him about Finn and about Anna. She tells him about what Finn did, how she can never forgive him.

And then she falls silent.

In her pocket, she has a little jar that she's kept since she was a girl. The glass is old and clouded, like the face of a watch left underwater, and when she brings it out flakes of snow immediately start to cling and drip down its curved sides. Inside, barely visible in the grey light, are the old blue chips of paint from Welty's bed that she'd collected from the floor of their room in the caravan. She's always kept it in her bedside drawer, but only this morning did she wish to bring it, so that she can now place it down, and return to find it still here. Something of his life that he too might be able to sense.

The snow is still falling, and when she looks down at her feet, she sees that the outline of her da's boots has gone. It'll just be her prints left when she leaves. She's been standing still for so long that the snow has gathered on her shoulders, is starting to cling to any part of her it can get at. If she were to stay here and not move for another hour, she imagines that she'd be completely covered.

She turns around. Through the winding sheets of snow she can see parts of her car, the dark rubber of the tyres and the black wheel arches. It's still the only one in the lot. The church looks to be closing in on itself, getting smaller and smaller. The sea is somewhere beyond it. It'll be snowing far out there as well, and it strikes her as a strange, sad thought to imagine all those flakes vanishing on impact as they touch the briny water.

She turns back to Welty and she stoops to touch the headstone.

I'll see you soon, she says.

Then she turns and walks back to the car. She can barely see it now, nearly all of it covered. The tyre tracks of her da's car are gone, buried. He's lost to her, adrift in the world, maybe never to be seen by her again.

The door is stiff when she opens it and climbs in. The windscreen is blocked white with snow and casts a pale blue light over her and the seats. She suddenly feels bitterly cold and tired. She clears the windscreen but then can barely fit the key in the ignition her hand is shaking so violently. She gets it in and turns it, but the engine offers nothing, not even the hint of a rattle or cough.

She turns again. The same. She does it over and over

until, finally, she admits that the silence is permanent, and she sits back in her seat, listening to nothing and everything all at once.

THERE'S NO OTHER FEELING that compares with holding Anna, this child that he's helped create. There isn't a time that he sees her when he isn't struck by the miracle of her very aliveness: the soft spill of her blonde curls, the smoothness of her skin, the way she moves and talks and is already a person in her own right, with thoughts and feelings and a way of receiving the world that might be similar to his own, or not, but will ultimately always be a mystery to him.

When she was only a few days old, he'd experienced an almost crushing wave of panic and pressure. This tiny body that he was holding every day and night, that fitted snugly in the crook of his arm and slept and woke to stare deeply into his eyes. Who was she? What was she thinking? What life was waiting for her to step into?

It was when he'd just finished bathing her and her hot little body was wriggling against his that it truly hit him: he was responsible for her. It was within his power to alter the course of her existence; it was up to him to instil in her the values and beliefs that he thought important, that he thought would help protect her, would help ease her passage in a world he knew could be relentlessly cruel.

But what did he know about life? What did he know about himself? What wisdom could he possibly impart? He'd had no father of his own, no template that he could work from. He'd loved his grandad – and since he'd died he'd thought about him with increasing fondness and respect – but the fact remained that there'd always been a distance between them, a bond that worked on the understanding that his grandad could offer advice, but with no obligation to explain it or tailor it to Finn's specific needs.

For Finn, the world had always felt too random and chaotic to achieve any real kind of judgment of it. He was only just coming to terms with it himself, its fierce, unrelenting pace, with the constant hum of other lives that were attached to his own or were just passing him by. Nothing had ever really made sense, and yet here he was, holding another human, one that was relying on him to explain it all.

He opens the door of his flat and places Anna down on the floor. Despite the cramped space and the general grimness, she seems to like being here. She finds it funny that his bed is in the same room as the kitchen. She likes how she can watch him from the sofa as he poaches their eggs and warms the beans in the pan; and rather than find it a chore to have to leave the room and go to the bathroom he shares with other tenants, she considers it to be a great adventure, prancing down the hall and weeing with great relish.

First, they go outside for a walk. He asks Anna if she'd like to build a snowman, but she tells him that she's already built one with Mummy this morning before they came. He suffers a brief pang at the thought of missing this thing, and he can't keep his mind from conjuring an image of the three of them, him and Keely and Anna, all at work in the snow, smiling and laughing.

He's fallen into this trap too many times before, when he's no longer in the moment enjoying the company of his daughter with the little time he has, but inhabiting some projected past or future that he can never have. It's a waste of his time, and he has to drag himself back into the present.

He always stops at the butcher's so that Anna can see Harry and be reminded of where her daddy works. He opens the door now and finds Harry behind the counter with a piece of chalk in hand, writing down some new cuts of meat and new prices on the blackboard. When he turns at the sound of the bell, his face lights up, his crooked teeth coming together in a wide grin.

He speaks to Anna as if she's an adult.

Are you keeping well, little lady? he asks. Are you making the most of your time with your daddy?

Anna nods.

I am, she says.

She thinks Harry endlessly entertaining, and she often asks him to detail all the different meats behind the counter. She shows no squeamishness about it. If she could, she'd have her hands in there, churning it all up. Before they go, Harry gives her a hard-boiled lolly, which Finn tells her she can put in her pocket and save for after their dinner.

Just as they set off, the first few snowflakes start coming down, and Anna chirrups delightedly, turning her mittened palm up for them to land on.

Where does snow come from? she asks.

From the sky, he says.

But how?

She often asks questions like these, questions that he feels he ought to know the answer to, but mostly never does. It makes him want to live in a library, to dedicate his life to the accrual of facts, so that they can always be there waiting for him, on the tip of his tongue, to feed his daughter's eagerly expanding mind.

Back in the flat, he flicks the heater on and the two lamps. They're both hungry, so he starts to make what he always makes for them: poached eggs and beans. He doesn't have a TV, but he's not sure Anna would want to watch it anyway. He knows she watches videos on the player he got her, because she tells him about them, but when she's here with him, she seems to be content just to watch him, as if he's great entertainment himself.

As they eat, and he mops the beans and yolk from around Anna's mouth, he sometimes wonders how much of their day Anna tells Keely about. Does Keely listen to what they've done and think him a poor father? Does she think him boring or unimaginative? Does she expect more from him but choose not to say? There was a time when he would have been able to guess correctly at anything she was thinking. Thoughts seemed to visibly pass over her face and he could read them there, as clearly as if she'd already voiced them.

Now, it's like she's a different person. He looks at her in those fleeting moments when she drops Anna off and picks her up and he has no idea what's going on behind her eyes. She's shut herself away from him. Something as solid and impenetrable as steel has separated her from his intuition. She's no longer his to know.

He has, in his weaker moments, contemplated what it

will be like if Keely meets someone else, another man that settles into the house to live with her and Anna. It has kept him awake, to think about how his role might change, how his presence in Anna's life might be diminished even further. He will be able to do nothing about it. He'll have to simply watch as this stranger handles his child and gradually builds a relationship with her that is stronger, more fundamental than his own.

After they've eaten on the sofa, with their food on their laps, and he's washed the plates in the sink, they move over to the small table. It's not a table they can eat at, because it's too high for Anna. The woman behind the till at the shop told him it's an artist's table, though he doesn't really know what this means. All he knows is that he likes to have it for his books and for making his notes and drawings.

The table is large enough for Anna to lie down on and do her drawing while he sits and does his own sketches. He opens one of the books Graham gave him and he finds something for them to look at, and then, without exchanging a word, they both settle and start their own little sketches of the vases and trinkets that are photographed on the page.

This is the only sound in the room, of pencil lightly scratching across paper. Finn lifts his eyes every now and then to study his daughter, to see how the tip of her tongue creeps out from between her lips, to marvel at the way her wrist is cocked as her fist grips the pencil. Sometimes she hums quietly to herself, or speaks aloud to her creation, announcing her intentions to it. But now she's silent, and he returns to his own work.

This is when he's at his most content these days. There's nothing else in the world but him and Anna. All of his worries and fears temporarily evaporate, and his life no longer seems to be the irreversible mess he so often believes it's become.

After half an hour, he asks Anna if she'd like some hot chocolate. It's a treat that he's been waiting to surprise her with, and when she claps her hands excitedly, he goes over to the fridge and gets out the milk, then reaches up to the cupboard for the powder. He sets the milk to simmer on the hob, and as he washes a spoon at the sink, he sees that the snow is falling thick and fast, much more so than it was yesterday.

He hears the milk start to bubble and he moves to take it off the heat. As he stirs the powder into the mug, he glances down at his watch. He never fails to be amazed by how quickly time passes when he's with Anna, how cruel it is that this is all he gets.

He suggests that they drink it while looking out the window at the snow. By the time they'll be finished, it'll be almost four. It's always around this time, nearing Anna's pick-up, that he feels compelled to start asking her questions. Some of them are stupid, but that's not the point. He just wants to hear her talk. He wants to savour her voice, wants to store up the sound of it so that he can listen to it when she's gone, replaying her words over and over again in his head before they start to fade, which they always do.

His watch tells him it's four o'clock. Keely's normally always early and will buzz up a few minutes before four. But ten minutes pass and he hears nothing. Maybe the buzzer has broken and she's stuck waiting downstairs. He picks Anna up and walks down with her on his hip, opens the door and stares out on to the street. The snow is swirling now, gathering on the cars, on the pavement, clinging to the stems of the lamp posts.

No sign of her.

They go back upstairs. He has a little wooden box of dominoes, which he gets down now from his one shelf. Anna still can't quite play properly, but she likes to patiently set them up in rows then knock them down or stack them as high as she can before they begin to teeter and topple over.

While Anna is playing, he goes to the phone and rings Keely's house number. No answer. He looks down at his watch. She's never been late before, not once. He places the phone down, goes back over to Anna.

Is Mummy coming soon? she asks.

Yes, he says, she'll be here soon.

When it reaches five and Keely's still not turned up, he knows that something isn't right. He needs to start acting. He can get a bus over to the other side of town and he can knock on her door, maybe even break in if there's any sign that she's had an accident.

He decides that this is what he'll do. He gets Anna dressed in her coat and hat and mittens, and he changes into his jeans and puts his own fleece on. He carries Anna in his arms down the street, making sure he keeps her pressed close to his warmth. There are very few cars out on the road, and those that are drive very slowly, their windscreen wipers going furiously, their tyres whispering slushily.

The lights of Christmas trees wink in the windows and Anna points her favourites out, the ones that she thinks have the most presents under them.

The bus shelter is a small stone hut. There are beer cans scattered on the seat inside and scrawls of black graffiti up the walls, names and hearts and obscenities all mingled together. Anna is starting to get sleepy. He can feel her head lolling against his shoulder, and when he asks her questions, she takes a moment before answering. He doesn't know whether he should keep her awake or whether he should just let her go. Keely has been annoyed before when he's let her drift off, because it's her that'll be up all night. He's suggested more than once that Anna stay over with him, but this has been dismissed. Where would she sleep? Keely had asked.

They wait for the bus, but after fifteen minutes there's still no sign of it, and he knows it's not coming. It must be stuck somewhere in the snow, or the service must have stopped altogether. He begins to search his mind for an alternative plan, for something he can do. Anna is now asleep, so he walks back to his flat, hoping that Keely's going to be there waiting, standing outside and looking up, stomping her feet impatiently in the cold.

But when he gets there, she's nowhere to be seen. He could ring the police, but what would he say? His ex-partner is over an hour late to pick their daughter up? They wouldn't take him seriously, even on a night like this. He wouldn't be able to articulate the tightening of the knot in his stomach, his feeling that something is wrong, and they'd end up telling him to just keep calm and wait another few hours.

But he's not calm and he knows that he can't wait. His mind is whirring, whirring, whirring. He has to do something, and it's then that he finds his feet taking him toward the shop that Keely used to work at. He remembers the night that Mr Lister had driven him to the hospital, and now he thinks that he can ask to borrow his car, and he can drive himself to Keely's house.

The little bell rings when he opens the door and it's Mr Lister who's behind the till, wearing a green cardigan, the same one that he'd had on the night that he'd taken Finn to the hospital to find Keely when she'd first learned she was pregnant with Anna. He looks up from reading something on the little clipboard he carries around with him. His moustache is greyer these days, and his hair is even thinner, down to the last few wisps. He stares at Finn and must see the worry in his face, because he immediately becomes flustered, moving out from behind the till and asking questions.

Finn does his best to explain. His words are all mixed up, but all he needs to say is that Keely is in trouble and Mr Lister is all ears. He listens as Finn asks to borrow the car, and then without a moment's hesitation, he moves over to where his coat is hanging behind the till and fetches his keys from the pocket, telling Finn that he can have it as long as he needs to make sure Keely is all right.

Finn hurries out to the car parked on the other side of the street. He turns on the engine and places Anna down on the passenger seat. He flicks the heating on full blast and straps her in, then goes back out. He pulls the cuff of his coat over his hand and goes to work, scrubbing the windscreen free of snow, dragging his arm back and forth until it burns. His breath comes out in pale rags and his nose runs, but he doesn't stop until he can see the vague shape of the empty driving seat and then Anna curled up on the passenger seat.

The snow churns in the air. It is bitterly, bitterly cold. Some more cars come crawling by, even slower than before. He waits for them to pass, and then climbs into the car. He places his hands against the air blasting out of the heater, but finds that it's barely started to warm up. He places the back of his forefinger against Anna's cheek, feels that she's cold. He needs to hurry and he curses the heater, loud enough that Anna stirs slightly, lifts one crooked finger to rest on the tip of her nose.

After a few minutes, a small patch of the windscreen starts to open up at the bottom of the pane. Finn ducks to look out of it, finds that he can just about see enough of the road. He only has to get across town to Keely's house, it's not far. He makes sure Anna is strapped in, and then he pulls out.

The wipers move with the same throb and pause as a beating heart. The windscreen starts to open up, so that he no longer has to hunch over so much. He steers the car as carefully as he can along the roads, and he moves his arm out to shield Anna whenever he's forced to brake. They don't have far to go. He convinces himself that Keely will be at the house. Everything will be OK. Whatever the problem is, he'll be able to help fix it.

But when he pulls up, he knows that she's not there. The car is gone and all the lights are off. He needs to think where she might be. He closes his eyes. The heater blasts loudly in his ears. He's thinking when he suddenly recalls what Anna had said the other week, something about a grave, and he starts the engine again, knowing where to go.

SHE STANDS BY THE side of the road, willing a car to come along, straining her ears to hear the chug of an engine. But nothing comes. It's too far to walk back to the town. Darkness has settled all around her but she can still see the snow veering across her vision. It swarms her voice as she calls out for help in just the same way the wind had on the night of Welty's death. She has one of Anna's blankets wound around her neck like a scarf but still the snow manages to insinuate itself down the collar of her coat, so that she can feel the trickle of water over her clavicle, seeking to steal yet more heat from her.

She's probably only been waiting for five minutes now but she can't wait any longer. The church had been locked. It was a risk to leave the car, and she knows that to stay out here any longer would be disastrous. She retreats, trudging back through her own steps in the snow that's now climbed halfway up her shin. Her feet are soaked, though she can barely feel them. She's already grown slower and weaker since leaving the car. Her head is bowed like an old woman's, her blonde hair now damp and clinging darkly to her brow. She wants to breathe more air in, but her lungs feel as if they've contracted, and every time she shivers she exhales more than she can bring in.

Her fingers can barely feel the handle of the door as she climbs back into the car. It's both dark and light inside, a kind of pre-dawn. Sometimes when she's in the bath with Anna, she dunks her head under and closes her eyes, and the thick silence is the same that surrounds her now, that plugs her ears and amplifies her every little movement.

She reaches and turns the keys again in the ignition, but there's no response. She thrusts her hands down her jeans, feels the slight tingle of heat in the ends of her fingers. She's read it in a book before, about someone who freezes to death, and she can recall thinking what a terrible way to go it would be, that even Welty's death would be preferable to such an end. All the waiting and the knowing. The slowness of it all, as if she knows that

he can't be sure exactly where he's going. He's only been to the cemetery that one time, which was a good few years ago now. It had been summer then. He remembers there being trees and birdsong. He remembers being able to smell and see the sea. He remembers the church and the rows of headstones, the whip of the wind through Keely's hair.

Anna's still sleeping, her head resting on her shoulder, her mouth open ever so slightly. The car is warmer now, but the snow is still coming down and he can't accelerate much over fifteen miles per hour. He's not seen another car on the road for a good while. It seems only to be them, following the bends of the road, peering out at a world that he almost doesn't recognize, a world that looks to him as if it could be ending.

There should be a sign, he can remember reading it. His eyes scan the road, darting from side to side. He knows that it must be near. He can feel it. He's looking for a narrow little track. He just needs to find it and then Keely will be there, he knows she can

smell Anna, the milksweet scent of her, on the blanket that's wound around her neck, and when she closes her eyes, she finds that she can smell an array of other things: the caravan and the staleness of the sheets on her and Welty's beds; the smokiness of the coal running off her body in the shower; she can smell Immy's mane and the sharpness of her dung when mixed with the salt on the air; the dishes that Ruth would bring round when her da was having one of his bad days.

Each smell carries with it an image, as clear and distinct in her mind as a photograph. This is her life. These are the days that she's lived, and they're crowding her now because there's some part of her that knows it could be about to end. Her whole body is shaking with the cold, and she doesn't even have the strength to open her eyes. Her world is now confined to her own head, because this is the moment that everyone must reach before they go wherever it is they go, when their life is presented to them, where it all must come together with the hope of there being a meaning that might be discovered, and the

turn comes upon him so suddenly that he brakes too hard and the car skids, the wheel passing through his hands like water, unable to find any purchase on it. He thrusts out his arm and feels Anna lurch against it, but his eyes are still on the road as the car continues to spin, the tyres growling at first and then whining, screeching.

They come to a halt in the middle of the road. Stillness and silence, the snow drifting in the beam of the headlights, falling against the windscreen. Finn's heart gallops and his temples throb. He turns to see Anna's eyes are wide and staring at him. A very thin trickle of blood is coming from her left nostril. A second or more passes before she starts to cry, her little face contorting, raging with the shock and confusion of it all.

She screams for him to help her, but he can't, not yet. If a car comes now, then he knows it will come crashing straight into them. He starts the engine again and he tries to crawl the car along toward the turn, making sure not to get stuck, talking to Anna as he does it, telling her that she's going to be OK as he looks furiously over his shoulder to check for any oncoming cars, to make sure that

she hears a noise, something other than her own breathing. She wants to open her eyes but she can't. Her ears strain, but she can hear nothing. Just the slow plod of her heart

the humped form of a car is in his headlights. Anna is still screaming, so loudly that his eyes are narrowed as he brings the car to a stop and leaps out. The headlights throw his shadow darkly across the snow as he runs. His feet make a hushed sound, a whispering. He clears away the snow, finds the handle of the door, heaves it open and

she feels it. She feels herself being pulled up, up and out, and there's a warmth to whatever's now carrying her. It is his warmth. It is Finn that she can feel spreading, spreading, spreading through her body, so that she turns and looks back at herself from somewhere, and she can see herself being held by him and

he has her in his arms. She's alive, breathing. This body that he's loved and that he loves still, with the snow swirling down and coming to rest on her pale hair, on her cheeks, on her hands that he cranes his neck to blow the heat of his breath on to. Her eyes open and close, open and close. She's whispering something, but he doesn't want her to speak. Not yet. They will, but not now. He wants her to save her energy. I have you, he tells her. I have you. He kicks through the snow toward the car, and even though he can't possibly know it, he does know it, and

everything falls away, everything that she's ever lived through, and there's only what's to come that matters, only the spread of days that are stretching out in front of them, for those in the dark and those in the light.

Acknowledgements

Thank you: Mum, Dad, Terry, Gail, Zoë, Erica, Ian, Irwin, Stu, Hattie. To Bobby, for their shrewd counsel. Milly, Eloise, Kate, Bella, Holly, Marianne, and all at Transworld.

A very special mention to Uma Baker – glorious addition to the world and all-round powerhouse.

Finally, to RN – for all you've given me, and for all that's still to come.

MY NAME IS YIP
Paddy Crewe

Yip Tolroy and his fiery Mama run the general store in Heron's Creek, Georgia. An uneventful life, until gold is discovered nearby and Yip is caught up in a bloody, grievous crime, forcing him to flee. On the run, friendless and alone, he meets Dud Carter, a savvy but unlikely companion. Together they embark on a journey that thrusts them unwittingly into a world of menace and violence, lust and revenge. As Yip and Dud's odyssey takes them further into the unknown – via travelling shows, escaped slaves and the greed of gold-hungry men – the pull of home only gets stronger. But what will they find there if they ever return?

'Murder, gold, lost fathers …
Paddy Crewe has a 24-carat gift'
SEBASTIAN BARRY

'Immersive and beautiful in unexpected places'
THE TIMES

'A rollicking, page-turning wild west adventure'
GUARDIAN

'A thrilling bildungsroman adventure,
full of reversals of fortune and getaways'
NEW STATESMAN